INNOCENT LIVES

GUARDIANS OF GRACE, BOOK 1

JULIE BONN BLANK

DEDICATION

For my late brother, Rick Bonn
(film creator extraordinaire, massive creative mind
and lover of Jesus).
Thanks for believing in my dreams.
The Sasquatch is for you.
See you again!

HEADS UP

Recommended for ages fourteen and up.
This book is not for everyone.
Please note that although it ends positively, content
is suggestive of kidnapping,
violence, substance abuse, and rape
in the effort to raise awareness and elicit change.

WHAT THEY SAID . . .

"Julie tackles a difficult subject. One that is hard but necessary to face. She draws you in fully to the lives of two different victims, crosscut stories, but also manages to show you where angels show up. She gives hope in the midst of the trials, and the encouragement to press through."

—Cheryl McKay (Screenwriter *The Ultimate Gift* and Co-Author, *Never the Bride*)

"In *Innocent Lives*, Julie Bonn Blank has artfully captured the heartbreaking story of child-human trafficking. This is a difficult subject, but one that must be known so action can be taken. These precious children endure more than we can imagine, and their hearts and lives are shattered . . . sometimes forever. I recommend this book to anyone who cares that such atrocities are being visited upon our youngest and most vulnerable. And I implore everyone to get involved any way possible. We must rescue our children!"

—Kathi Macias (www.kathimacias.com), award-winning author of more than fifty books, including *Deliver Me from Evil*

"Bravo! A powerful book on the heartbreaking issue of trafficking. I highly recommend this to everyone, especially those who have a heart for the wounded. Truly an excellent read."

—Carla Ashton, Counselor, Co-Founder and Director of Soul Restoration Ministries

"I'm not really a reader and tend to read slowly. However, one day last weekend I set my timer. I was going to read this book for fifteen minutes and then clean the bathroom. Well, I set the timer two more times after that. After that, I finally downloaded the book on my tablet and took it to the bathroom with me. I leaned it against the toilet to read as I scrubbed the bathroom floor!"

—Sharon Creaser, ARMS (Abuse Recovery Ministry Services Group Leader)

"This is a riveting story, which open eyes to the abuse that is so prevalent in our countries today. Expertly and discreetly told, Bonn Blank pulls the reader into the harsh lives of these girls while portraying a message of hope and faith."

—Julie B Cosgrove, author of the award-winning *Hush in the Storm, Legitimate Lies* and *Freed to Forgive* trilogy

"Truly He taught us to love one another;
His law is Love and His gospel is Peace;

Chains shall He break, for the slave is our brother,
And in His name all oppression shall cease . . . "

-O Holy Night

PROLOGUE

THEY WERE NO LONGER CHILDREN, and finally allowed
real fun.

Thursday at 7 p.m., Cienna and Jasmine's dads, Jimmy
and Ken, still wiped off the occasional sweat drop from their
foreheads and Mari, Jasmine's mom, complained about her
flushed cheeks as she gathered her hair into a ponytail. "One
of those days!" She grabbed a park brochure off the picnic
table to fan herself. "You should get going!" She waved at the
girls. "Back before dark, please!"

The parents sat in the cooler shade of the trees by the
roaring mountain river where they drank iced tea, an
occasional beer, and talked adult-talk (whatever that meant).

After playing along the water's edge for a while and
collecting some unique looking rocks they stowed away in
their tent, the girls decided to take their promised walk and
get ice cream cones. They met with some resistance from both
their mothers, who eyed the lowering sun. The girls
specialized in waiting too long on a regular basis. "We'll be
back in less than a half hour," Cienna promised. Jasmine
agreed, vigorously nodding. Cherry chocolate ice cream called

her name. Gathering and pocketing their change (with an extra five thrown in on the sly from Cienna's dad, Jimmy), they waved and started down the road.

"Stay together!" called Mari. The two girls, hearing her loud and clear, waved harder.

"They think we're babies." Jasmine tucked her long blond hair behind her ear. Cienna rolled her eyes. "They act like we're never coming back."

"Well I suppose Sasquatch could get us!" Jasmine laughed. Last night around the fire, Cienna's brother Kai had boasted that one karate chop would flatten the furry beast. The girls snickered. Now, hilarity beckoned while imagining Sasquatch grabbing them and stashing them away in a cave somewhere.

"What do you think he looks like for real?" Jasmine reached down to tighten her shoelace. "Maybe he would roll us up like a croc does before they eat you."

"Hmmmm. Maybe he would be polite and let us give him a shave!" Cienna nodded firmly. Thinking about his extreme hair issue elicited a new set of giggles from both.

"Do you think he has nipples for real? The postcards at the store with his picture all have nipples on him."

Cienna batted her on the arm. "Eww, Jazz. Who cares about that!?"

Jasmine shut up about nipples and talked about the new cute boy at school instead. Chad had wavy dark hair and extremely bright blue eyes. He must have colored contacts. Cienna constantly admired his arm muscles. Jasmine was so busy fighting stomach butterflies that she forgot to say anything when he was in the same room. She only blushed, and Cienna teased her about it endlessly afterward.

At the General Store, they giggled when they passed the Sasquatch postcards and headed to the soda case. Then finally, the ice cream counter. With their cones and cans carefully balanced in hand, they headed toward the door.

"I don't want to go back yet." Cienna whined. "It's boring. All they do is talk. Blah, blah, blah!"

"Let's go the long ways." Jasmine's cell phone was in her back pocket. She should text her mom if they were going to be more than a half hour. But maybe she should finish her ice cream and wash the sticky off her hands first. Her phone jingled so they closed the store door behind them and paused on the wooden deck on the front of the store. She passed her cone and soda can to Cienna.

What flavor did you get?

Mom. Jasmine rolled her eyes, wiping her other hand on her jeans. **Cher Choc of course.**

OK. The screen flashed back with a second message. **How about the dairy-free sorbet next time?**

Jasmine smiled and tucked the phone away. Her ice cream cone would start a major drip session at any time. And Cienna looked a bit impatient trying to hold everything.

"Got it." Jasmine nodded after Cienna handed her items back. "We really should go the long ways back. They won't even know."

"Okay." Cienna shrugged. They headed along the road, with the forest at their right and the river at their left.

Within minutes, they saw a road leading up into the woods and headed up the mountain instead. Jasmine wanted pics looking down on the river. "Why is the road so bumpy?" Jasmine tripped on a large rock and almost dropped her ice cream. "Geez."

"It's a logging trail, doofus. Only big trucks come up here to get trees to build houses and stuff. Don't you remember when we hiked it a couple years ago?"

It did seem familiar. The woods darkened while Jasmine continued to walk up, up, up, eating her ice cream as she went. It dripped on her hand. She licked at the sweetness. The tall trees mesmerized. Sometimes on their family exploration trips, she saw huge mushrooms. Once, a hole in a tree trunk that she'd climbed into. Her daddy, Ken, had snapped a photo. "Maybe you should be an environmental scientist. Since you love outside." He encouraged her. But as she was climbing out of the tree trunk, she'd grabbed a plant for support and immediately squawked. "Maybe I shouldn't. I just stuck my whole arm in a patch of nettles." Oops.

Finally, they reached a point where they could look down on the river if they veered off road slightly and out to a cliff area made of solid rock.

"Pretty." Cienna saw another cliff made of rocks across the river. "Do you think there's an echo?" She started howling like a wolf. Sounds rebounded back. Jasmine giggled. She finished her cone and joined in. They laughed and howled and laughed some more. Jasmine pictured a pack of wolves on the other side howling back at them but unable to reach them.

Jasmine's phone chimed. "Dang. We better get back. It's almost dark. And I didn't even take pics. Wait a sec." Both girls paused as Jasmine took some shots of the river, woods, one of Cienna sticking her tongue out. Then they took a selfie together, grinning like silly clowns. Her phone's camera flashed.

Howling again, they headed back down the logging road toward camp, crushing their soda cans. Halfway down, they tossed the evidence but instantly Cienna felt bad. What if animals tried to eat them? She picked them up and tucked them in her shirt pockets. Her half-eaten ice cream started to slide off its cone.

Jasmine texted her mom. **Almost back!**

They talked about school and Chad some more. And ragged on the teachers. "Mrs. Bloss is cool, but I hate Mr. G." Jasmine grinned. "What's his real name anyway?"

Cienna shrugged. "No one knows. It's probably on the class schedule but who keeps those? He just has 'Mr. G' on the board. Maybe he has a stupid last name."

"Maybe. Or it's too long to spell. Hey, you won't be there this year. What am I gonna do without you?" Jasmine pouted.

Cienna, who was moving on to high school, grinned again. "You're a goofball. What do you want to do tomorrow? Kai wants to fish but that's boring. Dad said maybe we should rent a boat."

"A boat would be fun." Jasmine picked up a stick and broke it in half. "But I just really want to know how many s'mores I get tonight."

The girls walked down the hill, sometimes sliding a bit on the incline and once with Cienna even landing on her butt. Laughter rang through the woods. They never heard the quiet footsteps following in their wake.

CHAPTER ONE
Cienna

CIENNA AWOKE GROGGY, her stomach churning. Her hands, stuck behind her back, refused to move. Whatever vehicle she was in moved fast. She bounced, her hips almost rising completely from the floor as it flew around corners. Her mouth felt dry and sticky. "Wha-" she choked out.

A nearby shadow came to life. "Shut your mouth, or I'll gag you."

She opened her eyes wider. Tried to focus. It looked like the back of a van. But it was dark, and she couldn't tell for sure. Tears filled her eyes. She swallowed hard.

"Where am I?"

A laugh, horrible and grating, erupted next to her. The man grew more visible as her eyes adjusted. She tried to back away. The wall behind her felt cold and unmoving.

Dark eyes stared at her. He sported a scraggly beard. His smell about melted her nose. He leaned toward her as she squirmed, suddenly only an inch away. He smirked. Holes lined his mouth between yellow teeth. Then he rubbed her chest with his grimy hand. She jumped, quickly folding her body up against the wall as tightly as it would go.

"Don't touch me, you creepy, disgusting thing!"

"Shut up." He slammed his hand over her mouth. Hard. "Or I'll hurt you." His vicious tone backed up his words. Mercifully, he then ignored her, and she soon grew sleepy again.

When Cienna awoke again, the van was slowing. It stopped. She felt a little stronger. When the disgusting man tried to pull her out of the vehicle, she kicked him with both feet as hard as she could. He grabbed her ankles. Squeezed them hard.

"A feisty one." He snickered. He wiped his nose with his sleeve.

He dragged her from the vehicle. Her shirt pulled up as she went. She landed flat on her back outside the van. Her head bounced painfully against the ground. Her hands, bound behind her back, felt like they might break. Dizzily, she looked up at barn rafters. The smell of hay wafted to her nose. Wincing at the pain in her back and arms, she rolled to her side. A flattened soda can slid out of her shirt pocket. She must have lost the other one along the way.

"Where's Jasmine?" Her voice squeaked through her dry throat. She tried to sit up.

A fist slammed into her face. Whipped her head back. Tears leaked down her cheeks. She knew a kid in school whose father hit him sometimes, but she had never, ever been hit. Her face burned.

Two men stared down at her. Like she was a piece of merchandise.

"It'll do." A man with a smooth face adjusted his red baseball hat. "It's older." He kicked away the soda can. It bounced off the wall.

It? What would do? Afraid to move, Cienna caught the words "payment" and "office." She drifted in and out of consciousness. Would she ever see Jazz and her family again?

A bit later, the disgusting man with the beard left in the van. The man with the smooth face and baseball hat knelt next to her. "I'm sorry." He reached toward her face. She jerked her head away. He patted her shoulder. "I'll take ya home."

Her heart raced with hope. She slowly turned her head. "Do you know where Jazz is?" She whispered. For some reason her full voice hadn't returned.

He leaned closer. "No," he whispered back. "I'm real sorry. I'm Mike. What's yer name?"

"Ci-Cienna. Will you help me, M-M-Mike?"

He pulled her to her feet. Put his arm around her shoulder. Her head spun. She leaned into him, even though she didn't want to. He walked her to a large barn door, slid it open, and guided her to a battered, blue truck. He helped her in and released the plastic ties around her wrists with his pocketknife. He fastened her seatbelt.

Her hands cramped. Her heart soared. Whatever had happened, she was now headed back to the River Falls Camp.

Mike climbed into the driver's side and apologized again. "Roger roughed ya up too much. That wasn't supposed to happen." He reached over. Patted her knee.

She shuddered, then felt guilty. "What's su-supposed to happen?"

"He was supposed to take good care of ya," he growled. "Not yank ya out of the van like that."

"O-oh. But why am I even h-"

He reached out. Patted her knee again. "Enough for now."

Cienna laid her head back against the seat and stared outside. It was dark. How long had it been since leaving her family and Jasmine? Her head ached. Her cheek swelled where Roger had punched her. Her teeth hurt and felt loose. She sighed. Her phone sat alone under her pillow in the tent. She hoped Jazz was back at the camp and safe.

An hour later, they pulled up near a house. She sat up, startled. "This isn't the campground!"

Mike turned to her. "I know. But it's late, and I'm too tired to drive. We can stay here until morning."

"B-But what about my parents?" By now, they must be very worried.

"Oh, I told them yer safe. Don't worry. Ya can see them in the morning."

With a funny feeling in her stomach, Cienna grudgingly got out. She allowed him to lead her. This time to another barn.

"Aren't we going to the house?"

He shushed her, smiling. "I don't wanna wake Mrs. Mike. Ya gotta to sleep in here."

Inside the barn, a door opened into a room. Pitch dark. Her knees trembled. Stomach rolling, she jerked away and started flinging her fists at any part of his body nearby. He easily overcame her. Carried her to the middle of the room. With a rope, he tied her to a wooden pole that seemed to stretch to the ceiling.

"No-no! Let me go!" Cierra struggled against the rope. She screamed as loud as she could. He stood and crossed his arms. Smiled down at her. His hat was slightly askew. Beads of sweat broke on his forehead. Oddly, his blue eyes sparkled with amusement.

"All's okay. Ya can scream all ya want, but no one will hear ya out here. We're miles away from anyone else, and only the bear will come to investigate."

Bear?

She glared at him. Screamed again. "Help!" She screeched. Her voice was worn with fear.

Mike smiled again. He said goodnight and turned to leave. As he closed the door behind him, she heard the unmistakable sound of a board sliding across the door.

As the cold darkness closed in around her, she trembled violently.

CHAPTER TWO
Jasmine

JASMINE AWOKE TO FIND HERSELF lying on her side on a couch. Her hair stuck to her face, tears and snot leaked down. Her hands were tied in front of her. Her tee shirt ripped at the shoulder. She used the shoulder with the intact sleeve to try to wipe her face. Attempted a sitting position but failed. She fell back onto the couch, her head spinning. Whose couch was she on?

She forced herself to press her feet against the floor. Propelled her body into a sitting position and looked around.

"Ouch!" Her raw throat made talking difficult. Her head pounded.

"About time." A voice. From the corner.

Jasmine looked over and saw a heavy woman with jeans and a black tee shirt. She sat in the corner of the room. With the room on the darker side, she could barely make the woman out. But she could clearly see a small light and smell cigarette smoke. Jasmine fumbled for her inhaler in her pocket.

No inhaler.

"Where am I?" Jasmine used her shoulder to rub her eyes. "Where's Cienna? You need to put that out. I'm allergic!"

The woman breathed in on the cigarette, exhaling slowly. She stared. Jasmine tried to stare back. She quickly felt intimidated and looked away.

"Does your head hurt?"

"Why do you care?"

The woman laughed. A raspy, deep voice. "I don't really. I couldn't care less what it does to you."

Jasmine stood. She would use her best manners. Grand-mom had always said you could catch more bugs with honey than lemon juice. "I have to go now." She attempted an understanding and kind smile. "Would you know how to get back to the River Falls campground? My family and Cienna's family were camping . . . she and I walked to the store . . . " She wobbled. Sat back rather suddenly on the edge of the couch.

The woman laughed loudly. Somewhere in the house, a door slammed. "Sit down before you fall over. Man, some of you are hilarious when you're high."

"I'm not high." But Jasmine slurred her words. "How could I be high?" Her head pounded. She scooted back carefully against the back of the couch. This wasn't a dream. It was a nightmare. Woozy, she laid her head on the armrest. She surrendered to sleep again.

Sometime later, she awoke to find herself still stuck inside the same dream. She groaned as she opened her eyes. A strange girl with bright red hair and large green eyes was leaning against the doorframe of the room staring at her.

Jasmine jolted upright. Her lap was wet. "Ick. I can't feel my hands." The smell of pee filled her nostrils.

The girl frowned. "You're wet. We should clean up before you get in trouble. That might ruin the Trouble Couch. Wouldn't that be something? The new girl ruining the TC . . . "

Jasmine grunted. Tried to pull her hands out of the restraints. "I couldn't help it. I can't feel anything! How can I clean it up? I can't!" She wiggled around and tried to release her hands. The plastic ties bit painfully into her skin. "What do you mean by the Trouble Couch?"

The girl lowered her voice to a whisper. "TC is where we go when we get in trouble. You're in the bad room and not allowed out. You're lucky you have the couch. When I got here, I was on the floor."

Tears sprang to Jasmine's eyes. "How am I in trouble?"

The girl put a finger to her lips. "Shush. You'll get me in trouble too." She turned and slipped out of the room. Quietly closed the door.

"W-Wait! Please!"

Silence answered her. Jasmine began to sob. Her stomach grumbled loudly. After a few minutes, only hiccups remained. Was there no one else here? No one who could come to help her?

That girl had walked out the door. She could too. Jasmine stood, rebalanced herself and approached the door. With her hands still bound together in front of her, she reached for the doorknob. But it gave way before she even touched it. A hand slammed against her chest. She flew backward to the floor. Tried to catch her breath. The first woman she'd met, the larger one in jeans, lumbered over and smacked the side of Jasmine's head. She glared down.

"What do you think you're doing?" She leaned close. Her stinky breath blasted into Jasmine's face, making her queasy. "When in trouble, you stay on the TC. You were lucky. You should have been on the floor, but I do have some sympathy. And what's that smell? Piss?" She grabbed Jasmine by the arm. Dragged her back to the couch and pushed her again. "You made it. You can sit in it." She snorted. "Roger never said you was that much trouble. Said you was sweet as pie . . ."

Roger? Who was that? Jasmine squeezed her eyes closed. She sat in her own cold puddle. Where was she? Who were these people? And why was she in trouble? She buried her face in the arm of the couch again.

She started mumbling. Her knees trembled. She needed to eat. She needed to throw up. "Do-Do you know where my friend is? Where Cienna went? We got ice cream . . . took pictures." She felt her jean's pockets. "Where's my phone?!"

The woman placed her hands on her ample hips and glared at her. "I never heard of no Cienna." She turned and left. The door slammed loudly.

"Witch-devil," Jasmine muttered. Both names fit that monster.

Sometime later, maybe even a day, Jasmine still sat on the couch. Weak and shaky, she couldn't cry anymore. But at least her pants had dried and the couch, too. Mostly. It reeked like a diaper pail.

The door opened. The Witch-Devil entered the room carrying a bowl and a glass. Jasmine shook off her stupor and stared eagerly at the bowl while she struggled to her feet.

Without comment, Witch-Devil set it on the floor and motioned for Jasmine to put her hands out. She pulled a kitchen knife from her pocket. Cut the plastic from Jasmine's wrists.

Jasmine wished she could punch the woman and run out the door. But she realized her arms hung useless. For a moment, she didn't feel a thing. Then blood flowed. "O-Ow!" A million knives stabbed from her shoulders to fingertips. Her arms trembled uncontrollably. Spasmed at her sides.

"You're gonna shut up if you wanna eat." The Witch-Devil gave her an evil look.

Jasmine clamped her lips shut. Guess they needed to be tied, too.

"Shake 'em out."

Jasmine tried to obey. Her arms felt like weights hung from them. Suddenly lightheaded, she sat down hard on the floor.

The Witch-Devil left the bowl and glass on the floor and pulled a key out of her jeans pocket. She shook it at Jasmine. "It'll be locked this time. Your visitor is in deep crap." She grabbed the kitchen knife and left the room, slamming the door so hard it shook the nearby wall. The sound of the key locking the door from the outside made Jasmine wince. Her growling stomach refocused her thoughts.

Feeling inched back to her hands and arms. Jasmine devoured the soup and downed the glass of water. The soup was hot, and she burned her tongue. She barely tasted it. It was white so probably had milk in it. She was allergic. But she had no choice. If she reacted, she hoped it would be a stomachache versus not being able to breathe. How long ago had she had that dairy-filled ice cream instead of the dairy-free sorbet? The hours smeared together like gel ink on paper not given time to dry.

Even though her stomach rumbled with discomfort, her thoughts cleared. Her headache eased. But horror plagued her. How had she been bad? Did she hurt Cienna or her brother at the campground? Had her parents sent her here? She shuddered as she tried to pull up memories of her last sensible hours. Maybe this was a camp for bad teenagers. How would she ever survive? And where was Cienna? Her phone was gone too. "I'm so sorry, Mom. For whatever I did so wrong. Please let me come home."

Jasmine's arms ached. How long would she stay untied? Did she have time to explore? As she studied the room, she moved her arms in circular motions. A door across from the entrance looked like it led to a closet. To her relief, inside she discovered a toilet and very small sink. There would be no more peeing her pants if they let her move around. She used the toilet. Crammed her head under the faucet to drink as much as she could. Her brain still didn't feel quite right, but strength started to return. She had to figure out how to get out.

There were no windows in the bathroom. A small one lined the bedroom wall. Hope filled her heart as she rushed to it. Behind the curtain, there was glass. Behind the glass, a brick wall.

She pounded on the window in frustration. She let the curtain fall. Tears filled her eyes. Feeling her stomach give a final revolt, she rushed to the toilet and threw up. She sat on the dirty floor next to the gross toilet. "Breathe slowly, deeply. That's it." Her mom had coached many times when she was panicked or upset and sick. "You'll be okay, Jasmine."

She panted. Tried to focus on deep breathing. She needed to keep any food still left in her stomach there, or she would be too weak to even move. Maybe she could even die. What would that be like?

Later, sitting in the corner by the window-that-wasn't, she fell asleep and dreamed of the year it had snowed on Christmas Eve. Unusual in the Pacific Northwest.

At five, Jasmine had just started kindergarten when Mom woke her up and opened the window shade. Jasmine stared. Their front porch was covered with waves made of white stuff she'd only seen in books. Trees in their yard had turned white. The cold seeped through the window and she shivered.

She threw herself into her mother's arms. "Let's go play in the white!"

Mom laughed. "Come on. Let's find you some warm clothes."

Jasmine tugged her mom over to her closet and drawers. They picked out the thickest sweater and jeans they could find. Mom grabbed a long pair of thermal underwear. Banging noises reverberated from the hallway where her older sister and brother dug through the closet for boots. "That's mine!" Seth yelled. He sounded like he was buried in a blanket.

"His head must be inside the closet." Mom laughed. "These go on over your undies." She handed her the pink thermals decorated with tulips. "Same with the shirt, okay? I need to go check on things out there. I'll be back."

Excited, Jasmine pulled on the garments . . . backward. They felt a little odd, but she still pulled on her jeans. Or tried too. No matter how much she tugged as she hopped around the room, they wouldn't go up past her thighs.

"You must have got fat." Seth stood in her open doorway. His arms crossed at his chest and he wore smirk on his face. At nine, he knew how to dress himself.

Jasmine stuck her tongue out at him. "I'm not fat. At least I don't have boobs."

"Shut up, Jazz! I don't have stupid boobs either!"

She eyed his chubby figure and crossed her arms. She tried to stomp her feet. Unfortunately, with her jeans only halfway up her legs, she tripped and landed on her behind on the floor. Kicking at her closet door, she wailed. "Mom!"

Seth scooted out of sight right before Mom appeared, exasperation on her face. She helped Jasmine up and sat her on the bed, pulling the jeans off. "You're not fat. Just growing, and with the extra layer of thermals, these jeans don't fit anymore. Let's get another pair."

She found a looser pair of pants and helped Jasmine into them. She pulled the sweater over Jasmine's head and gave her a quick hug. "I love you, my Jazzy. Now let's go make a snowman and dance."

Later, Seth and Jasmine were tossing fairly friendly snowballs at each other. He helped her make enough snow bricks to make a cool wall while Mom finished the snowman with a carrot nose. At twelve years old, Amelie had grudgingly joined them, then decided to play with friends down the street and abandoned them.

Dad made popcorn that night and Jasmine sat in front of the Christmas tree in her warm, fuzzy blue pajamas with feet. She wondered how long it would be until Santa came.

Jasmine knew she was loved. She understood where she

belonged and loved her family with as much love as a five-year-old could manage. And as she awoke with her back pressed to the wall and her butt as sore as when she had fallen that day in her bedroom, her heart ached wondering what had gone so horribly wrong?

CHAPTER THREE
Melissa

MELISSA CHECKED THE TIME on her phone. The girls had been gone two hours, much longer than the half-hour they'd promised. She noticed Mari glancing at her phone as well. An uneasy feeling stirred. Catching up on each other's lives made time pass far too quickly. Sometime during their talk, ten-year-old Kai had slipped away and was sitting at a nearby picnic table playing with his handheld game system. It needed replaced. His parents insisted he save money for half of a new one first. With how fast his thumbs moved, Melissa was surprised the device didn't break. How did they make those systems strong enough to sustain the boy's battering?

Melissa stood. "Look at the time. It's pretty dark." She sent a quick text to Cienna. No answer. She hit the dial button. "Where are the girls?" She listened to the ring in her ear. It sounded louder than usual. The phone clicked over to Cienna's voicemail.

"Cienna doesn't have her phone." Kai didn't look up from his game. "It's in the tent."

"What?" Melissa's husband, Jimmy, gave their son a cross look. "How do you know that? And what are you doing

24

anyway? Don't you have a book to read? Something about nature, maybe?"

Kai shrugged. Eyes glued to the screen. "I found it under her pillow. She forgot it."

Melissa strode to the girls' tent, unzipped it, and plucked the phone off Cienna's sleeping bag where Kai had tossed it. Silenced. There were several texts from people Melissa didn't know. Conversations she couldn't follow. She pulled up the notifications from Snap Chat and saw that several of Cienna's "friends" had posted updates. And of course, there was her own text and missed call on the screen staring blankly back at her. Instagram had also been busy. She looked for Facebook and then remembered Cienna telling her she never used it anymore. Too many parents were creeping on it these days.

"I'll call Jasmine." Mari's usually calm voice raised a notch. "We texted a bit." Melissa glanced out of the open tent door. After a moment, she received a worried frown. "It went straight to voicemail."

"I guess we'll have to go get them." Jimmy stood from his camp chair, rubbed his lower back, and stretched. "Didn't they just go to the store?"

"For ice cream." Melissa exited the tent, still looking at Cienna's phone, confusion reigning. "How could she forget her phone? She never does that."

"Signal isn't the best here." Ken, Jasmine's dad stood. "That's probably why she left it behind."

"Come on, Kai." Melissa scurried around, grabbing her jacket, phone, and purse. "We're going for a car ride."

Kai mumbled. He stood and joined Melissa in the car. As soon as he'd buckled his seatbelt, he returned to his game, his thumbs flying over the keyboard.

They took two cars and drove two different directions in case the girls waylaid their route. But the town was small, and within twenty minutes they had circled the whole area, connected by cell phone. No sign of them.

They met on the side of the road near the campsite, and Ken walked over to Melissa and Jimmy's car. He shook his head slowly. "Mari called the police. She's talking to them now."

Her vision blurry with tears, Melissa buried her face in her shaking hands.

CHAPTER FOUR
Cienna

THE ROOM WAS LIGHTER when Cienna awoke. Although there were no windows in the barn room, she saw more of her surroundings. Startled, she noticed a small bed with a pillow on it in one corner. A sink hung on the wall in the other corner. Her body ached from her perch on the floor. Why hadn't he tied her near the bed instead? What an animal! Her stomach growled. She tried to yell, but her voice still wasn't strong. It probably wasn't even carrying outside the barn. Sasquatch had gotten her. And now what?

She pushed herself to sit up higher and move her neck around. There had to be something in the room she could use to get her hands free. With numb hands and any movement sending painful sparks up her arms, she tried to move her hands up and down and rub the rope against the pole to fray it. Like she'd seen in movies. With no feeling in them, she couldn't even tell for sure if they were moving. She grunted and wiggled in the hopes of getting some feeling back. Some feeling returned, painfully. Her legs weren't bound, so she wiggled them up and down and bounced her hips on the floor. If she moved enough, maybe the rope around her wrists would loosen.

Her bladder signaled that if she couldn't get to a toilet soon, she would be in trouble. She took a deep breath. Counted to five. Then she counted to five again. She took a deep breath and willed her bladder to hold steady. If she didn't think about it, the urge would stop.

But stop it didn't.

Cienna knew she was going to pee her pants any second. To her relief, Mike finally opened the door. Light poured in. She blinked. Suddenly, things seemed a little more hopeful. At least he hadn't hit her yet or tried to touch her chest. Maybe she could go back to the campsite now.

Mike had a mug in his hands. She looked at it longingly. It smelled like coffee. She hated coffee but was so thirsty, she would drink it anyway.

He stood over her and gave her a little smile. "How're ya feeling?"

"I have to pee. Can we go to the house now? Can I call my parents? Please? And I'm hungry too." She wasn't as hungry as she should be, but she was looking for any reason that might encourage him to loosen her. If reasoning was even possible with the man.

He paused, as if considering. "I'm not sure we're ready for that yet, sweetie."

"I'm not your sweetie." Her voice cracked. "I'm not." She was going to pee her pants right there on the barn floor door. How mortifying.

"Shh." Mike set his coffee on the floor. "Now, now. I think I might have an answer for ya."

He turned and left. She opened her mouth to yell again. He'd left the door open, so instead she tried to peer through it to see the rest of the barn, and hopefully outside. He returned carrying a bucket. "You can pee here."

She stared at him. "What?"

"I'll help ya."

The fear in her heart swelled, and she almost choked.

"No. I need a toilet." Maybe she should try talking softly to him. When she was on her feet, she would kick him in the crotch. Like her daddy had always told her to do. She reconsidered peeing in the container. If she did what he said, he would have to untie her. She could make a run for the door.

As if reading her mind, Mike turned and kicked the door closed. Sudden silence. "Where is Mrs. Mike? Can't she help me?"

He smiled as he went around the pole to untie her. "Mrs. Mike is baking today. Maybe I can bring ya something later if yer good. I've learned not to disturb her when she's baking." She could hear the grin in his voice. "That woman is a whirlwind in the kitchen. I don't get in her way anymore!"

He untied her and helped her stand up. He rubbed her arms briskly. Cienna wobbled and found that she could barely move her legs. She wouldn't be able to run anyway. Her face flushed.

Mike pulled down her pants and her underwear. Mortified, she covered herself with her hands and blinked back tears. He pulled off her shoes and her pants. The need to relieve herself was too strong. She refused to pee herself standing up. She sat on the bucket and released her muscles, letting a heavy stream flow. She covered herself the best she could and looked down. He handed her a handkerchief to wipe and then pulled her to her feet. "It's okay, Cienna. I won't hurt ya. Trust me. I'll help ya get dressed." He sounded moody now.

He again tied her hands behind the pole. She closed her eyes. He took his time and gently put her underwear back on and worked them up to her hips. He hummed the entire time. Once she was covered, she felt better and opened her eyes.

He gazed at her, his eyes sparkling. "So beautiful."

At his words, tears filled her eyes and dribbled down her cheeks. He liked her. She was in big trouble.

He immediately looked remorseful and reached up to wipe them away. "Honey, I'm so sorry. I don't want to make ya cry." He almost looked like he was going to cry himself.

Cienna was crying too hard to yell at him for calling her "honey." She wasn't his "honey." She was just a girl he kept tying up in his barn. Would she ever get outside again? Rage filled her stomach. Rose to her chest. Crowded her throat.

"Sh-shhh." Mike tried to comfort her. "Listen, if yer a good girl, I'll bring ya some food."

She managed to stop crying, but her stomach betrayed her and growled at the mention of food. "O-kay, okay."

Mike helped her sit up. Her pants still lay on the floor. He didn't seem to notice. He patted her head and sat next to her. He told her stories about how the bully next door growing up hurt him regularly. "I would never do that to anyone. How could someone do that?" He seemed lost in thought for a moment. "Maybe his dad was bad to him. I don't get it."

Cienna's stomach growled loudly.

Mike stood up. Looked at her directly in the eye. "If ya want food, ya need to thank me."

Cienna started to shake her head. Then realized he was serious. "Um-thank you for what?"

He puffed his chest out. "I saved ya from Roger. He was up to NO GOOD. And I brought ya the bucket and made ya feel better. Now I'm going to have a fresh cinnamon roll, and if ya want one, ya better thank me first." He breathed deeply. "Oh yeah. I can almost smell the ones coming out of the oven now. Mrs. Mike is amazing in the kitchen."

Dumbfounded, Cienna stared at him. After a moment of strained silence, she stammered, "T-T-Thank you."

"For?" He crossed his arms and tapped his foot, staring at her.

Cienna cleared her throat. Coughed. Almost choked. Her shoulder cramped painfully. He was serious. To get food, she had to thank him. Whaaaat? She took a deep breath. She wanted to kick him, but he was out of reach. She thought of her recent mortification. She thought of being naked when no other person had seen her that way. Cienna pondered him telling her she was going home but instead driving her to a remote farm. He had tied her to a pole and left her alone on a dark barn floor all night. "I-I thank you." She couldn't look him in the eye. She took a very deep breath. "T-Thank you for saving me from Roger—" She spoke the rest hurriedly, looking at the ground. "Bringing me the bucket."

Mike grinned widely. He came forward, and gently shook her shoulder. "That-a girl." Then he spun quickly and was out the door, slamming the brace across it, and whistling as he walked away.

Bastard.

CHAPTER FIVE
Rose

ROSE SAUNTERED INTO THE KITCHEN and eyed the table, the catch-all. It hosted dishes and piles most of the time and remained the main reason visitors had another entrance around the back of the house. One out of sight of the road and visible only after going down a thick, tree-lined driveway. At least that's what Kella claimed. Rose never could be sure when she and Sam lied. Constantly, she suspected.

"You're all a mess." Kella moaned frequently. The woman saw the house of girls as her cross to bear. So much to put up with! Rose almost smiled, thinking of the ridiculous groaning and the recitation that always followed. "Our guests deserve better. So, this is your area. You stay out of that side—" she hooked a thumb over her shoulder. "—until you're called to visit with them." And blah, blah and so forth. Rose learned quickly to tune Kella out.

The door to "that side" was near Rose now. The girls were let in and out as needed, but only by Kella's key. They avoided it as much as possible.

Rose joined Amber and Charli. They sat around the table eating stale doughnuts and drinking coffee. After Roger brought in a new girl two days ago, Sam had thrown her into the TC room.

"Maybe she ran away from home." Charli downed a cup of coffee. Rose pushed the doughnut box toward her. She waved it away. "Like Nia did."

"Nah." Rose tapped her foot and grabbed a doughnut. "I talked to her. She's scared spitless. Not everyone has a crappy home, Charli." At seventeen, Rose was the oldest of the group. She overheard them calling her "Mama Rose" when they thought she couldn't hear. One of the few good things about this place.

Two other pairs of eyes met hers. "You talked?" Amber laughed. "Why? You want a beating?"

Rose shrugged. "She's scared. Geez. Don't you remember? But then she got loud, and I had to go . . . " She didn't mention the second time she'd visited Jasmine to take her a soda.

"Stay out of trouble, Rose." Charli closed her eyes briefly and sighed. "Remember the last time."

"As if I could forget." Rose couldn't move for hours after Sam had taken her to the shed out back and beat her. Although the shed was at least forty feet from the house, the other girls claimed they'd heard the whole thing clearly.

Afterward, Sam threw her over his shoulder. Brought her back to the house. He tossed her on the TC. He locked the door, telling everyone that they would suffer the same fate if they checked on her. "Leave her alone!" He'd grabbed two beers from the fridge and slammed the front door behind him. His green van squealed down the driveway.

Kella took his threat seriously and stayed out of the TC room. Rose remembered hearing her screech several times over a few days. "Rose deserves to be in there! No one gets in the way of discipline. Sam was goin' after Charli and Rose should've stayed outta it!"

The girls found the key to the room and snuck in an ice pack, water and food . . . when Rose could finally eat. A fear hovered that Kella would find the key moved slightly out of place. All hell would certainly break loose. But Kella never figured out that Rose had a band of angels in the house.

The morning after the beating, the girls resourcefully halved and pooled some of the pills Kella made them take twice a day. Charli snuck in and helped Rose hold her head up to swallow and chase them down with water. For the first many hours, Rose could only lie on the TC and moan.

Another resident stumbled down the stairs and into the kitchen. At eleven, Bee was the youngest. She waved a greeting. Which was nice because lately she'd been sporting a real attitude. "Kella's coming."

The large woman stumbled into the room. Almost shoved Bee out of her way. She held a small, zipped cosmetic bag. The girls eyed it closely. Finally, time for meds. Sometimes, it was too long between doses, and they started feeling sick. Once Kella had run out completely. They felt gross for hours before she brought them more. Some threw up and had cramps and diarrhea. Amber went to sleep and was so hard to arouse, the girls panicked and finally splashed water on her face to make her wake up enough to take the pills that had just arrived.

Per protocol, they lined up. Rose, as the oldest, stepped to the front of the line. After struggling with the caps, juggling pills, and sometimes losing a few on the kitchen floor, Kella recently developed a new system. She now divided their doses into small baggies ahead of time. Twice a day, they each got one. The morning bag held a blue pill, a large white one, and a green one. The evening bags held another blue and white.

"Did the new girl get hers?" Nia entered the kitchen just in time to get in line.

Kella scowled. "That's none of your business. There's an order to things, you know." After handing out the baggies, she sat at the kitchen table and lit a cigarette.

"Why do you have to do that in here?" Bee scrunched her nose.

Kella glared. "Just for that, you get the crappiest jobs today, so you better shut it up unless you want more."

Bee glanced at the refrigerator, where the assigned chore list was already waiting. She fell silent. Glared back at Kella. Leaned against the kitchen wall.

"I have good news for you girls!" Kella tapped her cigarette on the side of the table. "So shut up enough to listen. We're gettin' better quarters!"

"What's that mean?" Rose rolled her eyes, then grinned. "Amber stole the last quarter I had." The girls giggled.

Kella drew deeply on her cigarette. She blew a mouthful of smoke in Rose's direction. Rose turned her head away. She'd been at the farm longer than any of the other girls, and sometimes Kella treated her like crap on purpose. Especially when Sam was paying more attention to Rose than to her. But Rose had long ago run out of ideas on how to fix that.

"We're building!" Kella bellowed. "You girls don't deserve it, so I don't understand what the heck Sam is thinkin', but we're making a second place down the road. So, you'll have visitors there in nice rooms with new furniture and beds. Also, hot-tubs and a nice bar. New TVs. You'll be spoiled sick. I tried to tell him you don't deserve it, but he says we'll get paid better. And then I suppose you all should have new clothes too." She muttered. "High class trash!"

"New clothes?" Nia eyes shone.

Kella pushed her chair back while the girls exploded into chatter about the new things they might see in a new place.

"I just want to go home." Bee mumbled this quietly, arms crossed as she leaned on the wall.

Kella jumped up, knocking the kitchen chair over hard on the floor. She stepped over to Bee, who had shrunk back further against the wall. Kella put her lit cigarette close to the girl's frightened face. Bee's eyes almost crossed as she watched it slowly move toward her nose. She turned her face to the side. "Well, I do." Her chin lifted.

Rose wished she could send thoughts to shush the younger girl. Would they put Bee on the TC with the new girl? She'd never seen two girls in the room before.

Kella swung hard, slapping Bee's cheek. Bee's lips quivered.

Her chest tight, Rose moved closer. "Bee didn't mean it, Kella."

Kella quickly swung around and focused on Rose. Bee ducked to the other side of the kitchen.

"Like I said, none of you deserve a new place." Kella shook her head, as if befuddled with the whole situation. "You deserve to live in that shed. Or maybe not at all! What do you think about that? Get this now and don't say one more thing." She huffed, her cigarette burning closer to her fingers, her face red. "This is your home. No one WANTS any of you because you are garbage. Garbage! You're lucky to have a place to sleep. And what about your pills? No one will give you those but me, but, by golly, you don't even appreciate it! Maybe I should make you go without those again for a few days. Now get!"

The girls scattered.

CHAPTER SIX
Cienna

WHEN MIKE VISITED AGAIN, he carried a cinnamon roll in a napkin and a large glass of water. After he untied Cienna's arms, she wolfed down the roll and drained the glass. No baseball hat today. Just clean jeans and a white tee-shirt. His hair curled at the ends. Cienna studied him. To escape, she needed to learn more. But in the meantime, her body protested about her hours of crouching on the floor. She intended to do something about that first.

"Thank you for the food and water." It startled her when she realized that she truly was grateful. Surely being tied in a barn earned her basic needs. But he could have just as easily ignored her.

Mike beamed. "Well. A fast learner, aren't ya? I told ya that I would take care of ya, didn't I?"

"Okay." A beat of silence. "Would-would there be a way that I could . . . get a longer rope maybe? Sit on the bed sometimes or go to the sink?" Perhaps he would let her gain some freedom one small step at a time.

He grew thoughtful and sighed. "I'm not sure we're ready for that yet."

Cienna wanted to scream at him. Ready for what exactly? She would still be under his control, and obviously, she wasn't getting out of the barn anytime soon. What the heck was his issue?

Another tactic, perhaps? "Will you tell me a story? Tell me more about when you were growing up. Or tell me what the house and farm look like. It's lonely out here." The last sentence she choked out and immediately grew anxious. He might take that to mean he should visit more often.

Mike grinned and slid to the floor, his back against the door. "I'm sorry about that, darlin'." He grinned. "Being lonely was not the idea."

"Well, what was the idea?!" Cienna immediately regretted her words. Why did she always have to say her first thought? Her dad said she was impulsive. She really did need to keep it in check.

"I want to be friends. I think we get along real well. And ya know, sometimes I git lonely too."

"Wh-What kind of friends?" She wasn't dumb. Everyone knew that most abductions didn't end well for the one taken.

Mike grinned again and scooted forward until he could touch her foot. She resisted kicking him. "I guess we never got yer pants and shoes back on. But maybe that's a good thing."

Her heart skittered. What did he mean? "Are-Are you going to rape me?" Her greatest fear, finally out in the open. She knew a girl in school who'd been raped. Her life had spiraled out of control and then she tried to kill herself.

Mike's head snapped up. His jaw dropped. "Oh no. I have scared ya." He shook his head, looking regretful. Reached out and gently cupped her cheek. "Sweetie, I saved ya from that Roger because you are worth far more than what he intended. I will keep ya safe. Don't be afraid."

Cienna forced herself to not cringe and met his eyes. Maybe if she did that enough, he would start feeling guilty.

Still maintaining the eye contact, Mike picked up her foot and started massaging it. "There now. Everything will be okay."

She jumped at first, but then relaxed. After forced and cramped positions on the floor for many hours, her muscles welcomed the touch. She tried to seem indifferent or even pull her foot away. But now she felt sleepy. Closing her eyes, her head leaned back slightly against the captivity pole. A huge sense of relief came. Things definitely could be worse.

Cienna barely felt it when Mike set her foot down and picked up the other one, starting another massage. But eventually the need to use the bathroom woke her up fully. She opened her eyes. "I need to pee." She used an apologetic tone so as not to upset him. "Real bad."

He gently set her foot down. Looked her in the eye. "Would ya like to sleep on the bed tonight?"

Her heart leapt. A mattress! Pillow! Warmth! "Y-Yes!" It popped out more enthusiastically than she intended. But she had shivered throughout the night, her muscles complaining the whole time.

Mike smiled. "Then let me help." He released her arms, grabbed the clean, empty bucket from the corner of the room, and pulled her to her feet. She wobbled a bit and started toward him. She would let him help without complaint if it meant she could lie on the mattress that night. She would cover her privates with her hands again and close her eyes. Everything would be all right.

She pulled her underwear off without help. This time, he helped her settle on the bucket. He backed up slightly, his eyes averted. Her heart pounded loudly. She was sure he could hear it. She closed her eyes tightly, and got it done.

When they were finished, he led her over to the sink and allowed another glass of water. She gulped gratefully, managing a "thank you" afterward. How long had it been since she had downed that soda with Jazz? No idea.

Mike grew impatient. He jerked her back over to the
pole and tied her arms behind it again without letting her put
her underwear on. He left the room, slammed the door, and
slid the board in place.

Cienna was left alone with her thoughts . . . and her fears.

She later heard his truck engine start, and as soon as it
was quiet, she yelled as loud as she could. She pulled hard at
her restraints. Hours later, her voice hoarse and her wrists
welted from her struggle, she heard the truck return. She fell
silent, but tears gathered in the corner of her eyes. Mike came
back into the barn room and untied her silently. She wanted
to hit him but her arms were numb. He saw the welts on her
wrists and rubbed them gently while shaking his head. He
didn't seem angry, and she was grateful.

"Can I have my underwear?" She kept her voice sweet.

"No. Yer more beautiful without them."

Now those stupid tears ran down her cheeks. Shame
filled her. No one had ever seen her like this. Her body was no
one else's business but her own.

He led her to the bed, tied one wrist to a metal loop on
the wall, and let her lie down. It felt like a cloud as she sunk
into it, and the pillow comforted her sore shoulders and neck.
With her free arm, she pulled the blanket up to her chest and
instantly felt better.

Mike had brought an ice pack for her cheek, still swollen
from Roger's slaps. He held it there for several minutes while
he looked at her gently. "Please stop hurting yerself."

As weariness overcame her, she found herself agreeing
with him. She fell asleep.

Cienna dreamed of her parents, Jazz, and her brother.
They were on a raft, and despite her dad's best efforts to slow
them down, they approached the falls quickly. There seemed
no way to avoid them. Jazz screamed and jumped overboard
as Cienna cried and reached for her. She grabbed empty air.
The rest of them teetered on the edge of the falls before tilting

enough to rush down. Cienna watched her brother fly off the raft, then her mom. The whole time, Roger stood on a cliff above them, laughing and laughing. She woke up, sweaty and disoriented. She jerked her hand. Realized it was fastened securely to the wall. Oh yeah. She was in a barn room with a friendly but crazy man sitting in a house nearby. Still, things could be so much worse.

"Thank you," she whispered. "Thanks for saving me from Roger."

Chapter Seven
Jasmine

JASMINE'S HOURS BLENDED. Her only highlights were the occasional quiet talk with Rose, who came in to check on her, and the food that appeared twice daily. Most days. The Witch-Devil, whom Rose said was really Kella, brought her milk. She tried not to drink it. When she did, hives broke out on her arms and chest and the big woman yelled at her for scratching. But she couldn't stop, especially not in her sleep. Rose caught sight of them once. After that, she snuck Jasmine a soda once a day or so.

After the third time hives appeared, Jasmine refused to drink milk. Her epi-pen was back at the camp. She could stop breathing.

"You ungrateful brat!" The Witch-Devil's face reddened, and she yanked Jasmine's glass away. Milk sloshed down the sides and onto the floor. Jasmine bore the consequences of continual wrath as bravely as she could.

After the scary woman left, she drank a delicious soda hiding under the couch cushion and squashed the can, hiding it under the TC so Rose wouldn't get in trouble. But Jasmine was still always thirsty and poised her mouth open under the bathroom faucet at every opportunity.

The food helped make her strong, but also made her feel sleepy and sometimes dizzy. After each meal, escape came. She turned her face into the couch cushions and disappeared into a mostly wonderful dreamland. Both her stomach and brain looked forward to meals. Something must be in her food, and it kept her sane. Without it, she would probably die.

Jasmine often heard voices underneath the floor. Other girls? Was Cienna down there? And she heard the Witch-Devil yelling as well. Sometimes there were noises in the rooms around her. Laughing, music, thumps, swearing. She longed to get out of prison and join them.

At last, the Witch-Devil came back. Time to start her "training." Jasmine had just eaten, so her brain was fuzzy. What training did she mean?

The woman yanked on Jasmine's arm and pulled her up off the couch. She grabbed her chin, forcing her to look up into the evilest eyes Jasmine had ever seen.

"You and me need an understanding. If you misbehave, or you try to leave here, you'll get locked back in this room for good. Or maybe even better, the shed. You'll become a skeleton, and we won't give a crap. Understand?"

Jasmine nodded. "Y-Yeah. Okay . . . "

The Witch-Devil shook Jasmine's chin back and forth.

"Ouch!" She tried to pull away.

Sudden release. She stumbled back.

"Ouch?" The Witch-Devil sneered. "Ouch? You haven't seen ouch yet." She grinned. "You will, though." She threw her head back and laughed. Jasmine wondered how to answer. She seemed to expect one. What would Cienna say? Her friend would probably punch her in the face. Jasmine looked at the floor. Why couldn't she be more like Ci?

"And another thing." The Witch-Devil ran her hand through her short, dark hair. She scratched her rear end and yanked up the back of her slacks. "Your name is Bay."

"W-What?" Jasmine laughed. "No, it's not. My name is Jasmine! Sometimes Jazz . . . "

Her torturer shoved her against the wall and held her in place with her heavy body. Jasmine's breath caught. Her heart wanted to pound out of her chest. "I-uh-I . . . "

The Witch-Devil bent her face down very close to Jasmine. At the smell of her smoky breath, Jasmine recoiled. She couldn't move. She clamped her mouth closed and held her breath.

"Not anymore," She hissed.

Legs shaking so hard Jasmine knew they would barely hold her weight, she managed to nod. Bay. All right. Not such a bad name. And no escaping either. Got it.

The Witch-Devil held her there a few seconds longer. Her eyebrows squinched together. Then she harrumphed and quickly stepped back. Jasmine almost fell but caught herself and righted her body against the wall. Her arms trembled. She stared at the floor. Her face flushed.

"Don't get stupid on me." The Witch-Devil turned and lumbered out of the room. She didn't close the door behind her.

Jasmine nodded and took a deep breath. She sprang through the bedroom door behind her captor. Eyes wide, she noted a hallway with pictures on the walls, other bedroom doors, a big comfy chair near a window—a reading nook. She was on a landing. There were two stairways. One led downstairs and the other up to another floor.

In front of them, a door slammed. Jasmine jumped and almost ran into the Witch-Devil, who had stopped walking.

A girl about Jasmine's age stood in the hallway. She had thin, straight brown hair and freckles. She wore jeans and a button up blouse. It was too big—it draped down to her thighs.

"Uh- hi." She raised a cleaning rag and a bottle of glass cleaner. "I'm cleaning. Promise."

"Hi, yourself!"

Did the fat woman always yell? Geez. When the girl smirked, Jasmine tentatively smiled. She hovered behind the Witch-Devil, not sure what was next.

"What do I tell you about slamming doors?" The Witch-Devil said in a very-controlled, now non-yelling voice.

The other girl shrugged. "Sorry. Accident. Who's this?"

Roughly, Kella grabbed Jasmine's arm and pulled her to her side. "Amber, meet your new roomie. This here is Bay."

Jasmine rolled her eyes. Sighed. Amber giggled.

"Huh." Amber nodded. "I'm sure her name is Bay. What a stupid name. Is she going to clean windows too?"

"Shut up. She gotta clean herself up before you can bully her into your work."

"Yup." Amber held her nose. "Phew-ee. You stink. The bathroom's back there." She pointed behind Jasmine to a large bathroom with a black and white checkered floor.

"She sure does." The Witch-Devil snorted. "You go find her a change of clothes." She turned and shoved Jasmine into the bathroom. Closed the door behind her. "Hurry up. I ain't got all day."

Alone in the bathroom, Jasmine took a deep breath. There was a window in here, too. Hope fluttered in her heart. She hurried to it and peered out. She seemed to be on the second floor of a large, white house. Was there any way out? The roof sloped down out of her sight. How long was the slope? How far was the drop to the ground?

A movement caught her attention—a man on a ladder in the front yard cutting branches off a tree. As if sensing her, he turned, grinned, and waved his pruners in the air.

"Help." She mouthed the words, hoping he'd read her lips. But understanding suddenly dawned. The man wasn't surprised to see her. He knew she was there. She gasped and backed away. Did he know the girls in the house got locked in rooms and slapped? Went without meals and water? Had drugs in their food?

The bathroom window was not an option right now. She quickly pulled the curtain closed, glad there was one, and used the toilet and shower. She knew her captor hovered in the hallway outside. Jasmine shuddered as she remembered being held against the bedroom wall by the sheer weight of her.

The warmth of the water brought tears. Grateful for the running water that covered the sounds of her sobs, Jasmine struggled to wash herself when all she really wanted to do was curl up in the corner of the shower and stay in the warmth of the water forever. She could live in the shower, couldn't she? And would it really matter if she ended up dying there too?

CHAPTER EIGHT
Cienna

CIENNA AWOKE TO FIND disgusting Roger standing in the doorway and leering. She screamed. He slammed the door behind him. Walked over to sit on the bed and slapped his hand over her mouth. "No one can hear you, girlie. Shut up."

She remembered well when he disciplined her in the van. She narrowed her eyes instead of telling him where to go. They spit fire.

"Feisty whore."

She gasped and stared up at him.

"Yeah, I thought so." He ripped her blanket off.

She lay there exposed, withering under his gaze. Her free hand twitched. Could she manage a left-handed punch? If he made any more moves to touch her chest again, she would knee him in the chin.

He nodded. "I see Mike is showing you what you really are." He put his nasty, dirty hand on her thigh.

Her heart raced. She couldn't breathe.

He was staring at her . . . *there*. "I'm gonna show you for real." He reached to yank up her shirt. "I'm gonna—"

The door opened, and Mike strolled in. "Knock it off,

Wyatt. It's not yer turn yet. And ya better leave now unless ya want yer nose up through yer brain."

Roger laughed, but he stood up. "Well then, you better get busy. Rules are she's mine for the taking if you don't."

Cienna whimpered. Roger had not been fooled. He knew Mike hadn't really touched her. The safety of Mike standing in the doorway beckoned her. Realization dawned. Time to be on stage. Swallowing hard, she blinked at Mike. "There you are. I've missed you. You've been gone too long. Come lie down, please . . . "

Mike grinned and strolled forward. She willingly scooted over toward the wall, and he lay on the bed with her.

Roger snickered as he left the room.

They were alone.

"Thank you." Her voice caught thinking about what might have happened.

Mike nodded. He seemed distracted as he placed his hand on her stomach, now bare, and moved it around in circles. His hand was warm, her stomach cool. Her insides clenched just a bit. He stilled, and then draped his arm across her stomach. She didn't move. Didn't complain. He had just saved her from Roger. By his side, she felt safe for now. Plus, she owed him. Cuddling for a little while couldn't hurt, could it?

Later, when she was alone again, with an extra lock Mike installed on the outside of the door to keep people out—now even he would need a key to get in—Cienna's thoughts whirled.

How had Roger known how to find her? What "rules" was he talking about? And, most troubling of all, why did Mike tell Roger that it wasn't his turn yet?

CHAPTER NINE
Melissa

THE TWO FAMILIES CONTINUED TO SEARCH. Although sympathetic, the campground owner grew unhappy about the publicity over two girls disappearing from the supposed safety of his land.

News crews lingered. Business dropped sharply.

He asked the families to leave the campground. He offered to place their missing posters at several places throughout the area. If the girls returned there, they would at least know how to reunite with their families. The families checked into a hotel.

Jimmy and Ken returned home for a short time. They gathered the girls' fingerprints from the Lost Child Kits completed at the Fair a few years ago and found recent pictures. They extended arrangements for their pets and gathered more clothing for their families. They contacted their supervisors at work, who thankfully understood and wished them well in the search. Melissa worked part time, but she didn't even bother calling her boss. She didn't care if she lost her job. Finally, on day five, after encouragement from Jimmy, she sent him a text.

He replied quickly. **We saw about Cienna on the news. Very sorry. Take all the time you need. We got a temp replacement. See you when you get back.**

That would never happen. Melissa would never leave Cienna's side again.

Each time she was near an outlet, she plugged in Cienna's phone to keep it charged. When not plugged in, it was in her pocket or her purse with the sound on loud. Nonetheless, she checked it constantly. She scoured her daughter's social media sites, hoping to find a clue. Any clue. The forensic policeman helped her turn on notifications for all the sites. Their team also monitored Cienna's accounts. Mari and Jimmy had so far kept Jasmine's accounts and time on social media limited. There wasn't any activity there to check—that they knew of. Melissa wondered if their daughter had found a way to override their rules. They had likely met a predator online.

Melissa sighed heavily. "It's an unsafe world and you two stepped right into it. Please come home!"

She posted the girls' pictures everywhere she could think of, online and off. She used savings to post advertising on the largest social media sites. And asked for shares. The ad with the girls' picture now had fifty thousand interactions and shares. That better keep going up. She authorized another budget increase on the ad. Every penny spent was well worth it.

Melissa and Mari helped search every day until they were too weary to move. What if the search team missed something? And what if that something was the key to finding them? They tailed along, sometimes forging their own trails, and always thanking the people in the town who helped. They wouldn't have made it without help.

A church in town started providing meals for their families, community searchers, and law enforcement. The Rydals hadn't attended church in recent years. Now she felt guilty. But they needed a miracle. If those people prayed for the girls anything like they prayed before meals, a whole host of angels must be at attention. "Now someone up there better make it happen." She nodded her head in determination.

"What, Mom?" Kai looked up from his game. She refocused on her son.

"Nothing."

She patted his head. He leaned against her shoulder. He'd returned to toddler clingy mode since Cienna disappeared. "Is she dead?" He asked once loudly in the General Store. Startled, Melissa turned her head so that he wouldn't see the tears springing to her eyes. The torment on her face. People stared then seemed to catch themselves and averted their eyes.

"I think she-they-got lost. That's why we didn't find them when we drove around. But lots of people are looking for them. In the meantime, we're taking a longer vacation."

Kai smiled hesitantly. She tried to smile back, knowing that if the girls could return, they would have long ago. Her heart felt like a brick.

Families from the church offered to watch Kai. And as much as Melissa hated having him out of her sight, she let him visit several homes for short times so she could search more. She walked around River Falls and asked questions, the whole time terrified that Kai would disappear too.

Without these kind people, Melissa would have forgotten to eat. She was never truly hungry anymore. Her jeans hung loosely. She asked Jimmy to bring her some from the box in the back of her closet, one size down.

Sleep became more difficult. Dark thoughts invaded dreams. The bleakness woke her. Often, she awoke with tears on her cheeks. Sometimes, she thought Cienna disappearing was a dream. She tore around the hotel room and even looked outside for her until Jimmy came out to get her. Reality hit hard then. She spent the rest of the night crying herself to sleep in his arms.

Guilt reached in. What could they have done differently? Why did they not insist that the girls stay at the campground on that hot evening instead of walking to the store for ice cream? It was all their fault.

Anger and blame also sent out ugly tentacles. The torment visited hourly.

"This is your fault," Melissa shouted at Jimmy after a particularly stressful day, one when they thought they had some clues that ended up completely unrelated. "You make us go camping every year. We should have all stayed at home and everything would have been fine."

He winced and yelled back. He left the hotel room, slamming the door behind him. Melissa sat on the bed and sobbed for an hour. Ridiculous. It was no more Jimmy's fault than her own. She spent the next thirty minutes texting him, trying to explain her anger, and finally apologizing.

She donned her hiking boots and headed to the campground to scan the familiar territory. After hanging at the campsite and reviewing the evening when their world collapsed, she sat by the river, now loud and scary. What had she missed?

When she awoke the next morning, Jimmy was curled on the floor. She cringed when she smelled him. "Getting drunk is not helpful."

"I know. It was stupid." He cried, and Melissa slid to the floor beside him. She cradled his head in her lap. "I miss her so much." He grabbed the tissue she passed him.

Her heart broke right alongside his.

On day six, a potential breakthrough came. Detective Miller called them early in the morning. "We found some items off the logging road, so apparently they went up that direction after the store. Can you come into the station?"

They rushed into clothes, knocked on Mari and Ken's door, and took Kai to one of the helpful families' house. Four worried parents sped to the police station.

"What if it's body parts?" Melissa's hair stuck up crazy-style. "Why can't they tell us on the stupid phone?"

Mari gasped loudly while Jimmy shushed his wife.

"I'm sorry, I'm sorry." Melissa sighed. "It has to be good news."

They didn't have long to wait before Miller greeted them and led them to his office.

"Did you find the girls?" Melissa crossed her arms. How would that news come about anyway? Wouldn't he have just told them that on the phone? Or were there sordid details best delivered in person? Miller nodded at the chairs. They sat.

He shook his head. "I'm sorry. We didn't find the girls. But we did find some clues. A smashed soda can was found up by the logging road. Half of an ice cream cone, and—" he paused. "Jasmine's cell phone was there, powered off and tossed to the side in the bushes."

White-faced, Melissa gasped. Covered her mouth. The walls suddenly felt very close. Even breathing became more difficult. Mari looked pasty-white, like she might pass out.

"Darn it!" Ken stood up.

"Please sit down." Miller gave him a sympathetic look.

He sat but perched on the edge of the chair. "They were kidnapped." He gritted his teeth. Put his face in his hands.

Miller nodded. "Probably. Nothing like this has ever happened in River Falls. But it does seem that if the girls had run away, we wouldn't have found the cell. We are pursuing the investigation as an abduction now. The lab is working on getting the fingerprints off the phone and soda can. Also, we'll be looking for clues on the cell phone itself. You know, photos, calls, things like that."

"Can we do an Amber Alert?" Melissa wrung her hands in her lap.

"Sadly, I'm afraid not." Miller shook his head. "In cases like this, on the first day certain parameters have to be met to issue one. We need an idea of a person or vehicle involved to issue those. I'm sorry. I hope we'll get there. Of course, the

Critical Reach bulletin has already been distributed to all the agencies. They're aware and watching for the girls."

He cleared his throat. "We've sectioned off the area. We found tire tracks and are looking at those, so maybe we'll get more vehicle information soon. I'm glad it hasn't rained, as we found all this so many days after they went missing. We had no idea before that they headed up that trail, although some searching was done in the area. We're taking photographs and following up on each lead. I'm sorry."

Their worst fears confirmed, the parents thanked him for the information and left. On the one hand, knowing the girls hadn't run away helped. On the other, it was even worse. They were very likely in serious danger.

Surely someone, somewhere, had seen the girls and would soon come forward. They could only hope.

CHAPTER TEN
Jasmine

JASMINE WORKED HARD to integrate herself into the household while still hoping to get home. She viewed anger from both the Witch-Devil and Sam, whom she had met officially soon after seeing him pruning the tree. Both of her captors got angry at the drop of a hat. She understood the need to lie low. To stay out of situations where she might end up back on the TC. That room was currently empty. Her second day off the TC, they forced her to clean it. She made sure to grab the soda cans from underneath the stinky couch. She didn't want her friend Rose in trouble.

In the room they shared, Jasmine and Amber each had a twin bed. That was a lot more than a lot of bad girls got, the Witch-Devil told her. "All you deserve is a place on the hard floor."

Jasmine still struggled to understand. Why she was so bad and what she had done? She couldn't remember, but it must have been very, very bad. Angrily, she often blamed herself. Her parents must hate her. It was the only conclusion that made any sense. But no matter how mad she got during the day, at night she was very sad and missed her whole family. If she could just talk to them, she would promise to behave if they let her come home.

She kept her tears as quiet as possible since Amber seemed to get irritated at her easily. She wondered if Rose cried every night. Or Bee? She heard that Bee was only eleven, even though she seemed fourteen. It appeared that Bee was the youngest in the house. Surely, she must cry.

When Jasmine awoke each morning and realized she was still at the white farmhouse, she grew irked again. But if she had to be there, she wanted the other girls to be nice to her. She talked to them whenever possible. She often volunteered to complete their assigned chores. Nia sometimes called Jasmine "mouse," but Jasmine didn't mind. She never had been brave or strong like Cienna.

"Amber," she whispered in the wee hours of one morning. She wasn't sure where the green van carrying Amber, Rose, and Sam had gone that night, but they had returned about 3:30 a.m. Amber had just kicked off some very tall heels, slithered out of a very tight, short skirt and halter top, and climbed into a tee shirt before crawling into bed.

"What, Bay?" Amber sounded impatient. "Why're you awake?"

Jasmine shrugged, then realized Amber couldn't see her in the dark. "Who else is here? Sam, Witch-Devil, Rose with red hair. You, me, Charli, who's the shorter one, and Bee. And then Nia? She has brown skin . . . "

"You got 'em all." Amber's voice muffled in her pillow. "Six of us now. It's your fault I gotta share my room. Why do you even care?"

"I don't know. Just wanted to know. What's your real name?"

With the dim light from the very small window toward the top of the bedroom wall, Jasmine saw Amber sit up, glare at her, and then flop back on her pillow, pulling her blanket up to her chin. "Teresa. Again. Why. Do. You. Care?"

Jasmine sat up in bed, drew her knees to her chin, and wrapped her arms around them. "My real name is Jasmine. My friend Cienna and my family sometimes call me Jazz. Do you think we'll forget our real names?" She couldn't imagine. But sometimes she was even starting to look up and respond when people called, "Bay."

Now that felt weird.

Amber laughed into her pillow. "Don't be dumb. You'll probably forget lots of things in the next few months. But really it's better to not remember too much."

Long after Amber fell asleep, Jasmine puzzled over her roommate's words.

CHAPTER ELEVEN
Cienna

CIENNA DEEPLY MISSED HER FAMILY, friends, and cats. She missed school. She even missed her backyard and bedroom. Although she had argued with her mom about the décor and furniture for weeks, they had reached a compromise. Cienna had painted one black wall instead of four. It was worth it when she got to pick out a new, glossy-black bedroom furniture set.

At home, she could go out with friends, take a walk, throw lunch in the microwave, read a book, wave the stick with the feather at the cats, make them chase the pen laser light, cruise around on Instagram, make a few crazy Snaps, and job search on her computer. She could even watch shows pretty much whenever she wanted.

Here, boredom ruled. Her body complained of constant hunger. Her muscles ached. She worried about Jazz and her family. She constantly tried to think of ways to escape. So far, the only viable idea was to gain more of Mike's trust and get into his house. He had to have a phone or a computer. She could email her mom. Or maybe he would be more comfortable in his house, give her more freedom, and she could run. She might be able to drive the truck if she could get the keys. But how to make him trust her more?

Mike found her wiping away tears that morning. "Didn't Mrs. Mike's homemade soup help ya? It always helps me when I have the blues."

She shook her head a little and then remembered that she should feel grateful for the weak chicken broth she drank the night before. It tasted like the time she had poured soup from a can into a pan and then added too much water. "Yes. That was delicious. Thank you so much."

"Well, then, why are ya sad?" Mike strolled over to where she was sitting on the bed. He sat next to her as he did most times now. With the sudden dip in the mattress, she shifted toward him. She quickly straightened. Hot anger exploded inside her. Enough was enough. How could she get out? Mike seemed to care for her somewhat. He certainly hadn't acted at all like Roger. He had never hit her. He didn't touch her in places he shouldn't. She decided to take a risk.

"I feel like crap." That was true. "I'm so dirty. I've never been this dirty. I need a shower. My arms hurt so much from being tied up, and I'm starting to think you don't trust me. I'm so upset." Her tears started in earnest.

Shock raced across Mike's face. "Don't trust ya? What do ya mean? I do! You have a bed! Sometimes ya can use the sink! And I'm keeping Roger away. Boy, that man is up to NO good. Aren't ya glad for that?"

Cienna forced herself to regroup. "Yes. I'm safe, and I owe that all to you. Thank you, Mike." She looked at him and sniffed. Wiped a tear from her cheek.

Mike touched her cheek gently, and she didn't jump away. "I would do anything for ya."

She believed him.

"Okay. May I please go see your house? I just need a shower to feel better. And I wouldn't mind meeting Mrs. Mike to thank her. She has been nice to make me food and everything."

Mike instantly jumped to his feet and paced back and forth. Cienna considered him carefully. Decided to push a bit further. "At home I take a shower every day." She folded her hands primly in front of her. "I would like to be clean and smell good...f-for you." She swallowed hard. He would probably want to "help her." But she felt disgustingly dirty, and her oily hair and underarms reeked. Besides, if she met Mrs. Mike, maybe the woman would help her. Maybe Mrs. Mike had no idea there was even someone in the barn. Was it possible?

"A shower." She decided to push. "Just one shower. Please. Then I will come right back to the barn with you. And you can-you can . . . lie with me on the bed again. That was okay. I-I liked that."

He looked at her for a long moment, deep in thought. "Okay. Mrs. Mike has a meeting in town after dinner. I'll come get ya then."

Mike turned quickly on his heel and, on the way out, knocked his red baseball hat off his head. He grinned and bowed before he scooped it off the floor and placed it back on his head. She smiled at him, understanding that she should be grateful for the entertainment. Mike closed the door firmly behind him and slid the board into place.

As hope flooded her heart, Cienna breathed a sigh of relief. Once she was outside the barn, she could get help and go home.

***

It was much later when Mike came to get her, but she was just glad he showed. He had followed through on everything so far, and she'd spent the whole afternoon feeling hopeful. Wondering how to thank him. Maybe she could thank him first, then find the right time to run.

It was dusky outside when he led her out of the barn. She couldn't believe she was actually going. He held her arm tightly, and she breathed the air deeply. A goat nickered nearby. She saw some cows in a meadow down from the house. The beautiful green of the fields and trees surrounded her. She wanted to lie on the grass and roll around. Mike must have sensed her delight. After they climbed the steps of the house, which was not so far from the barn, after all, he let her pause, turn back to the fields, and fill up her senses even more. Instantly, as she breathed deeply, peace filled her. It felt like a warm blanket wrapped around her heart. She blinked back tears. She was stuck. But there was always hope. Right?

They turned to enter the house. Why hadn't she pulled away and ran? But then, where would she go? It looked like a very large farm. There was no other house or structure in sight. For now, it was probably best to comply and gain his trust. She followed him into a large, yellow kitchen, with bright wallpaper and a small square table with four chairs near the front window.

Mike seemed nervous as she surveyed the clean but not fancy kitchen area. The paint would fall off the cupboards if she flicked it with her finger. The ugly linoleum floor peeled in spots. But still, she was grateful. She quickly scanned the room for a computer or phone, and then saw a yellow phone on the wall. Bingo. Should she lunge for it?

Mike quickly stepped between her and the phone and grabbed her arm. He turned her away. "Shower time." He sneered. He yanked her arm, pulling her from the kitchen into a family room that had a woodstove, two couches, a flatscreen, and a recliner. A quick glance out the window showed another building, possibly a house, some ways away. Her heart quickened. Neighbors! She panicked for a moment, thinking she had spoken aloud. If she had, Mike didn't seem to hear.

Her heart pounded louder when he pushed open the bathroom door, which was on one wall of the family room, and shoved her inside. He quickly slammed the door shut. She fell against the sink, ramming her hip into the countertop. Righting herself, she hit the light switch. A dull light came on over the sink, and a ceiling fan creaked to life. She breathed a sigh of relief. Was it possible that he would go elsewhere in the house or outside and she could escape? She stepped close to the door and put her ear against it. Jumped when she heard movement on the other side.

"Don't make me come in there. Just get it done."

"Okay."

Panic started in her belly. Moved quickly up to her chest. She used the toilet. Shed her clothes with her heart pounding harder each second. She turned the water on in the shower, stepping in before it even turned warm. There was a small window near the shower, but it looked too small to escape from. Thankful for the grinding fan, she reached out to slide it open quietly, but it wouldn't budge. Tears dripped down her face, blending with the water. More and more, it appeared her only escape might be befriending Mike and Mrs. Mike and winning her way into their house more often.

She could have stayed in the heat of the water forever, but Mike would come in. There was no lock on the door. She quickly found a bottle of shampoo and soap. She used an overabundance of shampoo in her efforts to scrub away all the dirtiness that she felt.

The knocking at the door came suddenly. "Hurry it up!"

"Al-Almost done!" But her hair wasn't rinsing quickly. The water pressure seemed low. She'd added too much soap. It was taking forever. Her massive and tangled-with-dirt curls were not helping.

He knocked at the door again, louder this time.

"I'm coming!" She turned the water off. Outside the shower, she only saw a hand towel. She yanked it off the holder by the sink and dried herself as best as she could before wiggling her still-damp body back into her dirty, now-too-big clothes. They reeked. Gross. She glanced in the mirror and noticed the fading bruise on the side of her face where Roger had hit her. Touching it gingerly, she wished for her makeup bag sitting in her backpack at the camp. It would have been nice to feel slightly human again.

With the thought of camp, and her family, tears threatened again. "Knock it off, Ci. Stay smart. You can figure this out."

The bathroom door opened without warning. She stepped toward the shower to get out of the way. Mike leaned in the doorway and crossed his arms over his chest. "Ya look like a drowned rat." He grinned.

"Well, yeah. There was only a small towel and my dirty clothes. What did you expect? Don't you even have a hairbrush I can use? I don't even think I got all the shampoo out of my hair . . . "

He growled and reached in to grab her arm, yanking her out of the bathroom.

"I'm sorry. I'm very sorry. I'm very glad I got to shower. I do appreciate it."

Mike's grip on her softened, although his journey to the front door with her in tow did not falter. "This is stressful, ya know." He stopped in the middle of the family room. "I'm sorry too that ya make me do all of this." He pulled her out into the kitchen and out the front door. Halfway back to the barn he said, "There should be a book on how to do it."

Cienna stopped suddenly and tried to yank her arm from his hand. "On what? A book on how to do what?" What exactly was Mike doing with her? And quite suddenly, he released her arm. They faced each other. Mike's hands were on his hips, and anger filled his face.

Cienna realized she was detached for the first time.

She turned and ran.

CHAPTER TWELVE
Mari

THE NEXT DAY BROUGHT unrelenting sun. Mari Jensen glared outside of the hotel window. The brightness gave a her a headache, and not for the first time, she resented it. As a psychologist, she understood the need to not enclose herself in darkness. As a mother, she wanted to bury herself in the closet and stay there. Ken wasn't in the room. She hoped he'd gone to the coffee shop on the corner to get them both some needed caffeine after a fitful night.

Her cell phone on the nightstand buzzed, and she ran to grab it. To her disappointment, the name she saw was Amelie's. Her oldest daughter rented a house with other girlfriends and was enrolled in summer classes at a Seattle college. Amelie had visited River Falls right after her sister had gone missing but had since returned to school.

"Am . . . " she breathed as soon as she picked up the phone. "Have you heard from your sister?"

"No, Mom. It's still on the news, and everyone is looking at me like I'm a weirdo. They feel sorry for me."

"Are you kidding me, Amelie? Your sister is missing, and all you can think about is how they're looking at you?"

"No." There was a sudden catch in her voice. "I guess . . . I was just hoping for some news . . . "

Mari softened. "Me too. Have you heard from your brother?" Sixteen-year-old Seth had stayed home because he hadn't wanted to go camping this year. His texts had been sporadic.

"Seth?" Amelie laughed. "He and Joe are playing video games. You know they are. He'll just hide behind the screen with his online friends." They were both quiet for a minute.

"He maybe shouldn't be alone much longer. I'll talk to your dad. Maybe we need to go home. Or maybe we should bring him here."

She heard Amelia choke back tears. "But you can't go home. What if Jasmine goes back to River Falls? She won't know where to find you."

The implications hit Mari's heart like a brick. Of course, the townspeople and the police department would contact them. But would they care for Jasmine like her mother would? Would Jasmine think they had given up the search? Would she think they had stopped loving her? These were all possibilities.

"Should I come back now?" Amelie's voice wavered.

Mari suddenly felt tired and worn down. The past two weeks had been the longest of her life. Would Amelie's support help? She knew her younger sister well and could help with the search. But as a mother, could Mari insist that her daughter take a leave from college and risk her grades? No.

"It's up to you. We know you want to be here, and we'd love to see you. But you have school. And don't you have finals coming up? I'm sure Jasmine would understand." Then she blurted out news they had just learned that day. "There are fingerprints on Jazz's cell phone that aren't Jasmine's and Cienna's. They belong to a man . . . a man the police are . . . familiar with."

Mari heard Amelie gulp and chided herself. She was too young to hear that. No, she wasn't. At nineteen, her oldest was an adult. And yet who could ever be adult enough to handle the disappearance of her younger sister? Had she told her too much? Maybe in person would have been better.

But Amelie surprised her. "Jazz is okay, Mom. I feel it. She's gonna come home."

Mari sighed. "Yes. Listen, I'll talk to your dad. I'll let you know what he thinks."

"Okay, Mom. I love you."

"I love you more." Mari hated to hang up on the only daughter she could communicate with.

She texted her son.

Hey. How goes it.

No answer. Maybe he was asleep. Then a few minutes later, **Fine.**

Such a detailed, teen-boy answer.

What are your plans for today? Can I call you?
K.

Getting him to pick up the phone was a miracle. "Hi, honey. I saw your Snap. Were you and Joe at the park?"

"Mom."

Mari remembered Parent Social Media 101. Follow your teens, but don't admit that you are there unless something weird comes up or you need to check on their well-being.

She hastened to cover. "No biggie. I was bored and just scrolling through the stories."

"Anything new?"

Mari cleared her throat. "No," she managed, realizing she talked around a large lump in her throat. Youngest child was on the phone. Youngest child was all right. "Are you staying safe? Locking the doors when Joe's parents are at work?" She sounded harsher than she meant to.

She felt him rolling his eyes.

"Yes." His voice lowered. Solemn.

"Nothing new except . . . ."

"Except what, Mom?"

How much detail was appropriate? None, she decided. He was still too young to learn that the case was now being treated as an abduction. "Jasmine didn't take her cell phone."

"I know. I texted her some."

"Has anyone come by the house?" She glanced at her watch.

"You got a package yesterday. It's on the porch."

Her heart skipped a beat. A package? She didn't order anything before they'd set off on their camping vacation. "Um, who's it from? Did you walk over and get it?" Then she panicked. "Don't go get it. Don't open it." Could it be the kidnappers? A bomb? A ransom demand? Was Seth safe?

She took a deep breath. "Seth, just leave it on the porch."

She heard him setting the phone against his shoulder and his voice muffling as he moved. Then she heard their neighbor's screen door slam. She held her breath. Finally, he was back. "It's from Bayside Auto Parts." He sounded a little breathless.

She relaxed. Something Ken had ordered then.

"We're coming home today to get you." She suddenly wanted everyone as close as possible. "I know we'll find your sister, but school starts in six weeks, and we have things to do to get ready." Who cared if he was almost an adult? He was her youngest. He was safer within her sight.

"Ah, Mom! We were going to see the fireworks tonight."

That's right. Today was July Fourth, usually a family holiday. No wonder she woke up angry. She told him to pack some clothes anyway, and she would see him in a few hours. He grudgingly mumbled something and hung up.

When Ken came back through the door, balancing two coffees and two doughnuts, Mari sat at the small round hotel table that barely fit between the window and the queen-sized bed. Ken wore dark circles under his eyes. He had lost his camping tan and looked pale, like he was ill. His dark hair had grown and curled out awkwardly above and behind his ears.

"You need a haircut."

He paused to set the coffee and doughnuts on the table before giving her a tired smile.

"And you know I don't eat doughnuts."

"I would settle for news on Jasmine."

Mari sighed. "I know. Me too. I'm sorry for snapping. Happy . . . Happy Fourth." Her voice broke. She took a sip of her coffee and a couple bites of the doughnut. Her appetite was low. Ken would finish the rest.

In return, he went to his backpack, pulled out a banana, and started peeling it for her.

"Thanks." She bit into it. "I talked to the kids—" At the look on his face, she clarified, "To Amelie and Seth."

Ken tilted his head. "And?"

"Amelie wants to know if she should come back, and I think Seth should be with us now. He got a delivery for you from Bayside Auto . . . ."

"I didn't order anything from Bayside Auto." Ken put his hands on his hips. "I've never heard of a Bayside Auto."

"What? Are you sure?"

They stared at each other for a split second.

She grabbed her cell phone, purse, and keys. Ken put his shoes back on.

"Call 9-1-1," he barked. "Make sure they tell Detective Miller."

Mari tossed the keys to him and dialed 9-1-1 as they ran to the car. After explaining their concerns to emergency dispatch, she sent a quick text to Jimmy and Melissa. **Weird package at home. Called police. Going to get Seth.**

CHAPTER THIRTEEN
Cienna

CIENNA RAN FAST. Behind her, the pounding of Mike's shoes sounded closer and closer. She felt his shove and hit the ground, landing face first in dirt and gravel. Raising her head slightly, she spit out rocks. Blood filled her mouth. She lay there panting, squirming under the weight of his body. She heard him breathing, but he didn't speak.

What would he do to her now?

Mike moved back a little, and she tried to wiggle free. But he flipped her over. Pinned her arms up above her head. Her eyes met his. His flickered. Was he going to kiss her? Ugh. She turned her face to the side.

"Well, that was stupid." He shook his head. "And a waste of a good shower. And ya promised to lay on the bed with me, not the gosh darn road."

He stood to let her up. She scrambled to her feet, glaring at him. Blood dripped down her chin. Mike cradled both her cheeks in his hands and abruptly pulled her face closer to his.

"Open."

Cienna opened her mouth. Suddenly his fingers were in her mouth, feeling her gums.

She was too shocked to bite him.

"Uh-huh." He grunted. "Ya bit the heck out of yer cheek."

She yanked away. She should run again. She shouldn't run again. He would catch her anyway. She sighed. Rubbed her right cheek with one hand. If she was nice, maybe he would get her an ice pack. Probably the best she could hope for.

To her surprise, Mike gave her a sympathetic look. "Guess ya just had to get that out of yer system." He adjusted his red hat on his head and took her hand. "Maybe ya just need to get out a little more often."

"Yeah." She glanced hopefully toward the road as he tugged her along by the hand. He kept a firm grip. Not back to the house but back to the barn. She tried to hide her sigh of disappointment.

"Well, ya better behave yerself then." He grimaced. "Then maybe we can take walks. But not . . . " He stopped and shook her shoulders firmly. "Not if ya run away." Grabbing her hand again, he pulled her along, almost stomping his way back to the barn and flinging the door open with one hand. He pulled her back to the room where she'd been imprisoned and slammed the door behind them.

She felt a small rush of gratitude when he turned his head and let her use the bucket without helping her. She wondered again if he would try to kiss her once they were lying in the bed, but she no longer felt so afraid of that.

Her sore mouth stopped bleeding, and she drank a full glass of water that had been sitting there from the day before. As promised, when she lay down on the bed, she slowly scooted over and made room for him.

No rope this time...thank you.

Mike held her with his arms tucked firmly around her stomach, murmuring softly in her ear. "What if Roger had seen ya run, sweetie? He would have caught ya for sure before I could."

Cienna shuddered. Roger sometimes still leered at her in her dreams, and she knew that out of the two of them, Mike was the much kinder man.

Maybe it really had been stupid to try to run away.

CHAPTER FOURTEEN
Jasmine

A S JASMINE COMPLETED MORE than her own set of chores, she started noticing when the other girls disappeared for a while. Once she looked for Amber, who was supposed to be helping scrub the floors. They weren't allowed to use a mop but had to get on their hands and knees and scrub with brushes. It took hours to finish, but less time when two girls did the job.

Jasmine finally concluded that Amber was in the part of the house where Jasmine wasn't allowed. Was that the nice part of the house? Did Amber have her own room in there or somewhere to hang out without everyone else? She imagined a cozy room with a soft chair. Maybe it even had a refrigerator for cold drinks. Maybe it was a quiet room with no disruptions allowed. Maybe it was way to escape from the Witch-Devil's wrath. Jasmine determined to ask Rose more about the room that was always locked.

Grudgingly, after searching for her roomie where she could, Jasmine started scrubbing the floor under the windows in the office area. The other day, she had tried to open all the desk drawers. They were locked. Was that where they kept the keys to the TC room and the pills they took twice a day?

A loud voice caught her attention, and she peeked up from the floor to the window looking out over the banned part of the house. A tall man with dark hair and wearing a business suit walked beside the Witch-Devil. They stopped on the sidewalk, and although Jasmine couldn't hear what they were saying, she saw the man open his wallet and place a thick wad of bills in the woman's outstretched hand. The Witch-Devil smiled at him, then moved closer to him and bumped her hip against his leg. He gave her an indulgent smile, as if tolerating her, before walking to a fancy black car and driving off down the long driveway.

The Witch-Devil turned toward the part of the house where Jasmine was crouching, so Jasmine ducked down farther, her heart pounding. She wasn't sure what she'd seen.

Was her captor selling drugs? Maybe that was the guy who was building the new place?

Another car drove up the treed lane, a Jeep this time. She returned to scrubbing the floor.

Later, when the Witch-Devil came in, she announced that starting tomorrow, "Bay" would do outside chores on the farm.

Jasmine felt a bubble of excitement. She had only been outside once, shortly after her arrival, when all the girls were hustled to clean out the barn while bars were installed on all the farmhouse windows. But now she could see if there was a way out, and perhaps more of what was going on in the part of the house she wasn't allowed into. She had to know what was in there.

Why were the other girls allowed and she wasn't? So unfair. She wanted to start her new duties and figure out why.

Liveliness ruled at the dinner table. Everyone came, including Sam. He complained loudly that the girls should have been given macaroni and cheese rather than the chicken dinner Rose prepared for all of them.

"Rose ain't worth the money that paid for this chicken." When the plate came by, he took a double portion.

The Witch-Devil gave everyone a rare smile before her announcement. "Bay's gonna graduate to outdoor chores tomorrow."

Some of the girls smiled at Jasmine, but Nia sneered. "Why don't you tell her what's after outdoor chores?" She startled and glared at Rose.

Jasmine had felt Rose brush her leg by her own as Rose kicked Nia under the table. But why had she done that?

"Shush, Nia." Rose frowned. "Shut it up."

"You know the rules, girls." The Witch-Devil stared briefly at each one, and conversation stopped. "You better obey them. Sam's got no problem dragging all of your butts out to the shed tonight if you're gonna open your big, fat mouths."

The girls sobered. No one, not even Jasmine, wanted to go back to the TC and be locked in without food and water. Not to mention anything Sam would bring upon them in the shed first. Amber had been pushed into the shed a couple of days ago. She sauntered out a short time later carrying her shoes in her hand. Sam had followed, zipping up his pants. Amber had come into the house, gone to her and Jasmine's room, and lain on her bed to read a book. Jasmine had rushed into the room to ask her if she was okay.

Amber had rolled her eyes. "'Course I am. Mind your own crap."

Relieved for her roommate, Jasmine smiled tentatively. Amber's "transgression" had been to argue with the Witch-Devil when the piece of lard talked about replacing their pills with dope. It was apparently now legal in Oregon and cheaper than the pills. Arguing with the Witch-Devil landed her in the shed.

"You didn't even do all of your chores today." Charli looked across the table at Nia. "Don't forget. You owe Bay."

Nia frowned and glanced quickly at the Witch-Devil. "Not true." She stared down at her lap.

The Witch-Devil frowned as well. "That so? You need more work, Bay? I'm not giving you enough? You want to do everyone else's too? You been bored?" She laughed harshly. "Maybe we should move you on to other jobs besides the farm work tomorrow, huh?"

"No, Kella." Rose's voice held a note of panic.

Jasmine chewed her lip. "I can do more. No problem." Rose frowned.

"You." Sam shook his fork at Rose and chewed his chicken with his mouth open. "Don't start. You know better than to open your big, fat mouth."

Rose sighed, nodded, and gave Jasmine a quick, gentle smile. Her eyes flicked to Sam. "Sorry."

"When's the new place being built?" Charli piped up from the other side of the table.

Sam glared at his wife. "We were going to wait on that."

The Witch-Devil shook her head. "Wasn't me."

Even Jasmine knew that was an outright lie. She'd heard the news from Rose the same day the Witch-Devil had opened her big mouth.

"Not me."

"I didn't."

The other girls exploded with denials.

Sam shoved his chair back from the table and stood, suddenly a menacing presence. His face was red, and his gut hung out between his pants and his shirt.

Gross. Jasmine shrank back.

Sam leaned forward and pounded his fist on the table. The silverware jumped. "Who told you about the new building? No one's supposed to know. Tell me right now."

Rose stood up quickly.

Jasmine watched wide-eyed. N-No. Don't, Rose. Please, Rose.

But Rose walked right up to Sam and met him nose-to-nose.

Jasmine hadn't realized that she was almost as tall as he was.

"It wasn't any of us." Rose raised her eyebrows mockingly. "It was Kella. She's lying."

Sam slammed Rose on the side of her head, knocking her almost off her feet. When she regained her balance, her hand crept up to cover the side of her face. She moved close and spat in Sam's face, then turned and left the room.

"Girl!" Sam's face had never been so fiery red. "Get back here." He grabbed his napkin and dabbed at the spit dripping down his cheek. Jasmine stared at the table.

In the sudden silence, Sam cleared his throat, readjusted his shirt down over his protruding beer belly, sat down, and started eating again like nothing had happened.

The Witch-Devil calmly ate everything on her plate as some of the other girls started picking at their food. Gradually they started eating larger mouthfuls. But Charli's face was pinched with regret as she pushed her food around.

Jasmine stood up. "I'll be back to do the dishes." Suddenly feeling brave, she darted out of the kitchen to check on Rose.

Rose was in her third-floor room with her music cranked up, dancing to the beat. Jasmine poked her head in the door and saw Rose swaying to the music, a faraway look on her face.

"Do you want some ice?" Jasmine smiled at her.

Rose didn't stop swaying. She didn't even look at Jasmine.

"How about a soda?"

Rose smiled, and her beautiful long red hair swayed as she danced.

"Pills?" Jasmine was running out of options to cheer her friend.

"Come dance with me."

Jasmine glanced around. Rose's room was decent, and

she had space, including a larger bed, unlike the rest of them who were crammed into smaller rooms.

"Okay."

If Rose just wanted to dance, she would dance with her. It was the least she could do. Ignoring Rose's darkening cheek and eye, she stood and swayed to the music with her friend.

CHAPTER FIFTEEN
Cienna

CIENNA'S EYES POPPED OPEN as the barn room lightened with morning sun. Mike had pulled away slightly but was still there, his leg draped over her thighs. Two thoughts dawned almost at once. He had spent the whole night in the barn. And where was Mrs. Mike? Didn't she come home from her meeting last night?

With Mike in the room, the door must be unlocked. She briefly envisioned Mrs. Mike barreling in and waving her rolling pin, angry at them both. And then there was Roger, who apparently considered Cienna his own if Mike ever lost interest in her. Or didn't claim her in some way. Suddenly, an unlocked door seemed scary.

She poked his shoulder. "Mike. Wake up. I'm . . . I'm hungry." And she really needed to use the bathroom.

Mike awoke and rubbed his eyes. His hat lay on the floor, and he sat up and shoved it back onto his head. "Yeah, let's go."

Go? Go!

Cienna scrambled up and followed Mike to the house, trying not to show her excitement. After yesterday, she assumed that she would be banned from ever going into the house again. She didn't bother to take in the fresh air and scenery this time, just bounded up the stairs of the house, right on Mike's heels. Once in, she ran to the bathroom to use the toilet. When she came out, he was cooking eggs on the stove and throwing white bread in the toaster.

Her stomach growled in response to the smell. He grinned at her.

She found herself grinning back. "Good morning." She sat down at the kitchen table.

"Good morning." He spoke politely.

It seemed they were starting over again.

Soon there was a steaming plate of scrambled eggs and toast in front of her. She dove into it, not even caring that it was bland, and there appeared to be no butter for the toast. "Thank you." She spoke around the food in her mouth.

"Welcome." He ate quickly, shoveling the eggs into his mouth. He got up, went to the sink for a glass of water, and downed that too. "I need to make coffee."

"M-May I have a drink?" Cienna used her best manners. He nodded.

She got up from the table, pulled a glass from the cupboard, and also drank a glass of water from the faucet.

Mike took the egg pan off the stove and placed it in the sink. "I suppose ya should have milk. You're still growing after all." He smirked, then vigorously started scrubbing the pan. "Go take a shower. I'm going to get ya clothes today."

Clothes! She could finally get out of her stinky and too-large clothes. "But how will you know if they fit me?"

He grunted, finished scrubbing the pan, and rinsed it. "After that stunt last night, I can't take ya anywhere, so don't even think about it. Now go take a shower, or I'll strip ya and toss ya in there myself!"

Cienna hurried back to the table and shoved the last bite of egg into her mouth before taking the plate to the sink. She grabbed the toast. "Going." She skedaddled to the bathroom, cramming the toast in her mouth as she went.

After swallowing the dry bread, she drank more water out of the sink faucet. This time in the shower, she took more time. Mike wouldn't come in. Eating that much had made her drowsy, and she was relaxing in the pulsating hot water when he pounded on the door.

"Hurry up. I need hot water, too."

She almost told him to screw off but held her tongue. She didn't bother trying to open the window again, knowing it was useless. And now she was sorry she had tried to run away. If she hadn't, would she be going with him to get clothes today? She groaned. No matter what decision she made, it appeared it was always the wrong one.

She needed to call Mom and Dad. How long had she been gone from the campsite? A week? Two weeks? Were her parents even still there? Maybe when Mike went to get clothes, she could stay in the house, and use the phone. Mrs. Mike didn't seem to be around this time either.

Cienna missed her family and Jazz and wanted them to know that she was alive, even if she couldn't get back to them yet. And that she would keep trying, even though Mike kept her safe from Roger.

This time, a full-sized towel hung on the rack. She dried her hair and wrapped it around herself. She glared at her dirty, stinky clothes lying in a pile on the floor and kicked at them.

The door opened, and Mike stepped in. Again, she had to back up quickly to avoid being hit by the door. He stared at her.

He came in! She hugged at the towel closer around her. Yes, in the early days of her visit, he had seen parts of her no one had ever seen, but that had been awhile, and she felt pretty safe now taking a shower on her own. She no longer feared he might hurt her.

"I- uh . . . " Mike stopped staring at her and looked at the floor. Then he looked back up into her eyes, startling her with their intensity. "Just beautiful." He moved forward and wrapped his arms around her now trembling body. The towel shifted, and she pulled at it, trying to keep covered. "Don't be scared, sweetie. Please. I won't hurt ya, I promise."

He brushed her damp hair away from her neck and gently kissed her there.

She trembled. She knew he was nice. He wasn't going to hurt her. But this was beginning to feel weird. It almost seemed he liked her too much. He thought she was pretty. He saved her from Roger, and although in the barn bed, he'd had plenty of opportunity to touch her in what Mom would call "inappropriate places," he hadn't even tried.

Mike was okay. Strange, but okay.

Abruptly, he released her and stepped back, his face red. "Get dressed."

"I-I will." Had she done something wrong? She continued to hold her towel closed with one hand and searched for her pile of crap clothes with the other.

"No. I'll get ya something. A robe maybe." He left.

Still trembling slightly, her heart beating so loud she could hear it, Cienna sat down on the side of the bathtub to wait.

He returned with a man's robe and tossed it at her. She stared down at it. Wouldn't something of Mrs. Mike's have worked better for her? She took a deep breath. "Mike, where's Mrs. Mike?"

"Shut up." He abruptly left the room, shutting the door firmly. She halfway expected to hear a lock click, but nothing happened. She remembered the bathroom had no lock. She quickly replaced the towel with the robe. It was too big for her, and the part that was supposed to wrap at the front went almost all the way around to her back. She tied it tightly anyway. Standing up, she found it hung past her feet. No matter. It smelled clean and felt good against her skin.

After dressing, she sat on the edge of the tub. She glanced in the shower. Saw soaps and shaving cream for men. Recalled the chicken broth that was supposedly homemade but tasted like it came from a can. And Mike had slept next to her in the barn room all night.

A sudden thought burst into her mind that both scared and exhilarated her. Maybe Mrs. Mike didn't really exist.

CHAPTER SIXTEEN
Jasmine

"WHERE'RE YOU GOING?" Jasmine sat on her bed watching Amber dress in heels, a tight skirt, and an almost see-through shirt that evening.

"The club." Amber ignored Jasmine's questioning gaze. She tapped out of the bedroom, slamming the door.

Jasmine sighed and buried her face in her pillow. Amber hated her. Maybe she needed to do more of Amber's chores.

Jasmine heard the doors of the long van in the driveway slide closed. It drove away. Suddenly she felt very alone.

She wasn't alone for long. The Witch-Devil, who usually disappeared for most of the evenings, came into her room and hauled her off the bed. Jasmine blinked sleepily at her. She must have dozed off.

"What's going on?"

Wearing a wicked smile, the Witch-Devil slapped her. "Guess I can't do that for much longer." She sighed. "Clean up. Sam wants to see you. Although, for gosh sakes, I don't know why. You're just a piece of garbage. Of course, you are young . . . " She pulled Jasmine out of the bedroom and down the hallway. Shoved her into the bathroom. "Take a shower." She slammed the door.

Jasmine shuddered and glanced at the bathroom window, now covered in black bars. After the girls had returned from cleaning the barn, Sam announced that all the bad men would now be unable to get into the house. Then he laughed.

It was all her fault the windows now had bars. She shouldn't have looked out the bathroom window to see how she could escape. Now they were all stuck.

As she was showering, Jasmine heard the door open.

"There's clothes out here! You better shave." The door slammed. The room went quiet except for the quiet pour of the water.

What was happening? Jasmine's hands trembled as she scrubbed shampoo into her hair. Would she be going to the shed? Was she in trouble? What did Sam want to talk to her about? She washed quickly, feeling uncomfortable and so nervous that she nicked the skin over her ankle bone with the dull razor.

Once out of the shower, she looked with disdain at the waiting clothes. Mom would put her on restriction for life if she'd worn those at home. At the thought of Mom, Jasmine's eyes filled with tears. Why hadn't she picked her up to go home yet?

The cut on her ankle oozed blood and dripped on the bathmat.

Crud. She hurriedly grabbed a wad of toilet paper, pressing it hard against the wound. She had only started shaving her legs the year before after she complained to Mom about how embarrassed she was to be the only girl in the locker room with hair on her legs. Her mom had apologized, and that very night helped her shave, showing her how to maneuver the razor without cutting herself. Jasmine had proudly finished the task and then spent the next several hours marveling at the smoothness of her legs. She couldn't wait to get back to the locker room after that.

The blood on the bathmat caught her attention again. Trouble seemed to follow her. She grabbed a washcloth. Tried to rub it away. She was still rubbing it when the Witch-Devil pushed open the door. Jasmine snatched the mat off the floor to cover herself.

"WHAT are you doing?" The woman stood with one hand on her hip. Jasmine saw nothing in the hallway behind the Witch-Devil. Actually, the house had been very quiet this evening. Maybe all the girls had left in the van along with Amber.

"I-I'm sorry. I cut myself, and there's a little blood on the mat."

"You stupid girl!" The Witch-Devil bellowed and stomped into the bathroom. "You know what? Forget the clothes! You don't deserve them!" She grabbed Jasmine by the arm and yanked her outside of the bathroom. Jasmine cringed and tried to cover her nakedness as the Witch-Devil laughed at her. She pulled the girl down the hallway, down the stairs, and into the kitchen.

Jasmine gasped. A tear rolled down her cheek. The windows were all uncovered, except for the bars. It was dark outside. Was there someone out there who would see her? Her face hot with embarrassment, she barely realized that the Witch-Devil was pulling keys out of her pocket and opening the door to the forbidden part of the house.

She pulled harder on Jasmine's wrist. Yanked her through the door. Another hallway. Doors lined up on either side. They came to a small lobby area with comfortable-looking chairs and a coffeemaker. The windows were covered with dark drapes.

"Wh-What? Where . . . "

"Shut up." The Witch-Devil twisted Jasmine's wrist.

"Ouch!"

"I said shut up." The heavy woman slammed her against the wall.

Jasmine trembled, unable to get away. "Please . . . "

"Shut up right now." She laughed. "Not that it matters. This part of the house is soundproof, you know. And no one is here but you, me, and Sam."

Jasmine shuddered. She searched the dim room frantically. No one was even around to help her if she screamed. Or could even hear her.

One of the doors opened. Sam stood there, a grin on his face. Jasmine cringed. She tried cover her privates. The Witch-Devil slammed the girl's hands back against the wall. Jasmine trembled as Sam came over. He looked her up and down. His grin widened. "Well, it's about time. Get her in here, Kella."

Tears poured as the Witch-Devil slapped her hard. Pushed her into the bedroom that Sam had exited. He followed behind them. Closed the door. The Witch-Devil shoved Jasmine. She landed on the bed face first, stunned. Even more stunned when she felt the weight of Sam close in on top of her. With one cheek to the mattress, tears flowed freely. She saw the Witch-Devil sit in a chair and lean back. Smiling.

Fiery pain pierced her insides. Jasmine screamed. But as much as she screamed, cried, and begged that night, until she could do nothing but whimper into the mattress, Sam and the Witch-Devil hurt her for hours. Told her they owned her now. She no longer had any choices. She was to do whatever they wanted her to do and do it quick.

"She'll make plenty of men happy." Sam grunted, apparently satisfied with something before he punched her in the head yet again. He took a long swig of beer from the nightstand. Grinned wickedly. The Witch-Devil laughed.

It was almost morning when The Witch-Devil took Jasmine, bruised and bleeding, back to her bedroom. She shoved her on the bed. Jasmine cowered in the corner and groped around to find blankets to cover herself. She would have fallen three times on the way to the bedroom if not for the Witch-Devil's firm grip. Her teeth chattered uncontrollably.

Alone at last, she whispered hoarsely, "M-Mom? Amber? Is anyone h-here?" She pulled her blankets up tightly around her face. She hid in the darkness. Shivered so hard the bed shook.

She understood it now. She was in hell. And one other thing suddenly became very clear.

Jasmine was dead. She could never be Jasmine again.

CHAPTER SEVENTEEN
Mari

THE TWO FAMILIES NO LONGER HAD A CHOICE. Some needed to return to work or risk losing their jobs. Someone still had to pay the bills and keep a roof over their heads. They had other kids to consider, and school would start soon. At some point, life for the rest of them must move forward . . . as much as they could manage in their grief.

Ken and Mari had returned home to pick up Seth. Before their arrival, the local police department confiscated the package. Several hours later, the couple learned it was a car part sent from Ken's brother directly from the auto parts store for a classic car the brothers were restoring. Mari couldn't decide whether to be relieved or sad that there was no clue to the girls' location inside the box. At times, confusion reigned for the day. Other times, it all seemed devastatingly clear.

The girls were gone.

The sad group gathered at the police station before heading home to Beaverton. In leaving, a chapter would close. Days and hours and weeks had passed. The girls remained missing. The team of detectives continued working to learn more about the man who had left his fingerprints on Jasmine's phone.

After Ken and Mari decided to hire a private investigator, Detective Miller recommended a young woman named Mollie Leeser. She had experience finding kidnapped children.

Miller spent a few minutes giving them the updates the department could release. "The wheel tracks point to a van by a major manufacturer, but we can't be sure because tires can be changed. We're looking for that model anyway, just in case."

"Any more call-ins?" Jimmy tapped his foot impatiently.

"Yes. Nothing has panned out yet. We posted more flyers to a radius of about eighty miles out of town to extend the reach. And of course, all the departments have received the bulletin and are also posting those when possible."

Mari's heart sank. How far had their daughters traveled? Or had they really not traveled at all?

"I printed the pictures they took that night with Jasmine's cellphone." Miller held out the prints.

All four gazed. Some warily. Some longingly. The river— a view from higher up. Trees. A section of cliffs. Cienna, her tongue sticking out. The last picture showed the grinning faces of their beloved daughters as they posed for a selfie. Melissa cupped her hand to her mouth.

Jimmy looked immediately away from the selfie and stared at the wall. Melissa held it close to her face. Tears welling, she leaned on Jimmy's shoulder. Her hand trembled and the picture shook.

When Melissa placed the pictures back on the desk, Miller slid them back. "Those are yours. We have copies."

"Thank you." She took the small stack and hugged them to her chest.

A young woman knocked on the open door, and Miller waved her in. "Folks, this is Mollie Leeser, the P.I. I told you about. Mollie, these are Cienna's and Jasmine's parents." He nodded toward each couple in turn.

As petite, pretty Mollie entered, Mari wondered how in the world she solved any cases. Obviously not with the brawn.

"I'm so sorry about your girls." Mollie shifted her shoulder with a large bag. "Detective Miller filled me in. I have a lot of things I want to look at, and I'll be in touch with you at least once a day with updates. In the meantime, it would help me to learn more about you and them."

Miller escorted them to a nearby conference room. "I'll leave you here to talk while I take Seth out for a soda. I'm sure he's tired of waiting in the lobby."

"Let's get started." Mollie pulled out her tablet. "I want to start with the days leading up to the camping trip, the mood of the girls, how often they walked to the store, whether they knew anyone in town." She peppered them with a host of other questions, typing their answers into the tablet. Mari and Melissa knew their daughters' habits best, but Ken and Jimmy added some details, too.

Mari pushed the picture of the girls on the cliffside over to Mollie.

Mollie tapped it and paused with her finger still resting on the picture. "I know where that is. When we're done, I'm going to walk the trail and take their route. The detectives here are very good at their jobs, but I just want to make sure and look again."

"I hope you take someone with you." Ken crossed his arms and frowned.

Mollie grinned. "No worries. My German Shepherd, Coal, goes everywhere with me. He's waiting in the truck now." She turned off her tablet. "I have a lot to get started on."

As she walked from the room, the four parents sighed as if on cue.

"Now we wait." Melissa sighed.

The four-hour drive back to Beaverton in both cars was quiet, but a thread of hope wove its way through their hearts.

CHAPTER EIGHTEEN
Cienna

CIENNA DIDN'T GIVE UP her quest to escape. Mike seemed to want her to be his Mrs. Mike. She shuddered. Obviously, her family had no idea where she was, or they would have broken down the door by now. Even her little brother, Kai, who was a pain most of the time, would have found a way into the house to rescue her.

How could she escape? What were the available tools and weapons? The phone on the wall was one. Maybe the neighbors out back. She still hadn't seen a computer, and Mike didn't appear to have a cellphone. That gave her three options. Get to the phone on the wall and figure out how to use it. It looked a little like the phones in the school office. She'd manage. Or she could run to the house out back. Maybe she could somehow convince Mike to trust her enough to go along today to get clothes from the store. She could get someone's attention there.

Cienna jumped off the side of the tub and threw open the bathroom door. Mike sat in the family room watching the news. On the screen, she saw a picture of Jazz. She gasped, covering her mouth. Jazz! She was hurt?! And then the likely truth. She was missing, just like Cienna.

Was Jazz here at Mike's somewhere? Was she in the neighboring house? Had she been crying, and Cienna couldn't hear her? Tears sprang to her eyes. Could Jazz be dead?

Mike frowned at her and clicked the remote to turn off the television. Looked her up and down. "That robe's too big." He grabbed a pen and a notebook from the table beside him and tossed them at her. They landed at her feet. "Make a list."

Cienna shook off thoughts of Jazz. She would try to gain Mike's trust. Taking a deep breath, she shuffled to the recliner. Sat at his feet. With one hand on his knee, she looked him in the eye. "You look nice today, Mike. I like your shirt." She actually did. It had blue stripes with some purple woven in. He also wore nice blue jeans with what looked like hiking boots. His red baseball hat was missing.

His eyes landed on her face. After a second or two, he smiled. "Ya ain't coming with me."

She smiled back. Patience. She was ready to be more in charge of this situation. But it might not happen quickly. "I want to talk to you." She took another deep breath. God help her now. Time for bluntness, rarely a problem for her. "I don't think you're married, Mike." At the startled look on his face, she added quickly, "and that's okay. In fact, I prefer just you and me."

He gave her a challenging look. "Why do ya think that? She just had a meeting in town last night."

Cienna straightened her posture and rubbed his knee a bit. He didn't move away. "Is town close by?"

Mike chortled.

"Okay, okay. I understand." She worked for an agreeable tone of voice. "You're right. Who cares where town is? But I do like the idea of . . . of having you to myself. Don't you?" Her eyes met his directly.

His flickered. The side of his mouth twitched. "And why would ya want to be out here alone with just me?"

Cienna thought quickly. She turned to face the now black flatscreen, leaning her back against his knees. She heard his breath hitch. His hands moved to her shoulders. She tensed, but he started rubbing gently. Even through the thick robe, she felt her muscles respond and relax. It felt good when he touched her. She hadn't hugged her dad in a long time.

"That feels so nice." She remembered to compliment him and be grateful. "Thank you."

Mike really worked her muscles. As she grew relaxed and tired, she determined not to forget her mission. His magic fingers found hard spots in areas she had never felt before.

Of course, the very nature of her mostly tied-up position in the barn might have something to do with that.

"Why would I like to have you to myself?" She tapped her chin, forcing herself to stay alert. "Hmmm, well, this feels pretty good right now. Thank-Thank you. And I could cook for us, Mike. Wouldn't you like some real homemade soup? Or spaghetti?" She could do spaghetti and a few other dishes. Maybe even learn some new ones.

"Huh. Sure, but soup is better in the fall. Don't ya know how to make anything else?"

"Ice cream." They made it at home with a machine. "Salads. And muffins."

"That sounds good. So, make a list, and I'll pick things up today."

She wiggled around to face him and raised her eyebrows. "You need a hairbrush." He grinned.

She laughed. Yes, her curls were a wild mess. And drying messier by the minute. "Do you have a hairdryer?"

Mike grunted. "Somewhere. And maybe some hairspray. Girls like hairspray, right?"

Cienna never used hairspray except when she had snuck into Mom's room to borrow it on a few occasions. But she nodded enthusiastically. "Yes, please. Then I could look nicer for you. And maybe a little makeup? Razors for a girl?" She continued to press a little bit. This conversation needed to continue on this positive slant. Build his trust. Making him laugh didn't seem like a bad idea either.

Mike nodded. "Okay. Make a list. I'll git it done." He leaned forward and cupped both her cheeks in his hands. "Baby." Suddenly serious, he blinked twice. "Mrs. Mike has been gone a long time."

She stared. He dropped his hands. He looked at the ground, sadness etching his features into a frown.

Instant regret filled Cienna's heart. "I'm so sorry, Mike. What happened?"

He sighed and looked up with a tear in his eye. "She died."

Cienna's heart jumped. How sad. No Mrs. Mike to save her.

"I like to pretend she's still here. But of course, that won't bring her back."

Cienna was silent for a few moments. From her floor position, she reached forward and rubbed his arm. She felt sorry for his loss. She sighed and turned back around, leaning against his knees. He placed his hands on her shoulders again.

"I'm so sorry." Cienna remembered a couple of years back when Grandma had died. She thought her heart was cut in two. And that she would never smile again. And yet she realized that she had. It just took time.

Mike apparently needed time to deal with his grief and feel like life was normal again. Perhaps she could help him in the short time she would be here.

"Do you...have any friends? You know, to help you and to go out with and have fun with when you need to be around people?" That helped her when she was sad at home.

Mike sat quietly.

She didn't say anything, either. Had he heard her? Should she repeat herself?

He stood up and stepped over her. She ducked. Mike retrieved the notebook that she hadn't picked up. He kneeled in front of her and handed them to her. "I hope I do now. Now, make a list."

Now that Cienna knew for sure she wasn't going to town, she couldn't put it off any longer. Darn it! She didn't even care that she was wearing a bathrobe. She would have found a way to draw someone's attention. But there was no hope of that now. She sighed. That left the phone and the neighbor's house out back. Only two other options.

Dutifully, she grabbed the pen and made a list that included clothes with her sizes and groceries. She planned to run after he left, but she didn't need him guessing that. As she thought, jotted notes, and tried to look deep in thought even more, Mike moved about the room. She added hairspray. Wondered if she could spray him in the eyes with it. She watched him take his wallet out of a drawer by the couch and slide it in his back jeans pocket. He had to search a bit to find his truck keys but finally did. They were somewhere around the corner in the kitchen. She filed it into her brain.

When she was done, he grabbed her list and tore off the sheet from the notebook, cramming it into his front jeans pocket. He hauled her to her feet. To the stairway.

"W-Where are we going?"

"Congratulations. You've moved into the house." He pulled her up the stairs. Stopped at the first door. "Welcome to the guest room." He flung open the door. "If yer good, ya can stay here now instead of the barn. But ONLY if yer good."

Cienna nodded quickly. "No problem. I'll be good." Uh huh.

He pushed her inside. She balanced herself. The only window was boarded up. But there was a double-sized bed with blankets and pillows, a dresser in the corner, a closet and a rocking chair. Not bad. Hopefully from inside the house she could at least get to the phone while he was gone.

"What's your preference?" Mike pointed to the bed. Handcuffs dangled from the metal headboard.

She sighed.

"I can hook ya up there, or I can lock the room, and ya can actually walk around. Your choice."

Cienna sighed. "What if I go without the handcuffs?" She had no idea how long Mike would be gone. The memory of the painful spasms after being restrained in the barn frightened her. Surely without the handcuffs, she could still find some way out of the house. Or maybe get someone's attention. She wanted to go home. And what if he left and then forgot about her? Maybe she could break down the bedroom door.

"Well, there's a trade of course." Mike smiled.

She nodded warily.

"Free to move around means I sleep here in the bed with ya tonight. Handcuffs and I sleep in my room."

Cienna remembered earlier in the bathroom. He had hugged her for a long time. Now that she knew there was no Mrs. Mike, lying in the bed with him could be dangerous. She would just have to make sure she wasn't still in the room when he returned from the store.

"Now." She put her hands on her hips. "I have a condition." She added a sassy tone to her voice. With the huge bathrobe, she probably looked ready for a Halloween party, not a fight. But she didn't care. She would take another chance.

Mike laughed out loud.

She smiled a little, too. Then she bit back her smile and tried to look ferocious. "I stay in the room. No handcuffs. You sleep in here tonight, but you don't touch me. I mean, no more than a hug. If you do, I-I won't cook anything for you."

His grin was triumphant . . . and a bit contagious. "Deal. I'm goin' to the store now." He scooted out the door while Cienna stood there with her hands on her hips. As he closed the door, there was the unmistakable sound of a metal bar sliding across the outside of it.

She blinked back tears. Alone, stuck, and frustrated.

CHAPTER NINETEEN
Bay

B AY AWOKE TO ROSE SWEARING and pacing the floor.
Amber sat on the side of her own bed across the small
room. They were dressed in comfortable clothes. Light poured
through their small window.

"I knew it!" Rose whirled around from the wall and
headed the back toward the bed. "No other time would he
send me to the club with a black eye. But he wanted us all out
of the house. Why didn't I figure it out? And he didn't drive
us. He had that guy . . . "

Amber cleared her throat in warning. "I think she's
waking up."

Bay opened one eye. Started trembling again.

"Sorry, kid." Amber truly did look sorry. "But you'll be
okay."

Tears rolled down Bay's cheeks. She turned to the wall,
huddling as close to it as she could.

She felt weight on the mattress next to her. She
panicked, flinging her arms out. Kicking wildly despite logic
telling her that Rose would never hurt her.

"Shhhh." Rose placed her hand on Bay's shoulders until

she calmed a bit. "It's just me. Look, I have pills for you and some water." She helped Bay prop herself up.

Bay gratefully swallowed them. The girls must have stashed some away or found the key to the hiding place. She saw large spots of blood on the sheets. Pain racketed through her head. Her body felt like it had been squashed by a hammer. Maybe she would be lucky, and the pills would kill her. Apparently, that was the only way out of hell.

"I'm so sorry." Rose crooned and hugged her gently. "So sorry. I should have realized something was up. I should have fought to stay here with you and not left you here alone."

Bay could hear Rose's tears in her voice. "Not your fault." She turned to the wall, tucking in as close to it as she could. She slipped back into a troubled sleep.

When she awoke again, the Witch-Devil stood over her, a frown on her face, her spiked hair awry. "What is this mess?" She kicked at Bay. "You're disgusting. Get up and clean up."

Trembling and cowering, Bay sat up and pulled the blankets up to cover herself.

"You disgusting pig," the Witch-Devil whispered fiercely. "I hate you now. Do you understand?"

Bay nodded quickly. Looked at the floor. This actually made sense. Maybe the woman was angry at Sam for doing awful things her. But she had helped. Maybe it didn't make any sense at all. The pills had obviously dulled her senses and made her tired. Her pain seemed less, but her heart felt numb. She regretted waking up.

"I-I'll clean up." Her voice shook.

"You better pay attention to that roommate of yours." The Witch-Devil headed for the door. "She's the only one with her head on straight around here."

Apparently.

Bay watched her crazed captor, now claiming to be her owner, lumber out of the bedroom.

Where was Amber? Was she in the other part of the house? The torture chamber? Was Sam hurting Amber there now? She hoped not.

Light-headed, Bay slid out of bed, dressed, and changed her sheets. She threw the bloody ones away, then immediately wondered if she would get in trouble for it. She wobbled down the hallway to the empty bathroom and searched for something to block the door so Sam wouldn't come in and hurt her. There wasn't much to work with, so she crumpled up a corner of the bathmat, still stained with her blood from her shaving cut, and shoved it under the door. At least the door wouldn't open easily and might get stuck if someone tried.

Bay pulled the curtain closed on the window and sat on the toilet, still trembling. It was painful to pee. She cried. She climbed into the shower. Braved cold water until she shook uncontrollably, then switched to hot that stung her skin.

She thought of her home, her parents, and siblings, and Cienna, but stopped herself. "Not yours anymore. They were Jasmine's, not yours. You'll never have a family. You don't deserve them. You're garbage. Disgusting and rancid garbage." And she knew that she was. She would never be clean again.

Tears rolled down her cheeks unchecked as she finished cleaning herself up, dreading getting out of the shower. Yet knowing that if she didn't, she would be dragged out eventually by the Witch-Devil. As she cried, she eyed the razor. She wished that she was brave enough to cut her wrists, curl up in the corner of the tub, and die.

CHAPTER TWENTY
Amelie

Amelie stared at stacked shelves in the refrigerator and closed her eyes tightly. Neighbors had brought casseroles and other food. None of it looked appetizing. She slammed the door shut. Home for the weekend, she thought she would find comfort with her parents and brother. Instead, she felt like she couldn't breathe. The house felt like a hushed museum.

She wandered to the table where pictures of Jasmine lay. She took a picture of the table and uploaded it to Instagram. "Can't even sit here," she noted on the caption. "It's all about Jazz. Although I do miss her." She took an apple from the bowl in the middle of the table and went to scout out her brother.

"Seth." She spoke loudly to interrupt his video game.

"Huh." His eyes never left the screen.

"I go back to school tomorrow." She crunched a bite out of her apple. It slid down her throat with difficulty.

"Yeah. So?"

"So." Amelie kicked at a throw pillow on the floor. "Let's do something fun. I'm tired of it here. SO depressing." She pulled her phone from her pocket and saw several hearts on her last post. People could feel sorry for you, even online.

"Does it involve pizza?"

Amelie grinned and tucked her phone back in her pocket. That sounded too good to pass up, considering the current contents of the refrigerator. "Definitely."

"Need a minute."

Amelie watched over Seth's shoulder as he pulled up the chat box on the game to let his buddies know he would be stepping out.

"Yeah, yeah." Amelie left the room to find her shoes and jacket. It was going on evening and would be slightly cooler outside. Her parents were at the store, so she texted them, **Taking S to get pizza.** She tossed the rest of apple in the sink. She and Seth hopped into her Toyota, and she started the car.

Seth took out his cellphone and started typing.

Can't you put that away for a little while?" She focused on the road. In the corner of her eye, she saw him shrug, finish typing, and put the phone back in his pocket.

He stared out the window. "It's weird she's still gone. Do you think she ran away?"

"No." Amelie braked at a stop sign. "They found her cellphone, you know. There were fingerprints of some dude on it." She checked for cross traffic and drove on.

Seth gasped quietly. Amelie felt bad. Maybe she shouldn't have told him that.

"Some guy took her?"

Amelie shrugged. She tried to ignore the sudden pull on her heart. "Guess so. Cienna, too."

Seth swore, but Amelie didn't correct him. She didn't blame him and had thrown plenty of word bombs herself that her parents wouldn't approve of. "I'm sure they'll find her soon."

"That police department sucks. They would probably find her if they put the FBI on it."

"I think the FBI can only help when a case goes out of the area."

Seth slumped back into his seat.

"What kind of pizza do you want?" She flipped the turn signal as she neared the pizza place. At the same moment, her cellphone beeped. She glanced down at it in the cupholder. Mom. She motioned to Seth, and he grabbed her phone.

"It says we'll meet you there." He typed a reply. "I guess they don't want us kidnapped. We aren't allowed to go without them." He scrolled to his sister's Facebook account.

"Hey, get off my phone and knock it off."

He set it back in the cupholder.

"Flavor?"

"Pepperoni." She saw him turn his head to the window. When he looked back, he had tears on his cheeks. Poor kid. No wonder he hid behind video games.

"I got people looking for her. My friends are keeping an eye out."

"Friends . . . around here?" She pulled into a parking place and glanced back at the street. Maybe she could get some time actually talking with him before her parents arrived.

"Friends all over. They have her picture now too." He wiped his face quickly and looked back out the window.

Amelie opened her mouth but paused. Home rules always stated that no pictures went out to the internet in games and chat rooms. Ones on social media were also limited by their parents. Jasmine wasn't even allowed to have accounts yet, and Seth only when he'd turned fifteen.

But how else would they find her?

Besides, there were missing posters all over the place, and Amelie knew Cienna's mom was paying for online ads.

"Okay. That's good." Turning off the engine, she turned to face Seth. "Almost time for your school to start."

"I know. It's so stupid. Everyone's just going to stare at

me and feel bad for us. I think I'll be sick instead." Seth continued looking out the window. "Do you think she's dead?"

Amelie breathed deeply. "N-No . . . " But her voice broke, giving away her real emotions.

Seth unclicked his seatbelt. "Well, you sound convinced." He opened the passenger door, hopped out, and slammed the door.

Great. Although they'd all had emotional moments, as the older sibling, she needed to set an example for Seth and at least try to keep away the tears. Seth headed into the building, and she knew he would be waiting for her at the arcade. He likely needed five bucks to start anyway because the money he earned from odd jobs around the neighborhood always seemed to disappear. The folks had pretty much cut him off from doing anything without supervision anyway. If she were Seth, she would stomp into the arcade, too. Instead, she pulled out her phone and posted on Facebook: "Why is this so hard?!" And she added a word Mom would probably see. She didn't care.

"She's not dead." She took a deep breath as she joined Seth near the Skee Ball area. "I think I would feel it if she was dead. Come on. Don't you need a card?"

Seth followed her to the machine with the video game cards. She inserted her debit card and bought him some game time. Passed it over to him.

"Thanks." He walked away.

She let him go, then texted Mom to ask what kind of pizza they wanted. At the pizza counter, she gave their order, minus Jasmine's usual cheese-less pizza that the owner made especially for her. At the table, as much as she hated herself for it, she tried to keep Seth within eyesight. She tapped her fingernails on the table, got up to grab her waiting milkshake, and returned to her seat. Her heart ached. Her sister couldn't have a full milkshake, but Amelie would gladly have let her sip on hers . . . if only she could.

In a short time, her parents joined her at the table.

Mom bit her lip and looked around for Seth.

"He's right there." Amelie pointed across the room.

Mom's posture relaxed. "I just wanted to be sure."

"He asked me questions on the way." Amelie stirred her milkshake with her straw. "What am I supposed to say? I told him about the fingerprints on the phone."

Dad huffed. "We aren't telling him everything. You shouldn't either."

"I disagree. He's sixteen. And he's afraid."

"So you're making him more afraid?" Mom shook her head.

"No, Mom. Geez. He's afraid because he doesn't know it all. You should understand that."

Mom sighed. "I know. I do. I'm sorry. It's hard to know what to tell him and what not to tell him these days. We're all afraid."

"Do you even let him talk about it?"

Mom opened her mouth, then slowly closed it. Her eyes flashed a warning at her daughter, but she took a deep breath. "We're doing our best, Amelie. No one writes a book on how much to talk about when your daughter is abducted."

"I know, Mom." Amelie sighed. "No one writes one for the sister either."

"She may have a point," Dad quirked an eyebrow. "Maybe we should ask him if he has questions. I don't want him to feel like he can't come to us and ask us things."

Mom hopped up. "The pizza's ready. I'll get it, but first I'm going to get Seth."

Dad held up his hand. "I'll get the pizza. You get Seth."

As Mom walked away, she sent him an appreciative smile over her shoulder.

"Hey, Ken." The pizza parlor owner gave Dad a sympathetic smile . . . and an order of breadsticks. "On the house."

Dad paused for a moment. "Thanks."

Sitting back down with Amelie, he spread out plates and napkins. He glanced across the room and shook his head at Mom. She stood with arms crossed, speaking to Seth. Seth kept his eyes on the screen. "Now what?"

"He wants to finish the game." Amelie grinned.

"Yeah." Dad nodded. "Say, are you ready to go back tomorrow?"

They reached for the same slice of pizza and laughed.

Always mixed feelings there. Going back to school meant pausing many of her efforts in the search for Jasmine.

"Sure. Although I could do without calculus."

"Can't blame you for that." He smiled. "Thanks for coming home. We love having you here."

Amelie used her napkin to catch a stray string of cheese hanging from her lower lip, rolling her eyes comically.

"I'm glad you're enjoying that." Dad focused on his own slice. "Home next weekend too?"

She shrugged and swallowed her bite. "Actually, I think I'll go to River Falls."

Mom and Seth arrived at the table at that moment.

"Not by yourself, you're not." Mom snapped.

Amelie rolled her eyes. "Are you going to follow me back to Seattle too?"

"Of course not."

Mom sank down on the chair beside Dad but didn't take any pizza.

Amelie could see the struggle in Mom's eyes. Wonderful, capable Mom when it came to helping her clients. Not so capable when tragedy struck at home. They missed Jasmine's cheese-less pizza and, more importantly, missed Jasmine. How could they move forward without their Jazz?

CHAPTER TWENTY-ONE
Cienna

CIENNA LISTENED AS MIKE'S TRUCK roared to life. Soon the sound of the engine became distant. She waited on the bed, her heart pounding. There had to be a way out of the room. She hadn't used her yelling voice in many days, and it might be worth it. Would the neighbors in the back of the property hear her? Was there even anyone in that house? There must be. She would get to them, somehow.

But they probably wouldn't hear her through the walls and boarded up window.

She jumped up, almost tripping over the long bathrobe, and started searching the room. She couldn't see all the way under the bed, so she scooted underneath as far as she could. She swept her arms widely, encountering nothing. When she slid back out, she noticed the thick layer of dust on Mike's bathrobe.

He needed some serious help with housecleaning. She moved on to the closet.

Her heart leapt when she saw boxes stacked inside. There were two apple boxes, the thick kind with the lids that covered the whole box.

"Yes!" She grabbed the bottom one and yanked them both out into the room.

She wiggled off the top box's lid and peered inside. Photo albums. Huh. No wonder the box was so heavy. She considered looking through the albums. Certainly, there would be some of Mrs. Mike. If nothing else, she might learn something about Mike that would help her get home. For now, she needed to concentrate on finding something, anything, to get her out of this room.

She removed all of the photo albums, stacking them on the floor, to search the bottom of the box. Nothing. She turned it upside down and shook it, just to make sure. Sighing, Cienna restacked the albums inside, being careful to place them as they'd been stacked originally. She grabbed the lid and pushed it back down on the top of the box.

"How much time do I have?" Adrenaline coursed through her body. She felt shaky. She pushed aside the photo album box and turned to the next one. How much time had it been? She had no way of telling the time. For the hundredth time, she longed for the cellphone that she had hidden from her brother under her pillow at the campsite.

Why hadn't she grabbed it when she and Jazz went to the store? Because they were only leaving for a half hour. And Jazz had her phone. They both had felt safe. Did Jazz still have her phone, wherever she was?

Cienna grunted and drew in a sharp breath, remembering seeing her best friend on the news. Hopefully Jazz was safe and home now.

She started to open the second box, but the lid resisted her efforts. She pulled harder, only to fall backward. She tripped on the long robe and fell on her butt on the carpeted floor. She swore and pushed herself up, pausing to listen for any noises outside of the house. Nothing. Dead quiet. And if this was anything like a horror movie, a monster might break through the door anytime now. She laughed but quickly sobered. There actually were monsters out there. Namely one named Roger. She couldn't waste any time. She needed to go home, now.

Cienna tossed the apple box lid across the room. It landed against the wall with a bang and bounced off. She felt . . . satisfaction. Perhaps she would do that again sometime. In fact, she would do it now. She hurried over, picked the lid up and flung it as hard as she could against another wall. Thud. Bounce. Off it went again, this time bouncing off the headboard. And again. Against the ceiling. She ducked out of the way as it headed back down to her.

"Arrghhhh!" She yelled loudly. "You can't keep me here! It's against the law!"

She caught the lid again and, grabbing one end, repeatedly banged the other end against the dresser. Bam! Bam! "I hate you! And I want to go home. I want to go home now!"

Cienna didn't feel it when the first tears leaked and started down her cheeks. But she suddenly realized she was sobbing. And that the lid on the box was dented where she had relentlessly smashed it against the dresser. What was she doing? Mike would see a smashed lid. Know she was going through his things.

A flutter of panic that started in her belly worked its way to her throat. She might choke.

"I won't be here when he gets home." She forced a deep breath. Tried to calm down. "I'm leaving. I'll never see Mike again."

Cienna sat on the bed suddenly, feeling a little dazed. She would never see Mike again. Would he go to jail? She pictured him behind bars, sitting on a cot, adjusting his baseball hat and looking sad.

Confused thoughts filtered quickly as tears dried on her cheeks. What was the problem here? Mike had taken her from her family.

No, he saved her from Roger.

Mike locked her in a barn and lied about Mrs. Mike.

She excused him. He was hurt from losing his wife, and he only locked Cienna up to keep Roger away.

She threw the box lid at the wall again. "He did tell me the truth today." She gritted her teeth, defending him and trying to chase the weird thoughts away.

But had he?

Cienna eyed the remaining box, now open with its contents to the peak of their boundary. She looked at the closed one with the photo albums. What secrets did those photo albums hold?

Mike had locked her in this room. The war continued in her head. He would have used the handcuffs if she hadn't agreed to let him sleep in here tonight. But Mike was kind. He'd been sweet, and he was keeping Roger away. That was a big deal.

Cienna shook her head fiercely and covered her face with her hands. She groaned. She had to get out. Whether Mike was a good guy or bad guy, her family didn't even know she was alive.

Sobered, she slid off the bed and returned to the opened, unexplored box. She took out a wooden box with a bound set of letters in it. She fanned through them quickly but didn't take the time to read. She found a framed picture of Mike on horseback obviously in his younger days. Was the horse still on the farm somewhere? Or maybe it was another farm in the picture. She set the picture aside. She continued to rummage, removing one item at a time. She looked for something that might help her get out of the room and to the phone hanging on the kitchen wall. There was nothing.

Cienna searched the dresser drawers and turned them upside down. Had a sudden thought. Straight from a movie, probably. She relocated the framed picture and took the picture out. Placed the picture carefully back in the box. Then she took the glass out of the frame and carried it to the dresser. She dropped the glass on the dresser. It shattered. Good. It wasn't too thick. If she could get a piece, she at least had a weapon. And maybe if she had it to threaten Mike, he would have to let her out of the room.

She salvaged a pointed piece of glass about two inches long and tucked it under the mattress at the head of the bed. It was something. She felt a flutter of hope. She carried the empty apple box over to the dresser, held it under the edge of the dresser, and used the thick sleeve of Mike's robe to wipe the rest of the broken pieces into the box. She took the box back near the closet, returned the contents, and squeezed the lid back onto it. Of course, it looked trashed, and barely fit back onto the box. That one became the bottom stacked box now. Hopefully, he wouldn't notice.

Cienna didn't find a way out of the room that day. After the boxes were again stashed in the closet and the dresser drawers returned to their proper places, she heard the unmistakable sound of Mike's truck engine. With both a sinking heart and a flutter inside her belly, she heard him mount the stairs to the bedroom and slide the bar from the door.

"Baby." He looked boyishly eager as he entered the room with two plastic bags and kicked the door closed behind him. "Look, I found some clothes." He stopped. "Have ya been crying?" He dropped the bags and enfolded her in his arms. "Don't be sad, please."

He held Cienna firmly, and she took some comfort in it. Her tears dripped on his shoulder. Her emotions had been in turmoil all afternoon, and she didn't know what to think anymore. So, she lied.

"I was just lonely." Her voice muffled in his shoulder. "I hoped that you wouldn't forget me up here. No one would ever find me, you know. No one around except us." Maybe he would tell her there were actually neighbors nearby.

"Oh, Cienna." He led her to the bed and guided her to sit down, sitting next to her. "I will never leave ya. I promise." With his arm around her shoulder, he squeezed her gently. "But I'm sure sorry that ya were lonely. I missed ya too!" He jumped off the bed, grabbed the bags, and grinned at her. "Aren't ya tired of that robe yet? It's way too big."

She smiled slightly back. "Y-Yes. It trips me up." She sniffed and wiped her eyes and nose on the arm of the robe. "But I guess it works for a tissue."

Mike laughed loudly. "We have tissues downstairs. I'll bring a box up for ya. I want ya to be comfortable here. After all, as long as Roger is around, yer my guest. I'll take care of ya."

Yes. Roger. "Thank you for keeping me safe." She meant it.

Mike grinned and tossed her a bag. "I'm unloading the groceries now. Git dressed. What's for dinner?"

"U-Umm." She'd been so intent on escaping that she didn't remember what food she'd written on the grocery list.

"I got porkchops." He gave her a sweet grin.

Seeing that he wanted her to remember what she wrote and that she had made a commitment, she nodded. "Yes. And you remembered the stuff for salad?"

"Did I ever." He walked from the room. "Now, git dressed! Geez! Girls!"

As he headed downstairs, Cienna grabbed the shopping bags off the floor. She was relieved to find no lacy or frilly things that she might be expected to wear. Just regular clothes. Two tee-shirts, a pair of sweats, some shorts, and a pair of jeans. With an eye on the door, she quickly struggled out of the big heavy robe and ripped tags off one of the shirts and the jeans. It was a warm summer, but Mike kept the house on the cooler side, so these wouldn't be too hot to wear. And this way, she would be ready to run tonight as soon as she got the chance.

But where were her shoes and socks? She looked around the room.

Right. They would still be in the bathroom where she had undressed for her shower.

She moved quickly to the door. Maybe as he was unloading, she could use the facilities and slip her socks and shoes on. He probably wouldn't even notice. She crept down the stairs and to the right, where she quickly entered the bathroom. At the same time, she heard Mike whistling as he brought groceries in.

"I-I'm right here." Cienna called through the door. She didn't want to surprise him or make him think she was being sneaky. "I need to use the bathroom."

"Okay." He headed out the door again.

She used the toilet, discouraged when she saw that her old pile of clothes, socks and shoes no longer littered the bathroom floor. He'd probably thrown them away. They had reeked, after all. But at least she now had clean clothes that mostly fit her. Although she had provided Mike with estimated sizes, her waist was smaller now. She didn't know what she'd do about socks and shoes. There hadn't been any in the shopping bags.

When she returned to the kitchen, Mike was placing food in the refrigerator and pantry. Salad fixings and raw pork chops sat on the counter. She sighed. She had actually never fried porkchops. She tried to picture Mom frying them up. Or did she bake them?

Never mind. She would figure it out. And if it went awry, there was that piece of glass waiting upstairs under the mattress.

She busied herself exploring the cupboards, finding a frying pan, a large bowl, and a cutting board. Now for the silverware. She found a drawer. Knives. Right there were sharp knives. She could threaten him, stab him, do what she had to do. She could grab one right now, turn around, take a few steps toward him and . . . .

"Not much selection." Mike suddenly spoke in her ear.

Cienna jumped, red-faced. Had he known what she was thinking?

"We probably need a new set, don'tcha think?"

She nodded, grabbed a knife with wavy edges, and turned to the vegetables that waited by the sink. "Sure. A new set would be nice."

A new set would be nice?! Here she was, acting like she enjoyed living with the jerk who had locked her in the barn and kept her from her family. She must be going insane. As she chopped the vegetables, she eyed the bright yellow phone on the wall. But Mike stuck close to her side, and she saw no way to lunge for it.

The pork chops weren't hard to fry after all. She remembered now that Mom did fry them and also always cut them to check for pink before taking them out of the pan. She did the same and managed to slip the knife behind a canister on the counter. They sat down to eat, and Mike brought both beer and wine to the table. He excused himself to use the restroom.

Finally. A chance. Should she grab the phone or run out the front door? The last time she ran, he'd caught her. The phone then. Once she heard the bathroom door close, she scooted her chair back. Winced when it squeaked on the floor. Not daring to move it any further, she carefully maneuvered her body in the tight space between the table and the chair. She reached the phone. Grabbed it quickly. A surge of hope blossomed in her heart.

No dial tone greeted her. The phone was dead. "No." She pushed the nine and one and one anyway, hoping it would somehow connect. It didn't.

"Darn it!" She hung up the phone. She would make another run for it instead. Maybe she could grab the knife behind the canister just in case?

A hearty laugh from the doorway stopped her. How long had Mike been there, leaning on the doorframe with his arms crossed? "The phone don't work." He grinned.

Run!

She turned to the front door and flung it open. Ran out to the porch. She made it halfway down the stairs before he tackled her.

She landed on her side, hard, on the sidewalk.

Mike heaved her up and over his shoulder. She pounded his back with her fists as hard as she could. "Let me go! Let me go! Let me go, you bastard! I hate you! I want to go home!" Tears streamed. It took her a moment to realize that Mike was not carrying her back up to the porch. Instead, they headed toward the barn. "Nooooo. Noooo. Please! No. I'm sorry . . . I'm so sorry . . . "

Mike dumped her on the bed in the barn. He did not tie her up. She lay, flat on her back. And blinked up at him, terrified. Would he hit her now? Rape her? But Mike just looked at her mournfully. "Now I'm sad. I really did want to share that nice dinner with ya. But our trust is absolutely BROKEN. Look what ya did. This is your fault, Cienna. Wrong move. Again." He clenched his fists. The look on his face was sheer anger . . . and pain.

She had hurt his feelings. She was too upset to try to soothe him. Besides, it wouldn't get her anywhere tonight. She turned her head into the pillow. Refused to apologize.

Mike stomped out the door, slamming it behind him and locking it. She supposed he would forget about her now. Cienna cried herself to sleep.

For the first time since Roger had kidnapped her, she prayed a desperate prayer.

CHAPTER TWENTY-TWO
Bay

AFTER BREAKFAST, Bay started morning farm chores. She dreaded them now because it meant she saw Sam even more. Each time he leered, grabbed her chest or stared at her, she begged in her heart to be reassigned to house chores instead.

A mere two days after the first time he had hurt her, he cornered her in the barn. He took her to the shed while she kicked and screamed. He spent some time again showing her who her boss was. Luckily, it was not hours this time. Sam still had farm chores to do. But she could barely walk when he was done, and her body throbbed where he had hit her. He sent her back to the house.

"Not that you deserve it. But I'm feeling a bit on the nice side today. Go to your room and chill out."

Bay scuttled as quickly as she could into the house but not to her room. Rose hadn't been feeling well that day or the day before. Worried about her friend, Bay visited her instead. She sat on the edge of Rose's bed and stared urgently at her. Rose didn't wake up. Her cheeks sported red splotches like a child with a fever. "Apple cheeks," Bay had heard it called.

Huh. Who had ever called it that? Her memory these days was pierced with holes and the pain of the last several days.

"Rose." Bay's voice broke. She had not spoken in several days. She still didn't want to. The quieter she was, the less chance for trouble. She reached over and gently shook Rose's arm. Rose opened her eyes and smiled at Bay.

"You talked." Rose's voice croaked like a frog.

Bay shook her head fiercely. And shrugged.

"You don't have to talk. I get it. I really do. Jasmine's gone now, isn't she?" Rose sounded sad.

Bay tilted her head. Considered that. Jasmine. Yes, the girl must be gone now. Disappeared into a world of . . . a world of what? Bay shook her head quickly. She wondered if the Witch-Devil had upped her dose of pills. It made the world a bit fuzzy. But at least the pain was dulled. She could make it through. She shrugged.

Rose scooted over and patted the mattress.

Bay smiled. Lay down next to her friend.

"Sam let you go for now?"

Bay nodded. Sure. After she had finally seen the shed, which truly was just a shed with a lawnmower and tools—and a dirty mattress and restraints in the back corner. No more mysteries on the farm. She'd been to the forbidden part of the house. Now she'd visited the shed. Wait. There was still the van to consider. And wherever the van with Sam and some of the girls went every night. Guess there was some mystery left after all.

"I knew another girl once." Rose whispered. They lay on their backs staring at the ceiling. "She stopped talking too. And then she actually made another personality. Weirdest thing. So she had two names, and they were like different people."

Huh. Rose was full of interesting information. Bay considered this silently. When she next turned to look at Rose, her friend was again asleep. Sleep was good. Safe in Rose's room, Bay also soon fell asleep.

She awoke a couple of hours later. In addition to the week of farm chores, she had one week of cooking dinner for everyone. Twice so far, she had cooked but left the kitchen before even eating. Being at the same table as Sam made her sick to her stomach. But she'd learned there were some advantages to cooking, too. For some odd reason, she got a stomachache and itchy when she drank milk. She could make substitutes for some of that. And sometimes there were leftovers. No one complained when she ate those the next morning instead of cereal and milk. Sam rarely came to breakfast. He had already been at work on the farm for several hours by then.

She glanced at Rose's clock. She had to get started downstairs, or she would face the wrath of both Sam and the Witch-Devil. As well as a few hungry girls who were currently wrapping up their afternoon free time, whatever that entailed. The Witch-Devil was right in one thing. At least they were all fed. She supposed she should be grateful. But her last few days had come with a whole new level of understanding. What could she possibly be grateful for while living in hell? Her friendship with Rose was the only thing that she could think of.

She rolled out of Rose's big bed with a groan and checked on her friend. She carefully took the stairs down to the bathroom to refill Rose's water glass. At least her friend was drinking. With her body tender and sore, Bay had a hard time managing the stairs the second time. But Rose would need more water. She would bring her food later, too. What was good for "apple cheeks"? Soup? Bread? Hot chocolate? Bay shook her head. Rose should probably have cold food since she was so warm. Maybe crackers from the pantry. Maybe ice in her water.

What was on the menu for that night? The Witch-Devil made a menu each week but didn't really pay attention if things got changed or moved around. That was a good thing, because half the time Bay reached for the needed ingredients, they were gone anyway. Improvisations had to be made and sometimes quickly. In the kitchen, Bay pursued the menu on the refrigerator. Chili, bread, and corn. Two of those were in a can, and bread was in the bag with red and blue markings.

Rose was much better in the kitchen than any of them. But so far, no one had complained about Bay's meals. All of the girls missed Rose at the table, for sure. And the fact that she was usually there standing up to Sam or the Witch-Devil in some way.

Bay found the two large cans of chili in the pantry. Her stomach rumbled. The front door slammed. Bay froze. Was it Sam? No, it was Nia and Bee, bantering about some stupid book they frequently disappeared into, when they could find one. She breathed a sigh of relief and went out. Nia and Bee sat at the kitchen table chatting. She felt like an older and more mature sibling as she cooked their meal and listened but didn't speak.

Bay picked at her food, never looking at Sam or anyone else. Then she went again to check on Rose, who seemed to be feeling a little better. She took her some toast, thinking chili might not be so good on Rose's stomach. Of course, the crackers in the pantry were opened and stale. Rose ate half a piece of the toast and drank water. It appeared that Sam and the Witch-Devil had forgotten about her. To Bay's knowledge, she was the only one who checked on Rose.

To Bay's dread, Amber informed her of the evening's plans. Bay had to dress up and ride in the van to the club. She guessed her final questions would be answered then, the last mystery solved. She shivered.

"You don't have a choice, you know, if you want to stay alive." Amber hopped off the living room couch. Now, after experiencing some of Sam's wrath, Bay believed her roommate. "And don't worry about getting pregnant. One of those pills you get in the morning, the green one, is birth control. Saves them money when no one gets knocked up. Or rarely. And the great part is you never have to have a period either. That rocks. Although sometimes I get a short one anyway. But it barely hurts." Amber hurried upstairs.

Pregnant? Pregnant!

Bay hadn't considered that possibility. Of course, she knew about the birds and the bees. She had started her period that spring. Which meant, which meant—what if Sam had gotten her pregnant? No, she calmed herself. She trusted Amber, although her roomie was a little harsh at times. And one of the pills would prevent that. That was a very good thing. Of course, if she had her choice, she would never see Sam again. At least the Witch-Devil left her alone now.

The Witch-Devil apparently assigned Amber the task of making sure her roomie got ready. Bay changed quietly and obediently, hating that the skirt was so short. It had a zipper the entire short length of the back. Anyone could grab it and zip it down and the whole thing would fall off. She tried on the pantyhose and instantly put a hole in them that tore up her thigh.

Amber sighed. "Just forget it. You'll have to go without."

No problemo.

Heels were another matter. She toddled so badly in them that Amber helped her take her first couple of steps. Then she told her to walk around and "practice."

Bay stepped carefully around the room a few times until she had a better hang of it.

It was time for hair and makeup. Amber seemed rushed and impatient now, looking at the clock on the nightstand. "This is your fault we're running behind. I'm always ready by now."

Bay wanted to say that she was sorry, but she didn't want to talk. She stayed silent as Amber curled her hair for her, pinned some of it back, and helped her put on makeup. "I'm not doing this for you every night." She stepped back to admire her work.

When Bay looked in the mirror, she didn't recognize herself. She looked so much older. At least sixteen.

"Huh," Amber snorted. "Darn it. Sam might say you look too old. Oh well. We're out of time. Tomorrow you can go as a ten-year-old." She laughed.

Whatever.

Bay toddled out of the room as Amber pushed her along, but she stopped at the stairs going to the third floor. With a fleeting and rebellious glance at Amber, she kicked off her heels and hurried up the stairs.

She shook Rose's arm gently. Rose mumbled, then turned to her.

"Jas . . . . Bay . . . ." Rose's eyes widened as she took in what Bay was wearing. "Oh no, oh no." She groaned and covered her face. "I'm sorry, lovey. I'm so sorry. It's probably because I can't go."

Bay felt sudden dread. What did Rose mean?

Rose reached out and pulled Bay in for a hug. She hugged her as fiercely as she could in her weakened state.

"Bay." Rose's tone sounded urgent. "You need to know that you will be okay. No matter what happens, think about other things. Happy things. Think of the day you will get out of here, because I know you will. You're not weak. You are strong. Do you understand me? Someone upstairs is watching out for you, and you are so strong. You'll be okay, I promise." She pushed Bay to arm's length and looked her in the eye. "Do you understand?"

Bay nodded. She would try to be strong. It was nice that Rose was looking out for her from the third floor. She knew her friend meant it. She would try to be strong like Rose. Not weak, like Bay.

"Bay!" Amber yelled up the stairs. "We have to go now, or we'll both be sleeping in the shed tonight!"

Bay shuddered. She stood and waved at Rose.

"Be strong." Rose closed her eyes again.

"Bay!" It was the Witch-Devil now.

Bay looked one more time at her friend. She pulled the blanket up to Rose's chest and fled, shutting Rose's door firmly behind her, as if to protect her friend. She fervently hoped that Sam was leaving Rose alone to rest and get better. She hurried down the stairs where the Witch-Devil grabbed her by the back of her hair. Amber glared at her.

"You piece of garbage!" The woman screeched and pulled her by the hair down to the first floor and out the kitchen door. The van was waiting with the engine running and lights on, everyone loaded up except for Amber and Bay.

The Witch-Devil pushed Bay into the van. Bay landed on Nia's lap.

Sorry!

She reached up to rub her sore head, tears in her eyes. Amber climbed in behind her. They both wiggled into place on the bench seats that were too short for all of them. There was no way even to fasten seatbelts.

Bay ended up by the window and barely registered that the driver in the front seat was not Sam before the man turned around and looked directly at her. He had blond hair and looked as big as a football player. "Well, you ain't starting out so great. Now we're gonna be late. Whose fault is that?"

Bay shrank back in the seat. She remembered Rose's words, "Be strong." She lifted her chin and stared back at the man defiantly. Cienna would be proud.

"Mouse don't talk no more." Nia shifted and smoothed her hair.

The man grunted. Gunned the van's engine down the driveway.

Bay turned and stared out the darkened window. This would be her first time off the farm in . . . weeks? Months? It was still summer, so weeks. And all she could think about as they drove was that Sam was not with them. That meant Sam was back at the farm. Rose wouldn't be safe after all.

CHAPTER TWENTY-THREE
Mollie

MOLLIE PARKED AT THE CAMPGROUND OFFICE. Inside the small building, she introduced herself to the owner and stated her purpose for being there. He seemed all too eager to help her solve the girls' disappearance, a typical attitude in an owner whose business had suffered through no fault of his own.

Mollie thanked him and went back to her truck. She dug Coal's new leather collar out of the pocket behind her driver's seat. She snapped on his leash. "Come on, boy."

Coal perked up, stretched, and jumped from the truck. He jaunted alongside her as she headed to the campsite where the two families had stayed. She'd had to put off her investigation for a few days because of new campers staying there, but the spot was finally empty again.

Mari had drawn her a diagram of the campground and the area where they'd set up. A triangle indicated where the girls' small tent had been, a circle for the fire, a labeled square for the picnic table, two larger squares for the other large tents, and the river, indicated by a squiggle of lines. Mari had even included where they parked their cars.

Mollie observed carefully, scouring the ground. She didn't know what she was looking for. Never did when she began working on her cases. Being at the scene sometimes brought understanding and often provided a final piece to the puzzle later. She took pictures with her cell phone. By the time she finished and headed toward the General Store, using the girls' route, she felt like she had a pretty good feel of the campsite. Apparently so did Coal. He had lapped twice from the river, sniffed empathically under the picnic table and peed in at least three places.

At the General Store, after hooking Coal's leash to the hook on the outside wall, she paused by the rack of postcards boasting Sasquatch, river views, the waterfall, and forests of evergreens. She continued to the ice cream counter, where a young man in a white shirt was restocking ice cream cones.

"Excuse me. Hi. I'm Mollie, a private investigator. Were you working the night the two girls from the campsite disappeared?"

"Nah, not me. That was Shay. Over there." He tilted his head toward the girl on the other side of the store. She pulled small log cabins out of a box, placed a sticker on them with a pricing gun, and set them on the shelves. She appeared to be about eighteen.

"Thanks." Mollie walked across the room and stuck out her hand. "Hi. I'm Mollie. I'm a private detective."

"So I hear." The girl ignored her hand. She flipped her long brown hair over her shoulder. Perhaps feeling a little defensive? Mollie often dealt with that. "Yeah, I was working when they came in. Doing the ice cream counter that night."

"Great. Can we chat?" Mollie pulled her phone from pocket and opened her Notes app. "What did they do when they got here?"

"They looked at the postcards and laughed about the Sasquatch ones. Then they grabbed sodas before coming to the ice cream counter. I don't remember the flavors.

Two cones." She reached down to grab and unwrap another log cabin.

Mollie nodded. "Did you see anyone following them or waiting outside?"

Shay gazed out the window as if trying to remember. "Not that I saw. Is that your dog?"

"Yes, that's Coal. He helps me out on my cases."

Shay nodded and stuck a sticker on the newest log cabin before setting it on the shelf. She sighed. Her defensive mood turned to sadness. "I wish I could help more, but I really don't know more than that. I hope they're okay. Oh, I did overhear them saying on the way out that they should take the long way back."

Mollie nodded. "Yes. Thanks. That they did. If you think of anything else, could you let me know?" She handed the girl a business card.

Shay nodded and tucked it in her back pocket. "Okay."

"Listen, Shay." Mollie caught her eye, holding the girl's gaze. "Stay safe. Maybe keep someone with you on your way to work and back."

Shay nodded. "My parents have been dropping me off and picking me up. My mom is freaking out."

"Better safe than sorry." Mollie waved to the two young people and left the store. Coal jumped up from the sidewalk and wiggled enthusiastically. She paused to study the "Missing and Endangered" poster taped to the inside of the door. Touched it through the glass. With a promise to herself to find the girls, she glared at the Wanted flyer next to the girls with Roger Wyatt's picture on it. She would get that creep, too.

Mollie unclipped Coal and headed to what she thought might be the long way back to the campsite the girls had chosen. It would take her past the lumber road where the cell phone, soda can, and ice cream cone remnants had been found.

On the way, she passed the post office and a few small shops. Outside the shops, benches boasted visitors. Most watched her without a word, and she sensed a general quietness about the town. Of course, Coal caught some attention and paused to be petted. Then he wandered over to the water bowl someone had left outside a store and lapped enthusiastically.

Mollie talked to each person she encountered, hoping that someone could provide a tidbit. All in all, people still seemed shocked and upset that "this" had happened in beautiful River Falls. Many wanted to know of any updates on the case, which she did not provide.

When she couldn't learn anything more from those she asked, she decided on a different tactic. She approached the next person, an older man, and after telling him who she was, blurted out, "Do you know or have you heard of Roger Wyatt?"

He cleared his throat and shuffled his feet. Turned to walk away.

Ha! She'd hit a nerve. "Sir, this is important." She caught up and walked beside him. "Please talk to me. What's your name? Please?"

"Ben Tucker. Why?"

In past instances, Mollie had sometimes shared more information than she should have in the interest of solving a case. But desperate times meant desperate measures. This man knew of Roger, whose "Wanted" poster hung at the store. She took a deep breath.

"Roger is a wanted man. We think he has a connection to the missing girls. Do you know where he is? How do you know him?"

Mr. Tucker stopped walking and faced her. "Can't help you. Sorry. I knew Roger when he was younger. His family used to vacation here every year. In fact, they would camp at that same campground. But I don't know where he is. I heard a few years ago that he spends time in California and Washington. I think his folks live in California now. He always was kind of a weird one . . . "

Mollie waited a moment. "Please think hard. Is there anything else that you know about him? Has he been back as an adult?"

"Yes, yes he has. I saw him at the General Store a few weeks ago," Mr. Tucker said. "He doesn't know me anymore, really. Or ignores me if he does. Anyway, that's all I know except I'm sure sorry those girls got taken."

"Thanks. Yes, we're working on it. Listen, Mr. Tucker—"

Coal pulled on his leash, eager to move on.

Mollie tugged him back beside her as she reached into her pocket for another business card. "It's very important that we find him. You could save these girls, or others, if you would please keep an eye out for him. Call 9-1-1 immediately if you see him and please let me know if you remember anything else."

Ben took her card and nodded. "Good work that you're doing." He shuffled away, mumbling.

Mollie pulled up her phone's Note app and found her to-do list. "Find Roger's family in California," she typed in. Maybe Miller was already working that angle. She would have to check.

For now, she and Coal would investigate the logging trail up ahead.

CHAPTER TWENTY-FOUR
Cienna

CIENNA AWOKE, FREEZING COLD. Her head throbbed. She heard noise outside the barn. She was sure of it. She stilled to listen. Yes, a car door slamming, and then voices.

"Help!" She rolled off the bed and ran to the door. Pounded on it. "Help! Please!"

Footsteps. The door unlocked. And before she knew it, she stood face to face with Roger, who sneered at her.

"No!" She stumbled back to the bed and dropped down. The lock was supposed to keep Roger out. But it hadn't. He was going to hurt her again. She just knew it.

She crossed her legs and arms. "What do you want? And by the way—" This had occurred to her when she saw Jazz on the TV "—you kidnapped us both, didn't you? Where's Jasmine?"

Roger sneered again. He slammed the door and strode toward her. He shoved her back on the bed, placing his hands around her throat. Struggling, Cienna reached to try to pull them off. She couldn't. She kicked at him. Managed to get one foot high enough to hit him on his backside with her thigh. Weak hit. But still she struggled and kicked some more. With her hands, she tried to hit him. He warded off her blows.

He tightened his hold and leaned down. His face only an inch from hers. She spat at him. Spittle landed right on his nose. Time to die? She would go kicking and screaming.

Roger glared at her and pinned her flailing body with his own.

"Listen here." His voice was low. Threatening.

She stopped struggling. He lightened some of the pressure on her throat. Which was good. She'd begun to feel lightheaded.

"There's something you're going to understand today, because obviously you don't git it yet. Mike owns you. He bought you fair and square. Do you know what that means?"

Insane! Cienna squirmed again and shook her head.

"It means—" He gave her a wicked smile. "—I sold you to him. He picked you out from all the chicks, and he wants you as his own. It means he can do whatever he wants to you because you belong to him."

Cienna emitted a strangled sound. Roger loosened his hold a bit more.

Where was Mike? He would save her. He had to. Owned her? Like a dog? Humans couldn't be owned!

"That means you can't escape. Ever. You'll be here until you die. And if you don't knock this crap off, that'll be soon. And in the meantime, you better do anything and everything he says."

He let go of her with one hand and yanked up her shirt. Cienna started shaking. Mike had not bought her a bra. She was completely exposed to this scumbag. Roger used one large, rough hand to grope her chest until it was painful. Tears streamed down her face. They soaked his other hand still around her neck.

He leaned down toward her ear. "Mmmm . . . do you understand?"

She nodded quickly. Her heart tried to beat out of her chest.

His breathing grew heavier. "I'll show you how it works, you whore." He removed his hand from her neck. Used it to rip the button forcefully from her jeans.

Cienna gasped. Choked back more tears. "I understand. I'll do what Mike wants. I-I promise."

Roger apparently didn't believe her. He used the next few hours to show her just who was the boss when he was around. He told her repeatedly that each time she disobeyed Mike, he would be back to remind her. When it finally ended, he shoved her into the corner and left. He locked the door behind him. She huddled in the corner of the room, naked, broken, and bruised. She shivered so hard that her entire body trembled. After an hour there, she crawled to the bed and under the covers, grateful that for now, Roger was gone.

Cienna didn't see Mike again for a long time. Now she understood. She had hurt and offended him. Perhaps her savior would never come back.

Roger came back the next day. She longed for the piece of glass hidden under the mattress in the house. She wanted to stab him right in the heart as he again raped her, choked her until she was lightheaded again, and slapped her.

"I am the boss. Mike is your boss." He made her repeat it to him.

Cienna gritted her teeth and never stopped fighting him. When she was able to, she screamed for Mike.

When he left, she hobbled to the sink to drink. She had eaten no food since being returned to the barn. Weakness hovered. But it also made it easier to disappear into another world when Roger visited. She thought of happy times with her family and friends, vacation at River Falls, and even her brother. She thought of Christmas. Getting an A on her last report card in English. She remembered the waterfall. The sound of the rushing river. It had been a long time since she had seen the ocean, but she thought often of the roar of the waves. It helped block out the awful things that Roger did to her.

He could hurt her body. And boy did it hurt. But he couldn't hurt her spirit. Roger thought he was in charge. But Cienna was rallying. She would hurt him back someday. She spent several hours designing various scenes in her head. All ended with Roger dead and locked in the barn.

One day when Roger came back, she hardly knew he was there. All she felt was his heavy boot kicking her. All she heard was his cursing as the left the room. She fell asleep again.

She awoke to Mike stroking her hair. She couldn't focus, or she would have jumped away from his touch. Then she was sitting up, and he was spoon-feeding her soup and holding her head to up to help her sip a soda. After having some of each, she felt a little more clearheaded.

"Are you going to hurt me, too?" She pushed him away. Curled up in the blankets to go back to sleep. He left her alone and locked the barn door behind him.

She awoke again later, hearing the lock open. She fully expected to see Roger walk in. But it was Mike. He looked at her gently as he set a tray filled with food on the floor. Then he adjusted his red baseball hat and left again.

She heard his truck engine start, and she pushed herself up on one elbow. With Mike gone, she was safe from him. But where was Roger? And how had Roger come in anyway? Hadn't Mike installed the lock for that reason?

Hunger and weakness overcame fear. She managed to get out of the bed and eat, hunching over the tray on the floor and cramming rice into her mouth with her hands. Her muscles ached. There were vegetables, and something that resembled canned meat. She ate it all, even though she'd always refused to eat any type of canned meat at home. Her stomach revolted. She threw up all over the barn floor.

She found her clothes and dressed. Her jeans weren't easy on the sore areas of her body, but she was cold and felt

safer and warmer with clothes on. Regardless, it was no
barrier for Roger and she understood that now. He and Mike
were in charge.

She tried to fit her whole head under the water faucet,
attempting to wash herself. And she drank. She wondered
how she could break out of the barn but was unable to stay
awake. She didn't even make it back to the bed but instead
curled up on the floor and fell into a dreamless sleep.

CHAPTER TWENTY-FIVE
Bay

THE VAN PULLED UP TO A ONE-STORY BUILDING with no windows. It was ugly grey with a large flashing sign out front. Bay didn't catch what the sign said as the van quickly pulled around to the back and parked. The girls chatted the whole way there, except Bay, who just listened. She heard that this club was mostly for men who liked to relax. But not always. There were women who apparently came, too. Amber bragged that she had seen both women and men at once. Whatever that meant.

They piled out of the van. Nia and Charli strode ahead, swinging their hips. Bee hung back, and Bay stayed near her.

Bee sighed. "The first time here sucks."

Bay nodded. She wasn't sure that anything could top what she had already suffered. She was nervous for sure, because so far, all the mysteries of the farm terrified her. But tonight, she was more scared for Rose back at the farmhouse.

"It won't suck for Bay." Amber snickered. She had hung back in the middle of the group instead of prancing up ahead with Charli and Nia. "Rose told her she's strong."

Bay jerked her head up and found Amber's eyes.

Jerk. How dare she listen in and then tell everyone that. Not cool. Shaking her head, she ignored her. Bee smiled sympathetically.

The blond driver guy knocked at the back door. Another guy with very dark hair and a round belly let them in. He was smoking a cigar. "About time. You know I don't have to use Sam's girls, and he'll be missing a pretty penny if I find someone else!" His voice boomed. He let them in and motioned with his hands for the girls to file down a dark hallway.

"Yeah, yeah." The blond driver flicked a bug off the wall. "New girl held us up. She'll get the hang of it."

The man dark hair laughed loudly. "That she will. I want to see her up there in the first group. Everyone likes the new ones. Is she young?"

"Twelve."

"Young enough, then . . . "

Bay shuddered. Their voices faded as the girls moved down the opposite hallway.

The group turned as one, pulling Bay along with them, and entered a small, dark room. She heard noise through the walls. Rowdy voices. Shouting here and there. Claps and whistles. The occasional, "Hey, baby, come see me now," and similar. Bay's fear grew. She tried to back into the corner of the room.

A different man waited for them in the small room. He introduced himself as Eddie. He checked them all over, his eyes roaming up and down. He occasionally teased some wayward pieces of hair and adjusted skirts that had somehow slid and weren't centered.

"And what's your name, sweetie?" He smiled at Bay. He pulled her out of her corner and into the middle of the small room while Amber snickered. He was only about as tall as she was. She found herself looking him in the eye, but not able to say a word. "You don't talk?"

"She don't talk no more." Nia pulled on some boots with a zipper up the back.

"Ah, okay." Eddie put his hand out to cradle Bay's cheek. She jumped. He laughed. "Be careful, Eddie," he murmured to himself. "New one's jumpy. Well, not for long." Eddie wore a headset. He paused to listen. "Listen here, girls. Boss says the new girl goes out first, but she won't know what to do, so you and you go with her." He pointed to Nia and Amber. Amber rolled her eyes. He pushed a button on his earpiece and spoke into the microphone hanging on his cheek. "Got that, boss."

"Oh my gosh. I never get a break from her." Amber grabbed Bay's arm and pulled her up three stairs through a black curtain. Nia followed.

When she arrived on a platform, Bay froze. People cheered. Lights blinded her. She remembered how lights had blinded her when she was in a play. In a play? She shook her head. Bay had never been in a play. But somehow, she knew it was a stage. And from the calls and whistles, it seemed they had an audience.

Music with a rhythmic beat blared. Someone called out, "Let's see it, baby!" Her eyes adjusted a little. She saw a pole in the middle of the stage.

Amber grabbed Nia and they started dancing. That was the only way Bay could describe it. Not really dancing though, like at the prom, but moving in tandem, in beat to the music. The calls and whistles from the audience increased.

Bay froze. She looked back at the curtain they had emerged from. Could she make a run for it? Her eyes adjusting more, she saw the blond driver at a table near the stage, drinking a beer. He winked at her and lifted his beer as if toasting her. Her eyes darted to the other side of the audience as the man with the dark hair and big belly suddenly jumped on the stage.

"Sorry, ladies and gentlemen." He bowed. "Pardon the interruption, but apparently the new girl needs some help."

Some people in the audience snickered as he approached Bay, grabbing her by the arm. The people in the audience who had been distracted suddenly stopped to watch.

He dragged her to the pole. Nia and Amber continued dancing around him. Bay tried to pull away, but he pushed her up hard against the pole while whistles from the audience increased. He pushed against her backside, making a lewd motion back and forth. "Feel this, darling?" he said in her ear. "You work for me while you're here. Want some more? I see you have a handy zipper on the back of your skirt . . . "

Bay shook her head quickly. No, no . . . She trembled. On the stage? He would do this to her on the stage?!

"Then you better dance!" He snapped and released her quickly. She fell to the floor. Her skirt had pulled up a little bit and her underwear showed. She blushed. The audience roared as she tried in vain to pull the tight skirt down. She stared up as Nia came over to help her up. Nia had no shirt on! Her chest was completely bare! Bay shook her head in confusion. The man with the dark hair had left the stage, but no matter. To Bay's horror, every eye in the audience seemed to be on her.

"Come on, girl, you can do this." Nia danced closer.

Bay remembered Rose's words. "Be strong, you will get out. Be strong."

After Nia pulled her up off the floor, Bay wiggled her skirt down, and found herself up against Nia's chest and moving along with the music. Okay, maybe she could do this. Anything was better than that man shoving her up against the pole and working her skirt up again. Or anything else he might do. She breathed a little easier. Nia smiled at her. This was apparently what they were supposed to do. But then what?

Out of the corner of her eye, Bay saw Amber move to the front of the stage. There were people, mostly men, sitting in chairs in front of the stage. Amber moved slowly, shaking her chest, and several whistled. Then she slowly took her shirt off, dangled it at the end of her finger, and dropped it. Men, and one woman, leaned forward and tucked bills in the waistband of Amber's skirt, murmuring appreciatively.

Bay continued to dance with Nia the best that she could. Fortunately, the song was soon over. Amber and Nia took her arms on either side and together, they bowed. Nia and Amber waved at the audience. Bay stared at the bright lights.

"Shirt off, new girl!" one guy yelled, but Nia and Amber hustled her off the stage.

"Not bad." Nia admitted. "I thought you were gonna ruin it for all of us. But not bad at all." Bay breathed a sigh of relief. She blinked in the darkness. Now she couldn't see well. But it was a relief to be off the stage.

Eddie waited. He ordered them to sit down in a row of hard chairs with mirrors behind them while he hustled Bee out to the stage on her own. She was dressed in a short, sassy skirt and pigtails, with ribbons in her hair. The song that started sounded like one that would play for a princess in an animated movie. The audience roared.

Bay sat as she was told and ignored Amber, who had passed most of her tips to Eddie when she had arrived backstage but tucked a larger bill in her shoe when she thought no one was looking. Bay wanted to thank Nia for her help but couldn't. She assumed that they would soon be out there again. Someone would probably force her to take her shirt off the next time. After all, when the girls usually left in the van, they didn't come back until at least 3 a.m. So they must dance to more than one song.

Eddie listened to his headset. "You got it." He grinned at the girls. "You and you." He pointed at Nia and Bay. "Done for now. You're going VIP."

"VIP." Nia sighed happily and turned to Bay. "This is good. We'll probably be busy enough you won't have to dance again."

That sounded good. Bay got up and followed Eddie and Nia out the door and down another hallway. Eddie opened a door and ushered them inside. "Mr. Nettles. Nice to see you again. Here's your entertainment. Now, you girls have fun." He left, closing the door behind him.

"Hello, Mr. Nettles." Nia politely nodded her head and then looked at the ground.

"Hello again, Nia." He wore slacks and a button up shirt. He sat on a leather couch. Black curly hair framed his face. He scratched a short dark beard. "Your friend?"

"Bay. She don't talk."

"Doesn't," he corrected her.

"Doesn't." Nia repeated and tilted her head slightly. "Sorry."

"Well, she'll have to make up for that then." He rose. Poured himself a glass of wine. "Cheers. And let's get on with it."

On with what? A fast panic filled Bay's stomach. She might puke. She held her mouth closed, tightly. Just in case.

Mr. Nettles laughed. He sat back on the couch and rested his elbows on his knees, his wine glass dangling from one hand. "Yes, Miss Newbie. Get on with it. Take your clothes off and get over here."

CHAPTER TWENTY-SIX
Cienna

SUNLIGHT BLAZED THROUGH THE DOOR when Mike opened it. Cienna blinked rapidly, groaned, and closed her eyes again. What did he want? "Just leave me alone."

"Well. Have ya learned your lesson? No fun going back to the barn I suppose after all the comforts of the house."

She opened her eyes again. Raised her eyebrows and blinked. Her head ached. Tired of the fight. "The comforts of the house? Yeah. That's what I missed." Did Mike not know that Roger had abused her in almost every way possible? Anytime he wanted to? Each time, she thought she would die. Was it four times now? Five? The days blurred together like one long nightmare. She closed her eyes again. Pulled the blanket up to her chin and rolled over to face the wall.

"It was yer own fault." Mike laughed. "That phone hasn't worked in years. I got tired of the sales calls and turned it off. And ya know, if it had just been that, I might have forgiven things but then ya ran. AGAIN."

"Yes. I ran. Again." She turned back toward him. Pulled herself upright. Glared. Anger simmered and bubbled up like a volcano. She leaned forward. Her dirty curls swung over her eyes. She finally stood, wobbling. Why couldn't she be about ten feet tall about now? She felt about two. She probably looked like Cousin It. "You see, I'm not used to being owned. No one owns humans. It's wrong! You don't understand, Mike!" She spat on the floor. Why, she wasn't sure. She wanted to show her distaste in some way. But now not only Cousin It hovered—she might as well be wild George of the Jungle too! Check that, since she smelled like trash, she was definitely George of the Jungle. Living under a bridge! "Leave me alone! You aren't allowed to touch me, and neither is Roger." She swore loudly. Plopped back down on the bed, pulling the blankets up to her chin.

Mike shrugged. "Okay." And he left.

Cienna started crying as soon as Mike closed the door. Mike, her protector from Roger. Who hadn't hurt her, but had only taken gentle care of her needs. Surely, he would not start hurting her now. But what if he did? Did that even matter anymore? She was soiled trash. She disgusted herself. But Mike would always treat her better than Roger.

She suddenly wanted a shower. Wanted to wash away the scum of the last several days. Wanted a decent meal. Needed clean clothes once again. Ones that wouldn't remind her of the horror in the barn.

She limped to the door, realizing that the bar had not slid across when Mike left. She slowly turned the doorknob. Pushed hesitantly. The door opened. He stood on the other side. She gaped in relief. "Do ya want to come back to the house now?" He smiled gently.

She nodded vigorously. Tears fell in torrents. She covered her eyes with a dirty hand. Shrunk back, afraid.

"Come on." He reached out to take her by the hand, even though she was now the scum of the earth. He walked her out into blinding sunshine. To his home.

And Cienna realized, it was her home as well.

Inside, Mike gently pushed her into a kitchen chair. Right in front of the broken phone. Stupid phone. Her head hurt. She laid it on the table, cradled in her arms. Her curls stuck to her face. Snot covered her sleeve.

Mike made ramen from two packets and toast with strawberry jam, which she practically inhaled. And then he made them both a drink with juice. Out of the corner of her eye, she recognized a bottle of a clear liquid. The same kind her parents kept in their liquor cabinet. Vodka. Mike added it to both their drinks.

Cienna sipped hers and almost choked. She had drunk some once at a friend's sleepover when they were passing one around. After one burning sip, she had declined to drink more. But now she looked at the glass, swirled it around and observed how the sun's rays hit it. It made purple swirls with the grape juice Mike had added. Pretty. She took another small sip. Much better mixed with juice. And she was so thirsty. She took a large drink and set it back on the table. That was probably enough.

Mike sat down next to her. Drained half his glass. "That will help ya." He nodded at the glass. "Ya gotta be sore with those bruises."

Cienna glared. Bruises, indeed. She picked up the glass and drained it. Within seconds, warmth filled her stomach, went all the way to her toes, and reduced her pain. She felt sleepy, warm, and comfortable for the first time in days. She pushed her bowl and plate away and laid her head on the table. A bit dizzy. Mike quietly finished his drink, ate a bowl of noodles, and helped Cienna to her feet.

She didn't fight when he helped her into the bathroom. He turned on the bath water, looked at her with obvious hesitation, then added a generous amount of liquid soap bubbles to the water. It immediately frothed. He helped her take her shirt off, shaking his head sadly when he saw the bruises marked almost all over her chest and arms.

"Such a shame, sweetie," he whispered angrily. "It's like—it's like a monster did this to ya!"

Cienna whipped her head toward the door. Well, at least her body did. Her head seemed very slow to follow. She almost stumbled.

"Where is he? He can get in here, can't he? Can't he, Mike? You-You didn't protect me at all."

"Didn't protect ya! What are you saying? Protect ya from WHO? Silly girl. If ya had obeyed me in the first place, this wouldn't have happened."

Cienna ground her teeth but let him undress her the rest of the way. What did it matter now? He helped her into the tub and winced with her when the soapy water hit the sores all over her body. "Ow, ow, ouch." She closed her eyes, trying to be brave, but she couldn't help the outburst.

She apparently wasn't so strong, anymore.

"I know, I know." He spoke softly. "But we need to wash out the wounds. Then ya can relax. The drink should help." He reached to the shelf behind him, grabbed a washcloth, and started washing her wounds.

She took deep breaths, suddenly fearful. "I got it." She pushed his hand away roughly.

For a moment he looked angry, and the fear in her heart grew. But he stepped back and just watched her.

This was Mike. Not Roger. Mike wouldn't hurt her. Right? He hadn't. But she was to obey him, do whatever he asked, at least until she escaped. What did that mean to obey him? What would he require of her now?

Under the cover of the bubbles, Cienna washed herself all over. She dunked her head under to wet her hair. She grabbed the shampoo bottle while Mike sat on the toilet seat and nodded in satisfaction. He reached over to drain some water, explaining that she would need to rinse. She nodded back. Her head felt extra heavy and warm. The bubbles delightful.

Her movements felt slow. She hoped Mike wouldn't get mad at her for taking so long.

He ran clear water and grabbed a large plastic pitcher to help her rinse her stubborn curls. They always held more soap than needed. She couldn't help but think how it was at home. There, she would have drained the tub and taken a shower to rinse. But Mike appeared to be staying in the bathroom. If she did what was normal, her full body would again be in his view. What if that made him like her too much? And if he "liked it" like Roger did, perhaps Mike would turn into a monster, too.

She groaned as they finished rinsing her hair. Mike apparently took that to mean that the rinsing felt good. "Much, much better, baby. And now ya must never be dirty again." He looked her in the eye. "Do ya understand me? Ya were a disgusting mess coming out of that barn. Makes me very angry. Ya know I don't often git mad, but I'll have no more dirt on ya." He reached out and shook her shoulder hard.

Cienna wilted against the other corner of the tub. Okay. Clear instruction. This then was what Roger was talking about. And if she didn't obey, Roger would be back to hurt her for days on end or maybe even kill her this time. She shuddered.

Mike released her shoulder. "Git that?"

"Y-Yes. I understand." Tears filled her eyes at this new attitude of submission that had been beaten into her during those few days in a barn. "I- I'll stay clean for you, Mike."

His eyes softened as he observed her. She drew her knees up to her chest, huddled in the corner of the tub.

"Sweetie." He shook his head. "Ya must not realize how beautiful ya are. How else could ya have allowed this to happen? I'll never understand. Now, time to heal. No more bruises. No more dirt."

"I understand." She said it louder this time. Her thoughts swirled trying to make sense of it. Of course, she would be dirty after days in the barn. And Mike knew she had been out there because he had carried her there. But he hadn't come to rescue her. Had he not heard her cries and screams? She shook her head.

Weariness overcame her.

"Soak." Mike got up and left the bathroom, poking his head in only to leave her a small stack of new clothes on the side of the sink.

"Mike." Sleepiness overcame her. "Can't I get a bra?"

Even though all of her had now been exposed to both men, she felt safer fully clothed.

Mike laughed. "I hear gals are much more comfortable without that silly stuff." He grinned at her and then closed the door. Then through the door, "But maybe if ya are really good for a while, we can go shopping!"

Okay. Grateful for the clothes on the counter, she realized she couldn't stay in the bubble bath all night. She just hoped she would be allowed to sleep in the guest room.

Cienna dozed. When she awoke in chilly water, her mouth tasted funny. She wanted a large glass of cold water. She hurriedly pushed herself to her feet, noting the light through the window was dimming. How long had she been in the tub? Her body still hurt, but the pain decreased some. She started to feel human again, except for her fingers and toes, which now looked like Grandma's skin in the years before she had died.

At the thought of Grandma and her family, Cienna felt a little energy. She must never give up. She would obey, and she would do what she had to do to survive and hopefully never come across Roger again. But she would watch and listen and someday, somehow get out. She would gain Mike's trust. And not screw it up this time.

If she didn't keep working on that, she would die. And she definitely wanted to live, if nothing else than to make sure Roger got his due.

CHAPTER TWENTY-SEVEN
Bay

B AY WASN'T THE ONLY ONE QUIET on the way back to the farmhouse in the predawn hours of the morning. Everyone seemed tired after a long night of work. The stupid driver seemed tired too. He kept weaving into the other lane. He didn't bother with conversation.

The night seemed unending. She had puked on herself once, after the man in the room smacked her in the head for not obeying fast enough. He made her strip and take a shower in the bathroom to wash the puke off. He watched her until he joined her there. He gently washed her hair while murmuring softly. After that was through, she discovered he was no different from the other men in what he took from her. When they finally returned to the couch, Nia was asleep. He woke her up and put them both to work. Still feeling sick to her stomach, Bay complied. She knew worse would be ahead if word got back to Sam of her nausea or her complete stupidity on stage. He owned her now.

Bay hurried up to the third floor as soon as she could and saw that Rose had finished another glass of water. She cheered silently. Her friend was asleep, and Bay felt her hot forehead. She sighed. Sat on the edge of the bed. In the morning, she would talk to the Witch-Devil. Rose obviously needed a doctor. In the meantime, since the Witch-Devil didn't appear when they returned home, and Bay had no idea where she and Sam even slept, she went down to the bathroom and got a washcloth, running it under cold water. She took it upstairs and used it to wipe Rose's bright cheeks. She laid it across her friend's forehead. She sighed again. Someone downstairs was watching out for Rose. She would never stop. Rose had to hang in there and get better. Bay couldn't make it without her.

Exhausted, she fell asleep next to her friend. She wondered if she would ever get to bed at a decent hour again.

A few hours later, Bay awoke to the Witch-Devil shaking both of her shoulders and yelling in her face.

"Get out of bed, you, lazy piece of garbage! You aren't even supposed to be up here. You have your own room! This is out of control!" Pulling Bay by the hair, she yanked her to the door. Bay managed to turn her head and look back to Rose. Rose hadn't even stirred.

Rose needed water and a doctor. Bay hoped she had said it aloud. If so, the Witch-Devil ignored her. She gritted her teeth as the big woman pushed her down the stairs. She almost tripped but managed to keep her balance.

"Extra chores for you today. In fact, I think you'll really like today." The Witch-Devil shoved her into the kitchen.

Everyone else sat at the table and looked up expectantly. Sam was there too for the first time in several days. His eyes glittered as he eyed her zip-up skirt and skimpy shirt, still on from last night.

Bay sat miserably and stared at the cereal and toast that the Witch-Devil plopped down in front of her. Covered in milk, the cereal sloshed over the side. She pushed it away. They couldn't force her to eat, could they? She would either break out in hives or have to run to the bathroom all day.

That would get her in even more trouble, either way. And she wanted to save the toast for Rose.

"You missed med time cuz you were sleeping in a bed not yours." The Witch-Devil sneered. "You don't get no pills."

Bay looked at her lap. Her mode for coping with whatever the day brought was gone. And the birth control too. Somehow, she would have to make sure no men messed with her today.

The new building was coming along well, Sam announced. In a few months, the girls would work from there instead of the closed-off part of the house. It was closer to the highway, which would mean more business, so the girls should be glad for that. "Every room is like a penthouse. Clients'll pay a much higher price." He laughed. "Something had to change since none of you are earning your keep around here. I go in the hole just feeding you all and paying for utilities."

Bay stared at the table as the girls chattered around her about the new place. Then she stood and started clearing the table and filling the dishwasher. She dumped her cereal down the garbage disposal.

Suddenly the Witch-Devil was at her side. "You wasting food, girl?" She grabbed her arm.

Bay shook her head, but the Witch-Devil clenched her tightly. "Just wait. You wait 'til you see what's in store for you today."

Bay shuddered. The woman let her go suddenly. Bay stumbled but righted herself and continued scrubbing dishes. The fat woman moved away, and she finished washing them like nothing had happened. What could she do to get some meds? Could she break into the locked desk drawer in the study area? Was that where they even were? She scrubbed the frying pan as hard as she could, thinking only of how she could get some pills.

Before leaving the room, Sam came over and stood close to her by the sink. Her lower lip trembled. "Nice skirt." He barely even whispered. "Kinda showy, don't you think? But don't worry, it won't be on for long." Her cheeks flamed.

Bay bit her lip and concentrated on the dishes. The Witch-Devil grew angry when ignored. But sometimes ignoring Sam made him go away. She risked it.

He turned and left, slamming the kitchen door.

Bay felt the Witch-Devil staring. "It's not my fault," she wanted to say. But she couldn't. She scrubbed the dishes harder. When she finished, she wiped all the counters, cleaned the stovetop, and washed off the kitchen table. It would be stacked up again soon enough. She was going to the pantry to grab the broom when the Witch-Devil stopped her. "That's enough! Go take a shower. Your clothes for the day are on your bed. Your bed, not Rose's."

Bay changed direction. Her feet dragged up the stairs. She clearly remembered the pain after the last shower the Witch-Devil demanded. This time, there were no meds to dull it. What had she done to deserve this? Would she have to kill herself to get out of it? Every day, that seemed like more of a possibility.

But someone upstairs was watching out for her, right?

Yes, the thought of Rose on the third floor kept her strong. "You'll get out of here." With all her heart, Bay wanted to believe her.

She showered and dressed in the clothes the Witch-Devil set out in her room. She put on the makeup that was on the dresser.

Amber sat on her bed and sneered at her. "I got house chores today. But then again, I came back to my bed last night, and some people are too good for that."

Bay didn't comment. She finished putting on the mascara and the lipstick, and left the room, her head held high. Stay strong for Rose!

She continued the mantra in her head as the Witch-Devil unlocked the forbidden door in the kitchen and shoved her into the darkish hallway. Told her to go into the third door on the right. Trembling, Bay complied.

It was empty, with just a bed and a hard chair. She sat in the chair, pulled her knees up to her chin, wrapped her arms around her knees, and waited.

Within moments, the Witch-Devil brought the first client through the door. She closed it behind them.

And that is how the day continued. Bay lost track of the number of men that came through the door and vaguely remembered a woman as well. As the day grew longer, she grew nauseated from the lack of meds and food. She had to be let out of the room several times to rush to the bathroom in the hallway. But there was no break for her. As soon as she was done being sick, the Witch-Devil made her wash her mouth out with a strong mouthwash, brush her hair, and sent her back to the room to await the next client.

CHAPTER TWENTY-EIGHT
Mollie

MOLLIE AND COAL REACHED THE BASE of the logging road. She kept her eyes on the ground as they walked, a habit of hers to look for any possible clues. Anything weird, unusual, something the police detectives and searchers might have missed sometimes stood out to her. She stopped about halfway up the lumber road. Paused. Coal stood still. His nose tilted to the sky. Silent. Mollie appreciated his intuition.

This was where they had found the tire tracks. Jasmine's cell phone too. She knew they had also found fingerprints on the cellphone. But the department wouldn't tell her who they belonged to. Must be Roger's. Mollie let Coal sniff around before continuing up the trail. She wanted to complete the full experience and then spend more time at the crime scene on the way down. "Good boy." His tail wagged slightly but his intensity never wavered as he sniffed and explored.

Coal loped forward when a rabbit crossed their path. She unclipped him from the leash. They had no company. He was well trained. The dog took off after the rabbit, scrambled through some bushes and trees, making a racket. He reappeared a few minutes later with a disappointed look on his face. Mollie laughed at him.

Coal sighed and walked alongside her up the road. His sniffer started going again.

As they walked, stumbling on occasion on the rough, unused road, Mollie tried to place herself in the minds of the girls. What had they chatted about as they walked? School? She understood that starting this new school year, they would attend different schools. She wondered how Jasmine in particular was dealing with the upcoming separation. Jasmine had continued to text her mother while they walked. Mari had gladly provided them screenshots of the texts. But it was all casual conversation.

They reached the part of the road where the girls had veered off and found the cliffside. As Mollie peered down at the river, she suspected they had come for the view. A slight wind ruffled her bangs. She looked up and saw another rock cliff across the river. Here and there, trees stuck out of the cliffside at odd angles. Some looked almost dead. Others clearly thrived. Below, the river churned. She heard the rapids even from far above.

Mollie wanted to build a house right there at that spot. Perfect.

She sat at the edge of the cliff, again trying to conjure up what the girls might have been feeling. Coal sat next to her and laid his head on her lap. She stroked his ears as he relaxed.

"Maybe there'll be another rabbit on the way down."

He thumped his tail on the dirt. His ears perked as they both heard a furious rustling in the bushes. They turned to see a squirrel chasing another squirrel up a nearby tree. Nature at its best. Maybe even better than at the beach. Coal sighed in contentment and rested his head again on her lap.

Would Cienna and Jasmine ever see nature in its glory again? Mollie's heart ached. It was essential that she stay emotionally removed from the cases she worked on.

Sometimes that was very tough. Two young girls had already been gone for four months from home. She needed to find them. Her heart would not let her rest until she did. And if she couldn't find the girls alive, she at least owed it to their families to let them know what had happened.

Mollie stood up and tried to brush the dirt off her jeans. Coal sat up and wagged his tail, ready to go again.

"Got that, boy? We must find them. We have to." He tipped his head to the side. Coal understood. He would help.

They walked down the logging road and back to the crime scene. Mollie searched through the bushes and around the trees. Coal sniffed the road like crazy. Distracted by another rabbit, he rammed his head into a large wild blueberry bush next to the spot where some of the tire tracks had originally been found. Half his body disappeared into the bush. His tail wagged furiously.

"What do you have, Coal?" Mollie pushed back on the bushes to see better. The rabbit darted out the other side. Coal gave chase.

A glint caught Mollie's eye. She stared down at the dirt under the bush where the broken branches were now pushed aside. A credit card! Her breath caught. She looked closer. The card faced up. The name on it was Devon James.

She dug her phone out of her pocket to call to Detective Miller. "I think we might have an accomplice. I found a credit card at the scene. How soon can you send someone?"

CHAPTER TWENTY-NINE
Cienna

SINCE MIKE LEFT THE BATHROOM, Cienna showered to completely rinse all the bubbles off and ran her hair under the water again for good measure. No dirt. Not allowed. She would make sure no speck of dirt hit her again. Until she escaped. Then maybe she would find a mud puddle to roll around in like a pig. Or at least talk her dad into off-road four-wheeling.

She toweled off gently and carefully, wincing. She looked in the mirror, shocked at the misshapen face looking back at her. So ugly. She started to cry. Two black eyes and a long cut across her forehead that looked ready to bleed at any time. In a haze, she remembered Roger pushing her down on her knees on the bed. Then pulling her hair back and slamming her forehead down on the edge of the small wooden headboard. After that, her vision doubled for several hours. She noted bruises around her neck where he'd gripped her tightly. Her jaw was black and blue. It would take a long time, she suspected, before Mike would take her shopping with him.

Cienna bent down to dry her legs and noted bruises up and down both. With her fists, legs, and anything else she could think of, she had fought. She had tried so hard. She grimaced, realizing she had inflicted some of her own injuries as she struggled against him.

Still dizzy, she stood and grabbed the sink for support. She fought a sudden and overwhelming desire for Mom. But having failed them all, they might never forgive her. "I'm so sorry, Mama."

Hearing movement out in the family room and then the sound of the television, she quickly finished drying off. She dressed in the sweats, tee shirt, and socks stacked on the counter. She dried her hair with the towel as much as possible, then borrowed Mike's comb and tried to get the dark curls away from her face. When they snarled in the comb, she changed her mind and combed them forward to hide some of the bruising. She needed a haircut but didn't dare ask. She wouldn't tease and play with Mike anymore. Look where she ended up after trying that tactic. No, she would play meek and obedient. She would never be the same after Roger.

But she would survive. She would get home.

Cienna picked up her dirty clothes, opened the bathroom door, and found Mike in the recliner watching an old sitcom. He chuckled. Didn't he ever work? Maybe that's when he put her in the barn. She would ask. One of the many things she needed to learn to regain his trust . . . and get out of this place.

"Mike. Where do I put my dirty clothes?"

He laughed. "Well, ya wash them, doofus. Done laundry before?"

She lifted her chin. "Yes, I do my own at . . . I usually do my own."

Mike slammed down the footrest on the recliner, went upstairs, and came down with a hamper. "Come along. Ya might as well earn yer keep."

Cienna's heart clenched, and her jaw tightened instantly. Earn her keep? How about the last few days in the barn?

Hadn't that been earning her keep? How much more would these men expect of her?

Mike opened a door in the kitchen and led her down a shaky stairway. At the bottom, he flipped a light switch. The dim lightbulb was just bright enough to reveal a washer and dryer in the corner of the room, empty shelving on the other side, and various odds and ends like a wheelbarrow, tarps, a shovel, and old machinery.

Mike motioned her to the washer. She obeyed hesitantly, noting another pile of clothes on the floor in front of it. She knew they were dirty and now part of her job.

"Soap?"

He motioned to the cupboard above the washer. "Everything is up there."

She nodded. Began to sort the clothes. Including what he brought down in the hamper, the pile in front of the washer, and her own. Putting one load into the washer, she added soap.

Mike watched her with his arms crossed. She ignored him. Swallowing hard, she quickly threw in her handful of clothes Roger had removed from her and stuffed them in with the rest. The jeans had no button anymore, but they were the only jeans she had.

The lid plopped down with a bang.

Seconds later, Cienna heard a weird sound. A mew. A cat? She shook her head. Maybe she was going crazy.

"Start it already," Mike growled.

She looked at the dials, immediately confused. Two dials. She tried to think of the washer at home, but it had been so long since she'd been there. Her brain felt tired, and her head still hurt.

Mike reached around her and turned one dial to "regular" and the other to "warm". He pushed the "start" button.

Got it. Regular, warm and start.

He turned the light out and ushered her back upstairs.

"Now ya can make dinner." Mike smirked. "I'm thinking this will go a lot differently than last time."

With a deep breath, Cienna looked around the kitchen. It looked the same, but everything had changed. She felt better pain-wise. The vodka must have helped with that. But her heart felt heavy. "Yes." She sighed. "What do you want for dinner, Mike?"

He ignored her and returned to the family room, where the sitcom still blared.

"I see," she announced to the empty room. She bit her lip, wishing she could take back the comment. Fortunately, he hadn't heard her. As she looked around, Cienna remembered a movie from when she was small, *Beauty and the Beast*. Wouldn't it be nice right now if everything in the kitchen came alive, cooked dinner, cleaned up, and sang while they were doing it? She rolled her eyes at her weird thoughts.

She glared at the dead phone as she passed it to go to the refrigerator. Stupid phone. She didn't even think of running out the front door. Somehow, she knew Roger would be out there waiting. If she got caught, WHEN she got caught, she would have days of torture in the barn.

She found chicken breasts thawing in the refrigerator and leftover rice. Mom would say they needed a veggie too, but she didn't see any. She wondered where all the salad fixings had gone from the last shopping trip. Was she in the barn longer than she thought? There were apples in a bowl on the table. Those would have to do.

"Make all the chicken." Mike bellowed from the other room. "I want the leftovers for lunch tomorrow." Could he see her from there? Ugh.

"No problem." Despite his chiming in verbally, chances were pretty big that he would stay in front of the flatscreen now. They both knew she was very unlikely to try running away again.

But how to make chicken? She supposed it could be fried

up in a pan just like she had fried the pork chops. The pork chops she had gotten in trouble over and never had a chance to eat. Tonight had to be better. SHE had to be better.

She laid the three large chicken breasts out on a plate and sprinkled on salt and pepper and some fragrant-smelling spices she'd found in the cupboard. She put oil in the frying pan and added the meat. As it began to cook, the aroma filled the room. She started getting hungry. Should the rice be fried too? It looked cooked already. Should she ask Mike? She better not.

In the end, she microwaved it in a bowl and started chopping the apples. Boy, she could use her brother Kai's help. He liked to watch those cooking shows on You Tube and did pretty good in the kitchen. Thinking about him made her sad. He probably figured she was dead.

She glanced at the table. Was she supposed to set it? She'd set the table at home, but not always. Sometimes everyone just filled a plate in the kitchen before sitting down to eat. Once at Jazz's house, they had filled their plates and carried them to the family room to eat while watching a movie. She considered, then decided to set the table. After all, the night they were going to eat pork chops, they had planned to sit there. Right? She could no longer remember. And was she was supposed to set for two people? They had both eaten noodles at the table, so she guessed so. Or maybe Mike would want his dinner alone. She sighed.

While searching the cupboards for plates and glasses, she smelled something funny. The chicken was burning. She scrambled for a tool . . . spatula . . . anything, and finally used a fork to flip them over. They were charred a bit. Her heart raced. Would Mike be upset?

The microwave stopped running and started beeping. She rushed back to finish setting the table. This was hard work. And Mom did this almost every night. Cienna suddenly felt ashamed for not offering to help more.

Somehow, she got it all put together. Ten minutes later,

sweating with the effort, she told Mike dinner was ready. They both sat at the table. The microwave beeped again. She jumped up.

"Forgot the rice!" She burned her fingers trying to pull out the bowl. She finally found one oven mitt and a dishtowel and carried the bowl to the table.

Mike cut into his chicken. "It's pink." He threw his knife on the table.

Cienna jumped up quickly. "Sorry, sorry." She might cry. No, that was stupid.

How did that work? How could one side be charred and burned, but the meat inside still be pink? Maybe she had a solution. Her dad put his meat in the microwave when it was too pink for his liking.

"I can fix that." She grabbed his plate and put it in the microwave for a couple of minutes.

To her relief, the microwave did the trick, at least for the chicken. But the rice was dry, and Mike grumbled about that. And where was the butter?

She jumped up to grab butter and realized that she had forgotten drinks too. "What would you like to drink?"

"Beer." His red-rimmed eyes showed he was irritated. Had he continued drinking when she was in the tub? Maybe his juice and vodka hadn't been his last drink.

She sighed when she went to the refrigerator to get his beer and herself some juice. She hadn't dealt with a drunk Mike before. Maybe he would pass out later, and she could get herself out to the neighbor's house? Some people apparently passed out when they drank. Of course, she also knew some people got drunk and then really mad.

Her uncle was one of those. He needed to be driven home early from more than one family reunion. Last time, her dad had called him a taxi instead of driving him home and told him to get out of his face for good. But a month later, Uncle Brad was sitting at the kitchen table with her dad discussing the "good old days." Cienna had rolled her eyes and ran upstairs to her room in disgust.

What could she expect from a drunk Mike? Would he throw her in the barn again? She shuddered and picked at her food.

"Eat up." Mike chewed as he talked. "What ya made is what you get. Although it's not that bad." He savored his chicken in deep thought. "More onion. And better rice. If ya add water to the rice before ya heat it back up, it won't be so dry."

Oh. "Thank you." She kept her voice sweet.

Mike drained his beer and stood up. Cienna had barely touched her food. "Finish up. Maybe we can watch a movie. And then, my sweet, we're going to cuddle tonight. Maybe softly, since ya have some . . . uh . . . injuries. Ugly ones, by the way."

Cienna dropped her fork and stared at him. So this was it. Mike would now rape and beat her too. Her eyes filled with tears, and she looked at her plate.

Mike laughed. "Ya don't remember our deal?"

Deal? Her brain scrambled around, trying to pick up wayward pieces. Of course, the day before she had landed in the barn again was not very clear to her at all.

Mike stepped closer. She shrank back in her chair. He put his face so close to hers she could smell the beer on his breath.

"The handcuffs." He spoke slowly as if she was dumb. "Ya decided to cuddle instead of having handcuffs on while in yer room."

He left her sitting at the table. She stared at the dead phone on the wall. Was there a way to turn on the phone service? She longed to let her parents know she was hurt. And that she needed them.

She cleaned up the dishes, then headed to the basement to move clothes to the dryer and start a new load.

CHAPTER THIRTY
Bay

WITH HER DAY FINALLY THROUGH, Bay took an evening dose of meds. Within a half hour, she felt better and was able to sit at the table and manage some food with everyone else. Exhausted, she almost fell asleep on her plate twice. Charli elbowed her both times. She was grateful to learn that she would not be heading to the club that night but would be able to rest.

Maybe finding one thing each day to be grateful for would get her through this hell.

She'd not been able to look in on Rose all day and of course, couldn't plead for a doctor's visit either. But after dinner she had an idea. Sam and the Witch-Devil retreated to the office and closed the door. She quickly wrote them a note and slid it under the door.

Please help Rose. She's really sick and needs a doctor. Can you please call a doctor for her?

She hurried up to her room afterward and sat on the bed. She wanted to check on Rose but was scared to after the

Witch-Devil had yanked her out early that morning. What if the Witch-Devil sent her back to the club tonight anyway, refused her the next dose of meds, or had her go back to seeing clients all day in the forbidden area of the house?

Or all of the above?

She shuddered. She watched Amber getting ready to go to the club. Hopefully when everyone left, she could get food and water up to Rose.

Bay waited patiently, dozing and startling herself awake when her head dropped to her chest. Amber finished and headed downstairs. She heard the van doors slam. And then suddenly, a note was slipped under her bedroom door.

Rose is just resting. She doesn't need a doctor. Besides, she's too old to earn her keep anymore, so she is costing us too much money as it is! Stay out of her room, or you won't have a room to go to anymore. And I mean it. Kella

Bay crumpled up the note in her hand and threw it as hard as she could against the bedroom wall. She would check on Rose anyway. And she would do something more to get her better. There had to be something she could do for her friend.

She found sweats to change into and sat on her bed, waiting. Had Sam gone to the club, or had it been the other driver? And where was the Witch-Devil? The house seemed quiet, but it was only 8 p.m., according to Amber's little clock. She'd wait it out. Another hour max, and it should be safe to go give Rose some food and water and another cold washcloth.

Bay did not awaken when Amber came to bed at 4 a.m. She didn't wake up until 6:30 a.m. when their morning alarm went off. They both opened their eyes at the same time. She jumped out of bed, her heart slamming hard inside of her chest. Rose! She had fallen asleep! Rose had been without food and water all night long! And the day before too as Bay had been working in the torture chamber.

She rushed to get ready and ran downstairs. Surely after meds she would be assigned house chores for the morning. Then she could get to Rose.

Sam was at breakfast again and told the girls he had a sad announcement. Rose would not be joining them again at the table or at all, ever again. She just had been too sick to make it through.

He rose and left the Witch-Devil to deal with the girls' tears.

CHAPTER THIRTY-ONE
Cienna

CIENNA CREPT DOWN THE WIGGLY STAIRWAY, inching her way carefully, afraid to fall. She missed the bottom step entirely, almost fell, and swore loudly.

"Mew."

She stopped. And then, very clearly, she heard a thump. Not her imagination this time. Mike must have a cat down here.

A cat! Excitement bubbled up. She missed her cats. It would be nice to have one here to call her own. Maybe it was stuck somewhere and needed food.

"Kitty, kitty." She headed over to the washing machine while carefully looking all around the basement. The one small light bulb gave little light. Was the cat on the shelves? Hiding behind the washer? She stuck her head close to the yucky floor and called out, "Kitty?" Seeing nothing but cobwebs and grime behind the machine, she backed out quickly.

Hmmm . . . where could the cat be?

Forgetting about the clothes, she headed over to the area where the tools lay. The wheelbarrow was old, had a flat tire, and was empty. How did that get down there? She couldn't imagine someone pulling it down the staircase. She picked up a few tarps.

"Kitty, kitty, kitty!"

No answer.

Using all her strength, she moved a heavy chainsaw to look in a box behind it. The box was full of chains and equipment but no cat. "Kitty cat."

A thump sounded from the shelves to her left. "Ah ha! I knew it."

"What do ya think yer doing?" Swearing, Mike hurtled down the stairs and grabbed her hair.

"Ouch! Sorry!" Her teeth started chattering. "I-I came to do the clothes. I- I heard a c-cat. Do you-Do you have a c-cat? Ow! Please let go!"

Mike released her suddenly. She almost fell. He adjusted his hat. She backed away from him toward the washing machine, terrified of what he might do to her.

But his expression softened. "Baby." He reached out. "I'm so sorry. I-I drank too much tonight. I'm sorry I scared ya."

"Okay, okay." She continued to back up until she was against the washing machine. How dumb was that? Maybe she should have headed up the stairs away from him instead. She motioned to the machine behind her. "Uh, the clothes."

Mike sighed. "Yeah, the clothes. They go in the dryer."

"Uh, yeah. That's next." He seemed agreeable, so she risked it. "Mike, where's the cat?"

He blinked and lifted his hat. Ran a hand through his hair. "Uh, cat. Oh yes, the cat. It-It's a stray and I hear it too sometimes. But it's outside now. I think it's trying to come in the basement. Looking for mice, I'm sure! Seen a few barn cats too."

She nodded. She suspected that if a cat lived in the barn, she would have seen or at least heard it while in there. Well, if there was a stray outside, maybe she could pet it. Maybe Mike wouldn't mind if she befriended it. If he ever let her go outside again, which he probably wouldn't unless she was heading back to the barn over his shoulder. "Well, I-I should put the clothes in . . . "

"Yeah, yeah. Don't want them to get all sour." He watched as she transferred the clothes and turned the dial to sixty minutes. "Don't forget the dryer sheet."

Oh, yeah. The dryer sheet. She opened the cupboard where the soap had been, found a sheet, and tossed it in with the load. She started the dryer.

"I should start another load. There's quite a bit to do."

"Yup." He crossed his arms.

So he was just going to stare at her until she finished the job. Fine. She bent over to get the pile of lighter clothes and arranged them in the washing machine. Once at home, a load had become unbalanced. The machine made an awful racket. When she and her brother had hurried into the laundry room to check it out, the machine had moved six inches away from its usual spot. She smiled. Her dad had come in and fixed the horrendous noise by lifting the lid and rearranging the towels inside. He had moved the washer back into its usual spot. She learned to spread the clothes out as evenly as you could. And if something heavy like a towel was on one side of the machine, make sure the other side of the machine had one as well.

Mike ushered her up the stairs to the family room. That was fine with Cienna. "Cuddle time" in the bedroom could wait forever.

Once he was seated in the recliner, she perched on the couch. "What do you do for a job, Mike?" She remembered her dad talking about how some people chat too much when they drink. This might be a good time to fish for information. Mike was drinking another beer and had handed her one too. She set it on the coffee table, untouched. He wanted her to pick out a movie. She chose *Twilight*, even though she had seen it a million times. Mike said the freebies were the only option and rolled his eyes at her choice, but now he sat and stared at it like he might actually be interested. Or maybe he was just drunk.

"I teach." He took another long drink.

Well, that explained the time off. But recently she had noticed the leaves turning colors on the trees and the evenings getting chillier. Shouldn't he be back to work by now?

"What do you teach?"

He glared at her and turned back to the movie. Okay. He was still mad at her. And drunk, which apparently made him irritated. She would shut up, for now. She wondered if the knife she hid behind the canister was still there. Sometimes he seemed a bit dumb but other times seemed to know exactly what she was thinking.

"Mike, I'm sorry." She hadn't meant to say anything but changed her mind. "I'm sorry for disobeying you when you told me not to run away again . . . " With every word, she grew angrier, and yet she kept her voice even, knowing she should make peace. Her survival depended on it.

Mike glanced at her, his expression kind. "I appreciate it. I'm not sure why ya felt like ya had to beat yerself up so badly because of it . . . "

It took a second for his comment to register. Beat up? Did he mean the physical stuff? The bruises on her body?

Did he actually think he did that to herself? What!?

She groaned aloud, but Mike was watching the movie again and ignored her. He crossed his arms. Conversation closed.

She should bring it up another day. He was drinking.

But somehow, she couldn't let it go. She just couldn't. "You-You think I did this to myself?" Her voice rang clear and loud. "Mike, what are you thinking?"

Cienna jumped up from the couch. She should run and get that kitchen knife now. Maybe she wouldn't make it. But maybe she had to try. Mike was starting to sound like a psycho in one of the horror movies who was kind and sweet for a while, but somehow just a little "off" and then in the end, killed everyone.

"Sit down!" He bellowed.

The extreme fears and emotions of the past few days suddenly overwhelmed her. She sat and started crying.

"I'm not clear on what ya were thinking. That was stupid. But it's done with, and now we move on. Start over. Right?" He turned to her, his blue eyes clear as the summer sky. "Right? No more talking about what ya did to yerself. Got that?"

She nodded slowly, wiped her tears with her sleeve, and turned her eyes back to the movie. But she could no longer focus. Whatever his games, he had to know the truth. Right? Right?! Panic welled up into her throat. If he didn't get it, how could he protect her from Roger? Obviously, he already failed to do so once. But now what would stop it from happening again?

She grabbed the beer from the table, popped the top open, and drank it as fast as she could. She was dizzy and compliant a half hour later when Mike turned the movie off, picked her up from the couch, carried her up the stairs, and deposited her on the guest bed. He crawled in next to her and pulled a blanket over them both.

She fell asleep with him spooned behind her, his heart beating steadily, and his breath against her neck.

CHAPTER THIRTY-TWO
Bay

ROSE HAD DIED. And it was Bay's fault. She hadn't fetched her water or toast. She completely failed in getting her to the doctor. Her best friend, her watcher from the upstairs floor, now gone. Bay wondered where Rose was now, and she was so sad that she stared out of the windows when she was supposed to be completing chores. She found it impossible to eat. She couldn't bear to watch Rose's body being loaded into the long, black car.

That same afternoon, the Witch-Devil marched them to the third floor with cleaning supplies. Now they scoured the large bedroom. Bay felt a tightness in her chest each time she thought about Rose, but she had been unable to cry. It was all her fault.

Bee started crying after the Witch-Devil left, and Amber yelled at her to shut up. But Charli, now the oldest in the group at fifteen, gave Bee a tight hug, letting her cry. "Do you know where Rose is?"

"N-No," Bee gulped. Tried to wipe the tears streaming down her face.

"She's in a better place!" Amber snapped.

Charli glared at Amber. Turned to Bee. "Rose . . . Rose is in a rose garden now. It's beautiful there, and she's safe. She doesn't have to see clients or dance at the club. There's no Sam. No Kella. There's a lake . . . " Charli paused.

As one, they stopped cleaning and appeared to be visualizing this place of peace.

"She gets to feed the ducks . . . . and she's free. She can do whatever she pleases, anytime she wants. And there's always a Thanksgiving feast in the kitchen and a warm, soft bed where she can sleep alone anytime she wants to nap. I think she might even have a dog, a puppy that runs and plays with her and a cat that curls up on her lap. Yeah. She'd like that. There's even an angel-an angel that watches out for her."

Bee sniffed against Charli's shoulder. "That-That sounds nice."

And a few minutes later, she diligently scrubbed the window, as if the clarity through it would help her to see Rose walking in her rose garden.

Rose, Rose, Rose! Bay had screwed up. She was so sorry. She cried silently. Almost choked trying to keep the tears in. She gently pulled Rose's blankets and sheets off the bed to be washed. As she did, a folded over piece of paper drifted out and floated to the floor. And written clearly on it was a name: Jasmine.

A letter for Jasmine? Bay looked around hurriedly. There was no Jasmine at the house. And yet . . . and yet. Something seemed familiar. Still facing the bed, she folded the paper smaller and crammed it into the front pocket of her jeans. No one else noticed. After she read it, she would share it. Maybe. Suddenly, she wanted Rose's words to be for her, and for her only. This Jasmine lady could wait.

The girls boxed up Rose's few belongings. They found a notebook with some drawings and poems that they flipped through casually, a bit curious. But they knew the Witch-Devil would be watching the clock and checking on their progress, so they didn't spend a lot of time on it. They put it at the bottom of the box, then added her clothes, alarm clock, a teddy bear, shoes, and a suitcase she must have arrived with. Charli and Nia carried Rose's belongings downstairs and placed them by the front door. The Witch-Devil said her things would be sold to make up for some of the money Rose had cost them.

Back upstairs they went, this time with a broom, mop, and bucket. Bay carried out the bed linens, curtains, and a small rug to be washed.

With all of them working together and bonded in memories of Rose, the cleaning only took a little more than an hour. They gathered downstairs in the kitchen afterward, and the Witch-Devil informed them that they had the day off from the club and from clients.

"I hope you appreciate it!" Man, when the woman yelled, she screeched. Bay almost covered her ears but resisted. "We really can't afford for you to have a day off. Don't say I don't do anything for you!"

For once, they were silent. Without Rose, no one got in the Witch-Devil's face for yelling at them. She harrumphed and then assigned them house and farm chores for the day, with the evening off.

***

Today she was thankful for weeding the flowerbeds. Bay sat in the warmish fall sun. She yanked out weed after weed, adding them to the growing pile on the sidewalk. No clients. That was also something to be grateful for.

Immense sadness filled her, followed by a new thought. Words from Rose. In the house there were other words from Rose, buried in the bottom of a box in the entryway. She stood. Glanced around. Seeing no one, she hurried into the house. With her heart pounding, she shoved her hand in the bottom of the box. There it was. The notebook. She wondered how Rose had come by a notebook to draw and write in? Maybe there was room for Bay to add to Rose's words and leave it for someone else.

She stuck the notebook under her arm and hurried to her room. Tucked it under her mattress. The piece of paper belonging to Jasmine would stay in her jeans pocket for now, just in case. She slipped over to use the restroom, almost running into Nia on her way out. She smiled at her and went back to weeding out front. She waited for the Witch-Devil to stomp out and start screaming at her for taking the notebook. Nothing happened. Bay couldn't wait to read more from Rose.

CHAPTER THIRTY-THREE
Cienna

WHEN CIENNA AWOKE the next morning, she was in the guest room alone, the door locked. Her temples throbbed. Great.

"I have to pee!" She pounded on the door.

Mike didn't come. He must have left. She sighed. How long would she be locked in here now? And what about her chores? The cooking he wanted and the laundry she was supposed to finish up? She didn't want to get in trouble.

She slumped on the bed. She would at least have liked to get outside to find that cat.

Physically, she felt better from her days in the barn. The bruises were turning greenish, and her face and neck weren't so puffy. Thank goodness, the sore areas were healing. But instead of increasing her obedience, her injuries made her feel only more determined to somehow get away. But how?

She flipped up the corner of the mattress and discovered her shard of glass missing. Wrong corner of the bed? Wildly, she flipped up the other corners of the mattress too. Nothing!

"Noooo." She pounded the mattress with her fist.

Opening the closet, she noted one of the boxes was missing.

The one with the beat-up lid. She kicked the one remaining. Huh. The remaining one held the heavy photo albums.

Mike wasn't stupid. Unfortunately. He must have seen the glass missing from the picture frame and found it broken in the bottom of the box, including the missing shard under the mattress. He had cleaned up as well. His long robe now hung in the closet. Not on a metal hanger that she might have been able to untwist and do some damage with, but a safe plastic one.

Nice.

She frowned. Opened the dresser drawers. Folded neatly inside were some of the clothes purchased for her. She slumped on the bed. It was looking less and less likely that she could get out. He always leaned a step ahead.

Somewhere, there must be a weapon. This was a farm. She heard cows and a goat. Wasn't there a need sometimes to put a farm animal down? Did Mike have a rifle somewhere? She had no idea how to even load one. But somewhere, something in the house or barn had to help her. And what about a computer? He had to have one of those somewhere too. They had just chosen a movie on the television. Didn't that mean he had internet? He couldn't just live on a farm in the middle of nowhere with nothing.

What about his truck keys? He mostly seemed to keep those in his jeans pocket, so unless she could get really close . . . she shuddered and shoved down the thought.

She buried her face in her hands.

Minutes later, she heard the slide move away from the bedroom door and the door open.

"Thank God. May I please use the restroom?" Polite Cienna. Non-questioning Cienna. She wanted to gag.

Mike looked well-rested. He wore jeans, a tee shirt, and brown leather slippers. She noticed muscular arms as he leaned against the doorframe. He must be strong because apparently he had carried her upstairs last night. He had nice hands, too.

What the heck? Her headache had infiltrated her brain.

Mike shrugged. Motioned her out into the hallway and down the stairs. When she was through with the toilet, he suggested a shower. Always glad for one, she tromped back upstairs to get a change of clothes.

Obedient Cienna. Compliant Cienna. Happy Cienna. Happy? Well, one could try, she supposed.

After her shower, she stood facing Mike with her dirty clothes in her hands. "I know there's more laundry to do . . . " Time to go back to the basement. She wanted to find the cat. Needed a friend.

"Nah. I need help in the garden. We can harvest a bunch and not have to spend so much on groceries. Ya eat more than yer share. Peas and beans are ready."

Outside! Warmth spread through Cienna much like when she drank the alcohol. She smiled. "Great." She used a casual tone, as if it didn't really matter to her whether she went outside or not. "I am-I'm happy to help. Should I- should I get more laundry started first?"

Mike shrugged. Stepped aside. He followed her closely as she made her way down the stairs. "I guess I should fix these steps before one of ya gals breaks a leg."

Before one of you gals? Cienna almost stopped on the stairs. How many "gals" did he have here?

"I have a cleaning lady." He frowned. Seemed in a hurry to add that information. "She's in and out of here too sometimes."

Ah. Okay. Cienna nodded, disappointed. For a moment, she hoped there was actually another female in the house. A Mrs. Mike or whatever. She longed to talk to someone other than Mike.

But a cleaning lady? When his floors under the beds were a mess? She must not come that often. Maybe only to do windows or something. Could Cienna somehow get the lady's attention the next time she came?

She started a new load of clothes. Mike dug around in a box of chains. She listened for a mew or thump but heard nothing. Then she remembered that each time she heard a noise before, it was after she made a loud noise herself. That made sense. One of her cats at home only mewed when he wanted something badly or when someone talked to him first. This cat had responded after she had dropped the washer lid. When the tub was full of clothes and the soap was in, she slammed it down as hard as she could.

"Watch it!" Mike paused in his rummaging. "Ya break it, ya gotta fix it."

She listened. Heard nothing over Mike's loud comment. She would try it again when alone. "Sorry. Now what?" She turned and saw a chain from dangling from his hand. He grinned at her.

"Got what I need." He nodded toward the stairs.

Excited about going outside into the sunshine, she asked about her shoes. "Ya gotta do without. At least it's not winter." He laughed. Put on his boots and pulled the shoelaces tight.

It would be harder to run away without shoes. But she would figure it out.

The chain was for her. Mike took her around to the back of the house, where a garden flourished. They remained in full sight of the neighbor's house she'd once glimpsed. Telling her it was her own fault for running twice, he cinched the chain around her ankle. He used a plastic tie from his pocket to close two links together. He fastened the other end around a tree.

He laughed and pinched her on the butt.

"S-stop!"

Mike laughed again. Pinched once more. "Need yer hands free. Plus, ya understand now that I can do whatever I want." It was a statement, not a question. She took a chance and ignored him. When she scowled, he huffed and turned away from her.

Well, at least she was in view of the neighbor's house. If they looked out their windows, they would see her working. Of course, they were too far away to see her chained at the ankle, especially with the thriving and tall plants she recognized around her. But could she wave for help somehow? Get their attention? A tear threatened as she realized that help was so close. All she needed was someone to see something weird and call 9-1-1, right? The police would come to the house and check things out? So close.

She would not lose hope. And she would gain Mike's trust again. Which meant she would work hard and not try to run. At least for a time.

Mike returned to the house. Cienna tackled her assigned rows with a vengeance. She hated working in the garden at home, even though everyone had to help occasionally. Here, she was so relieved to be in the sun and outside that it no longer mattered. Give her the garden. Make her mow the lawn. Let her milk those cows. She would do it all. Her heart soared with hope. Peace filled her, despite the miserable chain.

She heard birds singing in the trees, chased off a couple of squirrels, and tried to get close enough to pet a rabbit that had come to check out the vegetables. She couldn't get to it, but she laughed as it hopped away and bounced over the garden's chicken-wire fence. Did Mike realize his poorly constructed fence didn't keep the critters out? Dummy.

She threw a couple of beans outside of the fence in case the rabbit came back. Soon after, she discovered an ants' nest under the tree to which she was attached. She watched fascinated as literally hundreds of them carried food and other injured ants and bugs to their hill. She broke apart a few beans. Tossed the pieces to them as well. They gathered, using teamwork to carry the heavy pieces. Fascinating.

In a couple of hours, she had weeded all the beans and peas, putting the weeds in a pile as Mike had instructed. Now it was time to pick. He brought her two buckets . . . and a lemonade. Nice.

Her stomach growled. Wasn't it time for lunch yet?

Mike eventually left in his truck, grinning and waving as he drove away, apparently confident that the chain would hold her for now. It would be a quick trip, she suspected. He didn't trust her that much and probably never would again. She yelled at the neighbor's house for a bit but didn't see any sign of people. A discouraging sign.

She cut herself trying to rip the plastic tie off the chain links around her ankle to no avail.

"Argh!" She swore a bit too, stomping her feet like Kai used to do when he didn't want to do something her parents insisted on.

Trouble would loom if Mike came back to no progress. She picked some vegetables quickly, putting the beans into one bucket and the peas into the other one. Hungry, she crammed a few handfuls of beans, and then sugar-snap peas, into her mouth.

Time for a break. For a bit Cienna sat at the base of the tree, still eating stray veggies and finishing her lemonade. She studied the chain to see how much it would let her explore. She would look for the cat. A cat might help her time be a bit more bearable. Maybe it would want to cuddle with her during her breaks at the tree.

She walked to the end of the chain and looked around, spying another entrance to the basement. She hadn't seen the other side of it inside. Maybe the cat was in there. She stepped carefully down the three cement stairs. Pulled at the door.

"Mew."

It was louder and clearer now. Her heart started to race. It was in there! A kitty cat!

The door stuck a bit. She put both hands on it and pulled hard, almost landing herself back on the stairs behind her. She peered inside. Her eyes adjusted to the dark.

Clearly, suddenly, she heard not a mew but a tiny, whimpering voice.

She screamed and stumbled backward. She sat on the stairs and panted, eyes wide. The open door swayed in the slight breeze. Inside the door was a small room with a dirt floor. In the corner sat a very small girl, naked, and trembling.

CHAPTER THIRTY-FOUR
Bay

Less than a week later, the van pulled up. Sam and his blond driver wrestled out two terrified, very young girls with large brown eyes and dark hair. Despite their bound hands and gags over their mouths, they fought and struggled. "Feisty again." The driver slapped one on the face. She cried out. Bay, sweeping the porch, gasped.

Sam answered. "They'd better be. Roger promised me that, for sure. I like it when they fight."

Roger. That sounded vaguely familiar. Who was Roger?

Bay followed behind Sam and watched from a safe distance as he shuffled the two girls into the TC room. He took off their mouth straps and groped one of them as he pushed them into the room. "Can't wait for that one." He laughed in his evil way.

The girl squealed and hurried into the room away from him.

Bay heard crying as soon as he left, but she didn't stop to listen at the door. Instead, she followed Sam quietly and enough behind him that he didn't know she was there. She watched from the corner of the stairway while he put the key to the room in a dish on top of the fireplace mantel in the living room. He left the room to talk to the driver, who was still standing near the van smoking a cigarette.

Bay took a deep breath. Sat on the stairs. The key to the TC room was in the dish. Did she dare unlock the door and check on them? They might both run out at once, and then what would she do? Better give them some time to calm down first.

The first few days would bring nothing but misery to them. And who was she kidding? Their entire time here would be miserable. They were young, looked like twins, and would be in high demand with clients. Sam had likely paid a lot for them.

And now Rose was gone. Rose could not sneak them food or soda. Couldn't stand at the door and chat. The thought made Bay sad.

She quietly finished her chores for the morning. The crying from the TC room had stopped, and all was quiet. She hoped the girls were sleeping. Hopefully the Witch-Devil would bring them food from dinner this evening. If not, Bay might have to fish that key out of the bowl.

A few minutes later, as she dusted the fireplace mantel, Bay glanced in the bowl. It was full of keys. Each one had a different colored rubber ring around it. Which one opened the drawers in the office where all the meds were supposedly held? Which one opened the TC room? Maybe the best thing she could do was take the girls a pill when they woke up so they wouldn't be so upset.

What would Rose do? Maybe Rose could tell her more. Maybe Rose had left some message in her notebook. And there was that letter to Jasmine. Bay sighed and moved on to dusting the coffee tables.

At lunch, which was peanut butter sandwiches, chatter circled about the new girls. By now, they had all heard various noises. Screaming, yelling in what sounded like Spanish and crying. Bay watched carefully but no one took the girls food or water. During lunch, the Witch-Devil slammed several dishes on the table and yelled at Charli for talking too much about the new girls. Bay decided to stay out of it. Maybe tomorrow she could find the right key and do something.

After lunch meant free time for the girls heading to the club that night, but there was no more break for the ones assigned chores or the ones working for the day in the locked part of the house. Bay still had chores to do. She got busy right away, oiling all the wooden surfaces in the house, including the kitchen cupboards and stair banisters, and scrubbing the bathrooms. Once done, she had free time. She went to her room and closed her door. Alone at last. Time to open the letter from Rose to Jasmine, even though it was really none of Bay's business. She missed her friend. Needed to hear her voice, even if it was through her written words.

She opened her closet door and sat on the floor to read Jasmine's letter, partially closing the door. That way, she would have more time to tuck it away if someone came. She felt no guilt unfolding the sheet of paper that was obviously torn from the spiral notebook Rose used. Bay wanted to read more of that too. But first, the letter. It was far more mysterious.

She settled on the floor, leaving the closet door open just enough to let in light. Unfolded the paper.

Dear Jasmine, I know you don't like that name anymore, but that is your name, and its beautiful. Did you realize that we have that in common? My name is Rosabelle, and yours is Jasmine, so we both have a pretty flower in our names. We are the only girls here with a flower in our names.

Bay smiled and continued to read. Jasmine was a pretty name, and so was Rosabelle. She was glad to know Rose's full name.

As you know, I'm sick. I'm pretty sure it's a kidney infection as I had one a long time ago and it felt similar. I don't think I'm going to make it out of this house. They aren't taking care of me, and they won't. I'm too old now to make a lot of money for them, and I saw this happen with another girl after I arrived here. But before I go, I need to tell you two things. First, I'm not afraid . . .

Bay felt her heart squeeze tightly in her chest. She wanted to cry, but she couldn't. Rose's next words were hopeful, and even sounded happy.

I'm not afraid to die, Jasmine. And that is because I know I will go to heaven. I've had angels watching over me. They are here in this house. That's why I'm not afraid.

The letter in Bay's hand shook slightly as tried to understand the words. Angels? Rose had angels?! What a thought! Rose went on to say that she wished for this same peace for this Jasmine girl and to please search it out.

I need to finish this and sleep, Jasmine, but I have a favor to ask of you. Out of everyone here I trust you the most to help me, even after I am gone, and I knew as soon as I met you that you were the one to tell my secret to. Please help. Before I came here, I had a daughter. It would mean a great deal to me if, when you leave here, if you could find her please. Make sure that she is happy and safe, and never ends up in a place like this. She's all I have now. Please help me. I know that you will make sure she's safe.

Bay dropped the letter, startled. Rose had a child! A daughter?! One she had before she came to the farm? What had happened to her? Where had she gone? Eager for more information, she picked up the letter again. Rose's writing was getting harder to read, but she had listed out her full name, her daughter's name, birthdate, and a birthplace of Silverdale, Washington. She recommended that Jasmine memorize the details and get rid of the letter so Sam and Kella didn't find it. Finally, she told Jasmine that she loved her, and that there is always hope.

I know you'll make it out of here. Someone upstairs is watching out for you. Love, Rosabelle. P.S. It's the green key.

Bay folded the letter back up and crammed it into her pocket, taking a deep breath. A daughter. Rose was dead, but somewhere out there, her daughter lived.

CHAPTER THIRTY-FIVE
Cienna

A T THE SAME MOMENT CIENNA LANDED on her butt
outside on the cement stairs, she heard Mike's truck. She
swore. "Gotta go now." She scooted backward. "Be quiet. I'll
be back." As she was quickly closing the door to the secret
room, the girl's cry grew louder. Cienna risked putting her
head quickly back in. "I promise I will. You gotta be quiet. Be
quiet now or the bad man will get us both."

Huddled with her arms around her knees, the wide-eyed
girl nodded.

Cienna slammed the door closed. Her heart pounded.
She ran up the cement stairs. Raced back to the bean row,
accidently knocking the bean bucket over in her haste.

Mike didn't have a cat. No cat. He had a girl locked up
in a secret room.

Her thoughts whirled. Her arms and legs shook with fear.
The girl was naked. She must be freezing at night. Had Roger
hurt her, as well? Was Mike saving her from Roger? If so, why
wasn't she in the house with them? She was tiny. Her green
eyes huge as she and Cienna stared at each other for those few
seconds. Obviously terrified. Cienna had babysat her

neighbor's girls a few times. They were seven. Twins and sometimes a handful. She shook back tears as she realized this girl was no larger than her charges.

"Get it under control, Ci." She gritted her teeth. Still shaking, she realized that Mike was rounding the corner of the house. She had to pretend. Fake Cienna. Lying girl. Brave Cienna. Yes. She had to be brave. She knelt. Quickly started scooping beans up with both hands and putting them back into the bucket. Then his hiking boots were right in front of her. She stared at the ground.

"Have a spill?" Mike drawled. "Looks like ya got some done while I got the mail."

Cienna looked up slowly and met his eyes She narrowed hers. With all her heart, she wanted to kick him in the balls. And then stomp on his head.

That poor little girl. She told herself to stop thinking about it. She couldn't handle anymore.

"Y-Yes." She looked back down. Continued to gather the wayward beans.

Mike's boot connected with her lower back. Pain seared. She fell forward, landing on her hands and knees. What was this!? He had never hurt her before!

Immediately, she grew scared. Should she move or stay put? Tears welled up. Dripped into the dirt, some splashing on and washing her dirty hands. Cienna had felt brave. She tried so hard. Roger's damage always lingered. Her physical wounds, once healing, now reopened as Mike added his. Why couldn't she go home? Hug Mom and Dad? Where was an angel when she needed one? Didn't she deserve help?

And now there was a little naked girl under the house. She couldn't go home either. For the first time, she wanted to die.

Mike bent down to the ground. "Oh, sweetie. Why did ya make me do that? Oh dear. Come on, I'll help ya up. So much work, and then ya had to go spill it." He sighed heavily.

"Never mind. Let's finish this up so ya can get started on dinner." He helped her sit.

Cienna groaned. Wincing, she sat criss-cross-applesauce. Rocked gently back and forth as Mike finished picking up the beans. He frowned at the bean row. "That's not done. What were ya doing while I was in town? Climbing the stupid tree? Trying to escape?" His voice pitched a bit higher.

Cienna quickly shook her head. "N-No. I- took a small break. We didn't have lunch, and I was hungry. So-So I sat by the tree and finished my lemonade . . . " She panted. Looked at the ground, expecting his boot again, dreading the pain of it. "I-I like it here with you, Mike." The lie soured her from her toes to her head. Lying girl. Surviving girl. "I- do." She managed to look up and smile through her tears. "Thank you for letting me help outside today. It means a lot that you let me do that. I- I can see that you care . . . "

Mike frowned at her, then shrugged. "All right then. I'm glad yer finally coming to your senses. It can be good here for both of us. I take care of ya. I keep Roger away." He grumbled. "I'm just glad to finally get some appreciation. Now finish this up." He grabbed the stack of mail he had tossed on the ground and stomped off toward the house. "Finish it soon. I'm getting hungry."

Still shaking, Cienna cautiously looked at the basement door. It wasn't even locked. But the girl obviously couldn't get out. She must be chained up like Cienna. She reached down and rubbed her ankle where the chain had bit into it all afternoon. Weariness washed over her. Would the girl even get dinner? Did she ever even see the daylight? Probably not.

Sad, she pushed herself up. Despite her aching back, she quickly finished the assigned bean and the pea rows. Unable to wait anymore, she squatted behind the tree to relieve herself. Two hours later, still sitting against the side of the tree on the opposite side of the ants' nest, she wondered why she had bothered to rush with the vegetables. She had loudly called Mike's name several times. But still she sat, chained. Finally, she laid down in the dirt next to the tree. A warm presence hovered as she slipped into a peaceful sleep.

CHAPTER THIRTY-SIX
Amelie

HOME AGAIN, AMELIE VISITED Dad's home office to call her almost-boyfriend, Mitch. Unfortunately, Dad's office was growing more and more crowded. She moved two stacks of papers and folders from the chair and used her arm to push away more stacks on the desk. She leaned back in the chair and crossed her ankles up on the desk. Kinda messy even for him. Cleaning the house was apparently low on the priorities these days.

Coming home or going to River Falls on the weekends sure was putting a crimp into her social life. Where did she and Mitch really stand? Before Jasmine disappeared, they'd gone on two dates. Even now, they continued to text and talk on the phone. But since she was in school on weekdays and rarely around on weekends, they had yet to really define things.

She pulled up her contacts and hit his phone number.

"Hey." He sounded glad to hear from her.

"Hi. Sorry I fell asleep while we were talking last night." Amelie had felt terrible about it when she woke up.

Mitch laughed. "No worries. I didn't feel bad hanging up on you since I thought you were out. What's new?"

She giggled, thankful for his understanding. "Since last night? Not much. Oh, wait. My mom actually let Seth out of the house today to mow the neighbor's lawn. Shocking."

"About time. It's been months."

"Yes." She sighed. "I wonder where Jasmine is."

"I wonder too. Do you still feel like she's okay?"

"Yeah, I do. Why?"

"I don't know. I was just . . . reading up on some stuff. Some trafficking stuff."

A slow burn crawled up Amelie's spine. She shuddered. "Huh?"

"Trafficking. You know. Humans. Slavery really. A lot of people are trafficked. Held against their will. Forced to work without pay or for sex. That kind of thing. I read that over a million kids each year are forced into trafficking."

"What?" Amelie almost dropped her phone. "That's crazy!"

"Yeah, and it's not just overseas. It's here in the good ole US of A, too. They just busted a ring in Federal Way. They were using hotel rooms for the girls and sending the men to see them there. Prostituting them. When they busted it up, they discovered most of the girls were minors and can't consent. Even the grown women had been forced into it somehow."

"Mitch, I know. I've heard of it. Crazy numbers though. Are you saying my sister is out there being trafficked?" Her voice hitched. Then she whispered, "Is that what you mean?"

"I just-I just wondered. I mean, they were both taken. We know that. We know some dude took your sister's cell phone, powered it off, and tossed it in the bushes, right? And there's been no sign of them."

"There are clues." Amelie's mind raced in a bad direction. "They're working on them. I talked to Detective Miller in River Falls last weekend. He never mentioned trafficking. But they do have clues. Wouldn't-wouldn't there be like no clues if they were taken by experienced traffickers? I mean, you would think . . . " She paused, denying the terrible possibilities. "They said it's a kidnapping for sure, but that's all, Mitch."

"But Am, why would they kidnap them in the first place? Take all that risk? There has to be a reason."

Amelie forcefully shook her head. "No. That can't be. Why are you thinking that about my sister? That's crazy! You think she's in some brothel somewhere, being beaten and used?"

Mitch sighed. "I don't know. It just seems to fit. I thought I would bring it up to try and help. Sorry . . . "

"No, no, it's okay." Amelie put her free hand against her forehead. Trafficking. Wow. Was it possible? Did the bad guys find victims in little River Falls, Oregon? Her head started throbbing. "Now I'm really scared."

He sighed again. "I'm sorry for mentioning it."

After they hung up, Amelie called Dad. She knew he was working extra hours over the weekend and they would spend time together on Sunday. But she couldn't wait.

"Amelie?" Dad's voice held a note of concern.

"Dad." She tried to steady her breath. "I was just talking to Mitch." Oh, shoot. He hadn't heard of Mitch...yet.

"Who?"

"Mitch. Sorry. A friend from school. Anyway, he's been hearing a lot about human trafficking and how people are taken and forced to work for nothing. Or forced-forced to prostitute. And I . . . I . . . do you think Jasmine might have been taken by traffickers?" She paused, realizing she had just opened a can of worms. "Dad?"

"I'm here. Look, Am, I . . . I don't know. Yes, Detective Miller mentioned that to us. Or maybe it was Mollie. Or maybe no one did." She could tell he didn't really remember. He sighed. "I don't know, Amelie. I hope to God that's not the case. You can't think that way. We can't. I mean, can you imagine? I can't. Jasmine is going to be okay, and we're going to figure all of this out. Where's your brother?"

"Mowing Kary's lawn." She felt sorry for interrupting his workday. "Mom let him. I think that's good, don't you? Dad, what if . . . ? What if? Poor Jasmine . . . " Thinking about her little sister and all she might be going through at this very moment, Amelie started to cry. And she cried for Cienna too. "I'm-I'm sorry. Dad, I'm not trying to make anyone sad or think things that might not be. But now I'm really scared that maybe that's what happened." She hiccupped. Grabbed a tissue from his desk to blow her nose. "When are you home?"

"Five. Sweetheart, take a deep breath. It's going to be okay. We can talk more later. Please don't mention this to your mother or to Seth, all right?"

"Okay." She hung up, then stared into space, fearful that Mitch might be right. She blew her nose and picked up her phone again. "Is Detective Miller available? This is Amelie Jensen." Told he was in a meeting, she declined his voicemail and called Mollie instead. "Hi, Mollie. Listen, my friend and I were talking, and we've been hearing about human trafficking cases. I was wondering about Jasmine . . . "

"Hi, Amelie. I can hear in your voice that you're scared."

"Y-Yes." Amelie gulped. "I mean-I mean I know she was kidnapped, and I know that doesn't usually end well. I . . . assumed someone might hurt her and hoped no one would kill her. But I never thought . . . she could be getting hurt all the time! And Cienna, too. Is it possible?"

Mollie's sigh reached across the miles. "I'm sorry, Amelie. Yes, it's possible. I think everyone assumes that it's a possibility. We just don't really talk about it. Sometimes kids are taken for trafficking purposes."

Amelie sniffed. Pulled another tissue from the box. "And . . . and are they rescued ever? Or do they end up in some foreign country in a brothel, never to be seen again? I hear they get killed sometimes? Or they die young just because of so much abuse . . . " She hiccupped, her head throbbing.

"Some are rescued. We're very close to having the information we need in your sister's case. We should know more soon. I can't tell you more, and I can't promise, but I do feel hopeful about finding Jasmine and Cienna."

Ending the call, Amelie let a little hope spring into her heart. She wandered to her Facebook icon and posted: **Did you know? Over a million kids are forced into trafficking each year!** She tagged Mitch, and let her phone fall to the desk, her heart heavy once again. If Jasmine was being trafficked and was rescued, how could anything be normal again? Wouldn't it be better for her sister to die and be at peace rather than face years more of abuse and possible death at the hands of her captors?

CHAPTER THIRTY-SEVEN
Bay

Bay cooked dinner that night. It was Amber's turn, but she gleefully gave up any and all chores to her roommate when Bay asked. She probably thought Bay was stupid. Bay didn't care. She wanted somehow to get leftovers to the little girls upstairs. That meant she either made extra or gave up her own portion. Sam had given his customary speech that no one was to disturb the girls in the TC room. Even the Witch-Devil had yet to visit.

But Bay knew Rose would have visited by now.

Throughout dinner, she considered what she knew about the room. The inside of it. The converted closet, of course, but what about the lock on the outside? It was a locked doorknob, and it also had a slider lock.

She supposed that kept everyone inside for sure. Even if they knew how to jimmy a lock.

She would have to wait until everyone was asleep or at the club, and be very, very quiet. She'd heard the new girls periodically throughout the day. Of course, they cried. They were so young.

The van eventually roared off to the club. Charli was busy working the locked side of the house with the Witch-Devil in attendance. Bay figured Sam must be at the club tonight, too. She carefully dished up leftovers and poured a large glass of water. She had already tucked the green key into her pocket minutes before. The girls would have to share the plate and glass. There was no way she could carry two of everything and unlock the door quietly. She tucked the large plastic glass of water in the crook of her arm, took the plate in one hand, and headed up the stairs. Paused at the top. Hearing no noises, she continued quietly down the hallway. The TC Room was the last room on the second floor, the farthest from the others.

She set the plate and glass down and managed to unlock the door, slide the lock bar open, and open it. The door squeaked. She froze.

Deciding no one had heard, she opened the door to see two brown-faced, very scared little girls sitting on the couch. Their hands were not bound, and they held each other tightly. She put her finger in front of her lips to tell them to be very quiet, then turned and reached back to grab the food and water. She brought them in and closed the door.

"Por favor ayúdame," one of the girls said quickly as Bay set the dishes on the floor.

She placed her finger to her lips again and glanced urgently back and forth to the door. Shhhhhhh.

The girls looked at the food and, after only a second of hesitation, climbed off the TC and came to the floor to eat. One girl shivered. Bay reached out and gave her a hug. Probably not the best idea. She didn't need the attachment and for them to think she could save them. But the girl clung to Bay and ended up sitting on her lap while she wolfed down the food. After they ate and drank, Bay showed them the closet bathroom. They nodded and thanked her.

Bay picked up the dishes and inclined her head toward

the door. She smiled gently. With large eyes and tears starting again, they watched her leave.

Outside the door, Bay sighed. Her heart pounded. SO scary! Had Rose felt scared when she was an angel in disguise to Bay? If so, it hadn't stopped her. When Bay was imprisoned there, she'd clung to those visits as her lifeline. And she had no idea things would only get worse when they let her out. Maybe it would have been better if they'd left her to die in the TC room.

She scuttled quickly to the kitchen, washed the dishes by hand, dried them, and put them away. The house was still quiet. When she passed the room she now knew Sam and the Witch-Devil slept in, she heard loud snoring. Good. He'd probably drunk himself to sleep early, so maybe he would leave her alone. Relief coursed through her. The jerk gave her nightmares.

She settled into bed and opened Rose's spiral notebook. She couldn't wait to read more of her friend's words. Absorb more. Become wise like it seemed Rose had done in her time here. And of course, as she did, she would miss her.

I don't understand. Please help me make it through this . . . and to help some of the other girls while I am here.

I want to make their lives easier in some way. Please help me to do that. To be their angel like the ones you have sent to me.

Bay read about halfway through Rose's writings when she felt sleepy. She remembered to tuck the notebook under her pillow before closing her eyes.

The next day, she was assigned to the locked part of the house for the afternoon and evening. She knew she would stay there for most of the evening and night, so she watched all morning for a chance to grab the key to the TC Room. As soon as she could, she visited and took a soda. She indicated smashing the can to them when they were done and putting it under the couch.

"Si." They nodded their heads, then hugged her before she left.

Bay hurried into her room to dress in the revealing clothes the Witch-Devil told her to wear. She tossed her jeans on the floor. She was running late. At the last minute, she grabbed Rose's notebook from under her pillow and hid it under her clean pile of clothes stacked on the closet shelf. She figured the more places she found to hide it, the better. The letter to Jasmine had also been carefully tucked into the pages. Treasured mementos Bay intended to keep.

Halfway through her shift in the torture chamber, Bay heard Sam bust into the locked hallway, yelling Kella's name. It was then she realized the key to the TC Room was still in her jeans pocket . . . on her bedroom floor.

CHAPTER THIRTY-EIGHT
Detective Miller

MOLLIE'S CALL FROM THE WOODS started a flurry of activity. Detective Miller sent an officer to retrieve and protect the credit card. He also told his assistant to start searching the name, Devon James, in their databases. Once he had the credit card in hand, he called the issuing bank listed on the back.

As he expected, the bank informed him that he needed a court order to access any information. Still, he had to try. Time was of essence for both girls. If this man was involved, they needed to find him as soon as possible. Roger Wyatt continued to dodge them despite the warrant out for his arrest.

The next step was to get an emergency warrant. Miller punched in the number for the Assistant State's Attorney. Gable didn't pick up, so he left a voicemail. "Hey, Gable. Hope you and the family are well. Look, I'm going to need an emergency warrant for a bank to get info about a guy possibly connected to those two girls who disappeared here. Call me back as soon as you can, please."

Mollie

After turning the credit card over to the cop, Mollie whistled for Coal and returned to her truck at the campground. Coal hopped up on the seat, turned around three times and settled down for a nap. She pulled out her tablet and started a search of public records for Devon James. Then she picked up her phone to call her friend at the DMV. Next, she headed back to the police station.

She sailed into the room and greeted Miller. "How's it going?"

He grinned. "Thanks to you, we're moving forward now. I can't believe we missed that credit card."

"You're welcome. But it was Coal," she called to his retreating back as he hurried to his next meeting. She just hoped she was in time.

She borrowed a small conference room to work on locating Devon James. In the meantime, she also pulled up records on Roger Wyatt and looked for his folks, who apparently now lived in California.

Detective Miller

In two days, Miller obtained his court order. Doing things by the book could be a lengthy process. They all felt the weight. What if the girls didn't have one more day?

The bank was served with the paperwork, so he headed to the closest branch two hours away. Making it just before they closed for the day, he met with the bank president behind closed doors. The man took one look at his badge and the paperwork and called his corporate office. The president provided him with Devon James's full name, address, cell phone number, social security number, transaction history, and more. In addition, they learned the card was reported lost and replaced with a new one on June fifteenth. The order was sealed, which meant the bank could not tell Devon James or anyone else that the records had been given out.

Back in his car, Miller pored over the transactions. "Got you." He smacked the steering wheel. "Here's one at the River Falls General Store on the day Jasmine and Cienna disappeared. Another one at the gas station." He started his car and gunned it back to River Falls.

"But how to tie you in? You and I both know you weren't there just hiking the trails. I think you are involved as they come, Mr. James." There had to be a record, some record of his contact with Roger, whose fingerprints were taken from Jasmine's phone.

Miller picked up his phone. Time for another warrant. This one for Devon James's cell phone history. And while he was at it, he would call old Mr. Henry at the gas station and see if he still had a video camera pointed at those pumps.

Mollie

"How's it going, Sally?" Mollie paused to chat with the officer who had front desk duty at the River Falls Patrol Station. "Seems a tad slow right now."

"It is." Sally finished writing on a form in front of her and tucked her hair behind her ear. "Quiet here except for the one case, of course. Detective Miller looks like he hasn't slept in days."

"Me, neither." Mollie pulled up a chair. "This one is killing me. We're so close. We have so much information, including the guy's address and that he was here at the time. We just need to tie him to Roger. I just want to go and march right up to the door—"

"He does have a warrant. We confirmed that this morning."

Hope surged in Mollie's heart. "He does? One they can move on?"

"Yes. Burglary. I hope it's enough."

"Interesting." Mollie stood and walked to the soda machine, inserting a dollar bill and some coins. "I found

Roger's folks." She sighed. "They claim they haven't heard from him in two years." The answering sigh from behind her indicated Sally's irritation with the slow process and her sympathy. They all wanted the girls to be safe.

The downsides of private investigating sometimes weighed on Mollie. Because she was a private citizen, not a cop, the police force couldn't share certain information with her. Sally had probably already said too much. Mollie didn't want to get her in trouble.

Mollie had talked to both girls' parents that morning but could only share a limited amount of information with them as well. She'd only said they were moving forward and seeking approval for another search warrant for records. She added a promise to call the next day.

She grabbed her orange juice and headed down the hallway to Miller's office. He saw her through the window in his door and waved her in.

"Mollie."

"Rob." She sat by his desk. "Don't we have enough yet? Please. There has got to be a way to get those girls soon."

"As a matter of fact, I just received what we need to move forward on the second set of records." He smiled. "My team is reviewing them now. Very soon, we should have enough to apprehend Mr. James and hopefully find them."

CHAPTER THIRTY-NINE
Detective Miller

A FEW MINUTES PAST SEVEN that night, Miller and patrol officers from the Portland Police Department surrounded a small home on 76th Street. They pulled in quietly with no lights or sirens. Although James's card had been found at the scene, they still had no real proof that he'd been involved. They did have proof of phone calls with Roger Wyatt. And they had a warrant for a past burglary.

They would push him to admit it all. Push him hard. Legally, of course. Miller put his hand on his holster and knocked at the door.

James answered the door. Bald and sporting a goatee, he wore jeans and a stained tee-shirt. He stared at Miller briefly, then started to close the door.

Miller stuck his boot inside as other officers moved forward to back him up. He pushed the door all the way open. "Devon James, I'm Detective Miller. You're under arrest for burglary."

James's face grew pale. "You got the wrong guy."

"That's what they all say." Miller started to handcuff him, but he struggled.

Two cops pinned him to the living room floor and completed the job while Miller recited his rights.

Determined to do everything by the book, Miller hoped he'd followed protocol and Gable's instructions well. They'd all seen criminals avoid prosecution due to "technicalities." But these girls' lives were likely at stake. He wanted an admission of guilt and information, and he wanted them quickly, even if he had to hound this guy all night long.

In the car, he texted Mollie that they were close to some answers. She replied she was already on the way from River Falls. **Don't call the parents yet.** He knew she wouldn't but reminded her anyway.

By 9 p.m., Devon James had been searched, photographed, and fingerprinted. He complained loudly during the whole process.

He sat in a chair in the Portland Police Department interrogation room glaring at the wall when Miller entered and set his file folder and notebook on the table. He sat down across from the perp, who stared unblinking at him.

Maybe he was a psychopath.

Both Gable and his assistant were outside of the one-way window and might text him while he questioned James. He set his cell phone down near his hand. "Our conversation is being recorded. There are microphones and video cameras around the room."

James shrugged.

"And to clarify, you do not want an attorney present?"

James rolled his eyes, stroking his goatee. "Don't need one."

"Mr. James, I would like to know your whereabouts on June 8th of this year. It was a Thursday. Do you remember?"

James scoffed. "I thought this was about a burglary."

"Where were you on June 8th?"

"I- I was on vacation."

"Oh? Where was that?"

James shrugged. "I was in Bend. Camping."

Miller raised his eyebrows. "By yourself?"

"Yeah."

"Okay." He made a note in his notebook. "What did you do while on vacation in Bend on June 8th?"

"I don't remember."

"Did you visit River Falls?"

"What? No." James shook his head and crossed his arms. "Not even sure where that is."

Miller leaned back and crossed his arms, too. He glanced at the text on his phone. **Mention the transactions but not calls with Roger.**

"You've never heard of River Falls, Oregon?"

James shook his head emphatically.

"Would you repeat that for the recording, please?"

James leaned forward and glared. "I. Have. Never. Heard. Of. River. Falls."

"I have records—" Miller tapped the folder. "—that place you in River Falls on that day. Financial transactions. Maybe someone is blackmailing you, and you can't talk to me? If so, I can help you."

James scoffed again. "What? A credit card? That thing was stolen. I reported it and got the number changed."

"Yes, you did." Miller kept his voice level. "In fact, your credit card was replaced with another on June 15th. But you used the original card in River Falls twice on June 8th."

"Wasn't me." James laughed. "That thing got taken back in May."

A text came through: **Signature on his intake form tonight matches signatures on the credit card slips in Bend and River Falls.**

Miller shook his head slowly. "All right then. I need a break. How about a soda?"

James shrugged.

Miller gathered his things and left the room. James's

bald-faced lies grated on him and wore him out. He didn't want that to come through in his questioning.

His sergeant handed him a soda. "We got confirmation from the video tapes at the gas station. Shows him and Roger Wyatt in a Ford van getting gas that afternoon. Running the plate now."

Miller stared through the one-way window as James stood and paced the room.

James was going to go down. Those girls would come home, one way or another. His energy suddenly returned.

Several hours later, Miller and James remained in the room. James continued to lie, and they all knew it. The team agreed it was time for the next step.

Miller removed two pictures from the file on the table and placed them in front of Devon. "Seen these two pretty young girls?"

An instant flush spread up James's cheeks. He looked away and stared at the wall again.

Miller crossed his arms and leaned casually back in his chair. "Roger Wyatt took these girls from a logging road in River Falls. I think you helped. Did you owe Wyatt a favor and he was after you to pay him back for it? He's a powerful man, and I totally understand if he was holding something over your head. He's known for that."

James paused and shrugged. He scratched his head and got up to pace the floor.

"Pretty girls." Miller tapped his pen. "Maybe they deserved to be taken. Maybe they were wearing clothes that just asked for it. Was that why you helped, James?"

"They did deserve it." James sneered. "Stupid chicks. They were laughing about Sasquatch and never even saw us coming up behind them."

A heavy silence permeated the room as James realized his mistake. Miller raised his eyebrows and shrugged nonchalantly, as if he could care less about the sudden admission after hours in the room. But his heartrate spiked like he'd just jumped off a cliff. In a way, he had. He hated this next part of his job. But he would do whatever it took to save these girls.

"Well, then. If you say so, they must have deserved it. And you must have had a good reason to help Wyatt out. I get it. I understand. He's a bad guy." He managed to laugh. "I wouldn't want to owe that dude a darn thing. That's just scary."

James sighed heavily, rubbing his forehead with one hand. "I need an attorney."

Miller couldn't argue with that.

CHAPTER FORTY
Mike

AFTER A FEW BEERS, Mike wasn't so hungry anymore. Chips from the cupboard helped too. He sat in front of his flatscreen, opened his few pieces of mail and flipped through the newspaper to see if there was any new news about his girls. Then he finally decided to check for leftovers. Speaking of leftovers, he should visit Penny tonight too. It had been awhile. She was probably hungry, both for him and for food. He chuckled. After providing for him, she received food. Tied up and naked all the time now, she knew the rules and would never hide from him again.

He ate leftover chicken and leisurely took a shower. It was nice not having to worry about where Cienna might be. Occasionally, he peeked out the back window and saw her asleep under the tree. May the ants crawl all over her. He chuckled.

Having her out there, however, dampened his plans to see Penny. After all, that was the route to the younger girl's room. Shoot. Having one in the barn and one under the house was supposed to keep it uncomplicated.

Penny had started in the barn and then later came to the

house. Mike struggled with her sheer immaturity. Although beautiful and young with blond hair and gorgeous green eyes, he found her weeping uncontrollably every night. Even after he hit her several times, she wouldn't stop. She refused to cooperate, hid under any piece of furniture or in any cupboard she could find. One night he found she'd cut her wrist with his razor from the shower. Fortunately, she was stupid too. She cut the wrong way on her wrist, couldn't go through with the second wrist, and all they had to deal with was some blood and her almost constant tears. Stupid kid. He beat her nearly senseless after that fiasco. She had finally shut up . . . for one night.

He had asked Roger for a trade-in. Roger laughed. He was a very rich man with this business and could afford to be picky. He looked Penny over, visited her in the barn, and decided he didn't want her back, no matter how pretty and how young. She was too weepy, and he didn't see a way to cure that outside of hurting her more, which didn't appear to help. He and Mike then had a serious discussion.

"I ain't taking her back. Get rid of her. Or maybe get her an antidepressant." Roger laughed. Some clients valued their girls enough to get them medicinal help of some kind. Most did not.

Mike shook his head. "I paid good money for her. Ya think I have money laying around? Since I don't have a missus, I really do need a girl. But this one ain't capable. She won't stop crying, won't help around the house no matter how much I show her who's boss. And she hides all the time. It's like freakin' hide-n-seek on steroids."

"Deal with it." Roger laughed again. "Get rid of her if you want. Guess she outsmarted you, huh? Maybe I can give you a discount on the next one that's a little more domestic. Or at least show her a thing or two if she doesn't get with the program." He waved Mike off, dismissing him.

Mike couldn't quite bring himself to "deal with it." So he

thought of another idea. He pulled out his savings ledger and decided what he could afford to give up. He'd sold several steers the year before and currently lived on the money. But he also had a few thousand in savings. He talked to Roger about a second girl.

"I cemented off the crawlspace under the house and put Penny in there. She only gets food after she pleases me and without tears. Yeah, she finally knows who the boss is." He grinned as Roger high-fived him. He was relieved to not hear the girl crying all the time. And the stupid hide-n-seek. Never again! She would have to stay in the crawlspace, even come winter. She just couldn't handle the full job. He kept her there for his own uses and fed her only enough to keep her alive.

They negotiated. Roger gave him a decent discount on Cienna. "But I get visiting privileges with both of them as part of the deal."

Mike happily agreed if he could say when and where Roger could visit. Now he had Cienna for companionship and help in the house and with the farm. The older ones were best for that, anyway. Mike wasn't really attracted to them so much.

Actually, Cienna was starting to grow on him a bit. Pretty when she wasn't all beat up, although not as much as Penny, and a hard worker. He enjoyed some leisure time with her, rubbing her shoulders while watching a movie and cuddling in bed. He'd never told anyone else about Mrs. Mike. Maybe they could be friends eventually. But was it his fault she had been jumpy lately and made him knock her to the ground out in the garden? No, siree, that was her issue, and he'd needed to set her straight. She was too stubborn. "I hope that she's getting it now." He laughed aloud. "Yer never going home, Cienna. Yer mine until I'm done." She would get used to him and, like Penny, would smile at him someday when he came in the door.

Mike had no choice but to collect Cienna from the tree and bring her into the house. It was getting darker outside, and in the past half hour, she had slapped away tons of mosquitoes as he grinned from the window. He pushed her into the bathroom and told her to take a bath.

CHAPTER FORTY-ONE
Cienna

"THANK YOU." Cienna thought she might be stuck outside all night. Relief filled her heart. A bath might help her back pain, and she was happy to get all the dirt out of her hair and off her skin before he noticed.

When she exited the bathroom, she found a bowl of canned soup waiting for her, ibuprofen, and another mixed drink. She was grateful for all three.

"Hurry up." Mike must be in a bad mood.

She ate and drank quickly.

"I left the buckets of peas and beans in the basement to stay cool. Ya can deal with them tomorrow."

When she was done eating, he practically dragged her upstairs by her arm and locked her in the guestroom.

Bewildered, she lay on the bed and tried not to think about the little girl under the house. She was young with electrifying green eyes. She must be freezing. Cienna shivered as she pulled her one warm blanket up tightly to her chin. Something to be grateful for. She had a room now, locked as it was, and a bed. If she behaved and didn't make Mike mad, she could live in the house with him and not be locked in the barn or under the house.

What had this little girl done to deserve being tied up there? A tear leaked down Cienna's cheek. She quickly brushed it away. For some stupid reason, she cried more easily when she had alcohol, although at first it made her feel braver and stronger.

She had promised to return.

Why had she said that? What had she been thinking? She couldn't go back. Mike would kill her. She couldn't even help herself, much less a little girl.

She pictured Eden and Evelea. She felt protective when she babysat them. She would kill anyone who tried to hurt them or restrain them or keep them against their will. That little girl under the house had parents somewhere . . . and a family... just like Cienna did.

She stared at the ceiling over her bed. And just like that, a cloud in her brain cleared. A clear voice in her head told the brutal truth. Mike was not protecting her from Roger. Mike had allowed Roger in the locked barn for several days while he supposedly "forgot" about her. And he pretended to know nothing about it. Mike allowed Roger to brutalize her more than once. Under his house, he restrained a little girl and kept her naked. He might even be hurting her now. How long had that poor little girl been helpless under the house?

She started sobbing. Mike was a very bad man. "I will be back. I'll get this figured out. And I'll save you, too."

CHAPTER FORTY-TWO
Melissa

MELISSA REFUSED TO RETURN TO WORK. Jimmy didn't push her. They could get by with just his paycheck for a while yet, even though the search for the girls had been hitting the savings pretty hard. Kai remained Melissa's constant companion. She homeschooled their son and didn't go anywhere without him. She even refused to let him visit friends without her nearby.

"I understand, Mel." Jimmy leaned against the kitchen counter. "But you realize it's not normal, don't you?"

"Just what about this whole situation is normal? Was it normal for Cienna to be kidnapped? What if we lose him too? He's-he's all we have left."

She left the room in tears and visited Cienna's bedroom, which she often did now. She lay on her daughter's bed and stared at the ceiling. Maybe she needed to go through her room again. What had she missed? A clue about someone she was in contact with? A reason to go up the logging road? What should she do? She would do whatever it took. Her only answer was to feel a push to keep hoping and looking, so she did.

Kai awoke her when he entered Cienna's room and lay down next to her. "Mom, when is she coming home? She's been gone a long time." He laid his cheek on her shoulder.

"I know, honey. Feels like forever." She stroked his hair. "I don't know."

"Are you in here hoping again?"

"Yes. I will always hope. Maybe it's helping somehow. I don't know. I sorta feel like wherever they are, they have guardian angels watching out for them."

"Where are the angels? In the sky?"

"Hmmm. I think more like all around us. Sometimes I feel them close to me. Do you ever feel that?"

Kai giggled. "What does that feel like?"

Melissa smiled. "For me it feels like . . . comfort. Like there's a warm blanket around me or I'm being hugged." She squeezed him to make her point. "Say, did you finish your spelling?"

"Yes. Those were easy words. I memorized them all already."

Good boy. Maybe she needed to move him to the next level.

"Will I ever go back to school?"

Melissa pondered.

"I think Dad wants me to go back." He whispered this cautiously. Glanced at the open door.

"What makes you think that?"

"He talks about when I go back to school."

"Hmmm." Melissa squeezed his shoulders again. "I don't know, Kai." She sighed. Perhaps she was fighting a losing battle. "I guess your dad and I need to talk more about it. Do you want to go back?"

Kai cuddled close. "I miss my friends."

Melissa's heart broke for him. "Sorry, buddy. Guess I'm not doing my best job these days. How about we call Caleb's mom and see if he can come play?"

"Okay." Kai got up and went to the door. "I'll get your phone."

Melissa sat up and swung her legs to the floor. Life couldn't stop for Kai. How could she do this better? How could she make sure he kept a life and friends, but not lose him too?

She knew she could lose him too.

The thought came from nowhere and terrified her. She wiped away a tear. She could fight it all she wanted, but she knew it was true. Kai could be taken while playing in the yard. Or someone could break into his room. It had happened. Losing one did not make them immune to losing another. She thought about a local family. One daughter had died from cancer, and months later, their second daughter died in a car accident. "Too Much Grief," the headlines had read. "More Than Any Family Can Bear."

She could only hold him tightly. And hope. And look for angels. She sniffled and grabbed a tissue from Cienna's nightstand. She whispered, "I don't know how I would go on . . ."

Kai brought her the phone. She wiped her tears and called to arrange for Caleb come over to play the next evening after school. Some friends had started avoiding them when they returned to River Falls, which hurt. Fortunately, Caleb's family still connected. She and Kai went to the kitchen. Chocolate chip cookies sounded perfect right then.

While the first batch baked, Kai took a bite of cookie dough to his dad, who was seated in his recliner.

"Yum, my favorite." Jimmy ate the dough and sniffed the air. "Smells so good."

"They'll be done in a few." Melissa entered the room and sat on the recliner's armrest. "Kai, go watch to be sure they don't burn."

Jimmy put his arms around her. "I know this is hard. We

want to hold him so close. But he needs to have a life. A good life."

"I know." She wrinkled her nose. "I'm sorry I struggle. Maybe, maybe we should look at him going back to school after Christmas? He seems to want to go. I don't want to smother him. I'm just so scared." Terrified now that she had said it aloud, she quickly added, "Maybe. I need to think about it, okay?" At the same time, she started thinking that if Kai went back to school and was safe, she might be able to volunteer somewhere. Like at the Family Peace Center, where they helped families every day overcome violence.

He nodded as he rubbed her neck. "I understand."

"Mom, Mollie's calling!" Kai bellowed from the kitchen.

Melissa hurried to the kitchen and came back with her phone at her ear. She sighed as she hung up. "Sounds like some progress with getting the search orders they need, but not much new."

Jimmy still stared at the flatscreen, but he'd switched from the news to an old sitcom. She didn't blame him. The news was depressing these days. There was only so much they could handle.

And what happens if they broke? It felt closer to that every day. She shook her head. They couldn't. Parents weren't allowed to break.

CHAPTER FORTY-THREE
Bay

As soon as Bay's client left, the Witch-Devil stormed into the room. Bay had heard her coming. She scrambled to pull clothes on but had only managed her shirt when the big woman grabbed her by the hair. Ouch! She yanked her down the hallway, bursting through the kitchen door. Half-naked, Bay tried to cover herself. Her cheeks reddened. All the girls sat at the kitchen table except for the newest arrivals. Charli had tears in her eyes and a bloody ear. Nia's face was red from an obvious slap. Amber looked no worse for the wear, but had her arms crossed. She glared at Bay.

"This is a lesson for all of you!" The Witch-Devil yelled. She pulled the green key out of her pocket. Waved it in front of Bay's face. "It's your fault. ALL your fault."

She pushed Bay into a chair. Bay groaned. Leaving the key in her jeans pocket had resulted in disaster. Each girl had suffered. Suddenly, they heard commotion upstairs, a combination of Sam's gruff voice and the new residents' rapid Spanish as Sam appeared at the top of the stairs, holding each girl by one arm.

Bay groaned. No . . . She buried her face in her hands. This was her fault, not theirs! They had no idea she wasn't supposed to visit!

"*¡Dejarnos solos! ¡Detener!*" one girl yelled as Sam dragged them through the kitchen and outdoors, heading for the shed. Those two little girls would never be the same again. Silence loomed after the door slammed. The girls looked at their hands or stared at the floor. Had Rose been there, she might have suggested they all tackle the Witch-Devil up and tie her up. Gang up on Sam.

But Rose wasn't there. And Bay couldn't do it. Heck, she couldn't even talk anymore. Tears held back for weeks finally dripped between her fingers and onto the floor.

As her punishment, in addition to working the rest of the day in the locked part of the house, Bay worked the club that night too. Exhaustion welled after seeing client after client, putting up with their whims and sometimes violence. Clients were told they could do anything unless it left a mark. Apparently, only Sam could leave marks. She barely had time to shovel some of Amber's dinner into her mouth and change clothes before being hustled to the van. On the way to the club, she fell asleep twice, her chin nodding against her chest. Getting out of the van, her legs felt heavy and uncooperative.

Eddie ushered her on stage. When she finally came offstage, crying and without her shirt on, he smiled sympathetically. "You're coming with me." He helped her put her shirt back on and ushered her to the VIP room. "Wait for your client. And dry those eyes. It's going to be just fine."

Bay sighed. She sat on the couch, wiping her eyes with her sleeve and wanting to curl up and sleep. She eyed the bottles of alcohol available on the counter across the room. Fortunately, the Witch-Devil had not withheld meds as part of her punishment today, or she would have been in big trouble. She might have tried to steal some booze. All she could think about were the poor little girls who had been dragged to the shed that afternoon because of her.

Bay wanted to throw up. At least on the stage, the audience provided some distraction. But there were no distractions to her dark thoughts in the VIP room . . . yet.

When the door opened again, Eddie ushered in a woman. Startled, Bay smiled tentatively. Sometimes women rented the VIP room, but not frequently. Someone who just wanted to talk? Possibly. Or it could be more. Eddie slammed the door closed. The wall jiggled.

She was pretty, with light brown wavy hair. She wore jeans, boots, and a light leather jacket. She smelled like a dog. She looked at Bay and smiled gently. "Hey, there. My name is Mollie."

Bay froze. If the lady wanted her to talk back, she was in trouble.

The woman sat on the couch. Bay automatically moved closer to her. Not only was it her job to make clients feel at ease, but there was suddenly a comforting presence in the room. Bay felt peaceful like she used to feel with Rose in her third-floor room. Mollie laid her arm around Bay's shoulder and talked in her ear.

"I have a story for you. And I really, really need your help. Can you help me please, Bay?

Bay nodded. Sure thing. She might be able to help. Maybe the lady was sad or going through a divorce or something. She would do what she could. As long as Mollie was paying, Bay's time belonged to her unless the club dude or Sam said otherwise.

"This summer, two families went camping by a waterfall. Every year they meet there to vacation. The girls from the families are BFFs."

Wait. What?

Bay twisted to look at Mollie. A puzzled look crossed her face.

Mollie sighed.

"This summer." Mollie stroked the girl's shoulder gently. "The girls went to get ice cream and never came back to the campsite. As you can imagine, the families are very, very sad."

Acid rose in Bay's throat. No . . .

Mollie took a deep breath.

Bay felt sick, but if she rushed to the bathroom, the manager would see. The other girls had told her there were cameras in the room.

"Bay." Mollie's quiet voice became urgent. "Their names are Jasmine and Cienna. They were taken. Have you seen Jasmine?"

Bay quickly shook her head, terrified.

Mollie pulled Bay in for a hug. Whispered in her ear. "I think you are Jasmine. You and the other girls are safe. There are policemen out at the farmhouse right now, getting ready to arrest Sam and Kella. And as soon as you and I walk out of here safely, there are police outside here, too, ready to come in. Please, Bay, tell me. You are Jasmine, right? I'll help you. You can go home."

Bay started shaking, her arms and legs trembling against her will. Jasmine and Cienna . . . Bay and Cienna . . . ice cream . . . . Sasquatch. Bay clapped her hand over her mouth as her teeth chattered. Panic welled in her stomach and chest. She was going to die. Right here with Mollie, she would die. After all she had survived, she couldn't do it anymore.

Mollie gently removed Bay's hand from her mouth. Bay softened at her touch. Still trembled.

"They're watching us now. Help me out a little bit." She smiled and squeezed Bay's shoulders again. "Your family misses you. What happened to you wasn't your fault, and they can't wait to see you again. Do you hear me? Nothing that has gone on is your fault."

Not her fault. Nothing was her fault.

Bay tried to process this. She remembered being locked

in the TC Room. Told that she had been a very bad girl. Was it possible that she had not been sent away because she was bad? But this woman had no idea of what she had really done.

Did it matter? If she got out, she could find Rose's daughter. Could she trust this Mollie? Was Sam waiting outside to beat her if she walked out? She suspected Rose would want her to walk out anyway.

Bay thought of the two little girls in the shed at the farm because of her. They were likely still in there, battered and restrained. Although she doubted Sam would kill them and ruin the chance of getting money for their services, she knew now there were fates worse than death. There were police there right now who could save them. And it was all up to her.

All. Up. To. Her.

But she had killed Rose. Could she now save those two girls? Light broke through the darkness. What would Cienna do? Bay smiled slightly. Cienna would grab this woman's hand and flee.

Rose had claimed someone upstairs was watching out for her. She suddenly realized that maybe Rose hadn't meant herself. Maybe, just maybe, Bay had a guardian angel. Maybe this angel had sent Mollie. Was Cienna out there too, waiting for her?

She was strong.

"I am s-strong." After weeks of not talking, her voice was tiny. "I am strong." She repeated hoarsely. She turned to Mollie. "Hi, M-Mollie." Her voice cracked. She grabbed her new friend's hand. "My name . . . my name is Jasmine. I like to go by Jazz . . ."

CHAPTER FORTY-FOUR
Cienna

CIENNA'S RISKY PLAN REQUIRED TIME. She hoped that Penny had some time, but she wondered how much. Who knew what Mike did to the tiny one? What if Roger had visited her too? Cienna worked outside as much as she could. She tried to build more trust with Mike and looked for moments to visit under the house. Her plan included getting Mike drunk until he passed out. She would steal his truck keys, release Penny from her bindings, and they would drive away as fast as the wind. She had never driven before. But she would figure it out. She had to.

She hated Mike. She was onto his games even though he continued his charm. Every time she found herself a little drawn to him, she remembered the little girl under the house. Then she bit her lip and did whatever she had to do to make Mike happy. Whatever it took.

In those weeks, Mike slept in her room several times a week. In those weeks, he decided at times he wanted a physical relationship. And although she cried in her heart, she allowed it. She worked on gratefulness—most of the time he was gentle, and the time differed dramatically from the experience with Roger.

Since the incident in the garden, Mike had not hurt her again. No kicks, hits, or slaps. She wasn't sure she could say the same for Penny. She saw bruises when she visited her in the small space that measured only about eight feet wide and four feet high. Stoic and quiet, Penny obviously didn't trust in Cienna's promises about a rescue. Most of the time, she didn't even seem to care. Cienna grew frustrated. She took great risk to feed her and provide company. Most times the little girl barely acknowledged her presence.

Cienna continued cooking and cleaning. She worked in the garden every chance she got, even when chained. She snuck vegetables to Penny a few times and managed some other food that wouldn't leave scraps or bones behind. She really wanted to bring Penny a blanket or at least a sweater, but if Mike had any clue that Penny was receiving help from Cienna, they would both be dead by Roger's hands, she was sure.

One time, Cienna saw Roger leaving from the door by the garden and seethed for days. But she couldn't do anything about it. Spared from Roger's administrations for now, Cienna remained wary. If she angered Mike, he would lock her in the barn room again, and Roger would visit.

Hardened and matured beyond her years, Cienna rarely showed emotion anymore. The last time tears came was the first day she'd promised help to Penny and had lain in her room feeling overwhelmed and at a loss. But tears had no place in a rescue plan, and it was up to her to make that happen. She would do it. She would get them both out.

Recently Mike had allowed her a bit more freedom. Once he let her answer the door when a delivery came, and he was busy.

She opened it with a grin. It was nice to see someone from the real world. "Hi."

"Hi." The white-haired man handed her a box.

Their eyes met.

Could he help? There was a little girl under the house who needed help. She opened her mouth to say it and froze.

Suddenly Mike was behind her. "Hey, Dave. I'll sign for that."

Dave handed Mike the handheld device with the black screen and an attached pen. Mike signed with a flourish and passed it back over. "Thanks, man."

Then to Cienna, "Just put the box on the table, honey."

"Have a great day, you two." Dave waved as he left, spinning his big brown truck quickly out of the driveway.

Cienna placed the box on the kitchen table and hovered at the window after he rounded the corner in the driveway, hoping he would return. Would Dave realize that something was wrong? That she didn't belong there? Would he return and save her, or at least call the cops? He didn't, of course.

Mike seemed moody and drank several beers that night. Cienna wanted to ask him what was going on, but he was snippy with her. She tiptoed around instead. Again, he locked her in the guest room early. In fact, she didn't even get dinner. Her stomach growling, she stared at the ceiling as she lay on the bed, glad to be alone, even though her stomach wouldn't let her sleep. Hours later, she finally slept and dreamed of being home and arriving late for school because she had been bad and locked in her bedroom.

When Mike went to take care of the cows the next day, Cienna slipped out of the house to take food to Penny.

"Penny, Penny." She quietly entered the chamber, not wanting to startle the girl. "I brought you some food."

Penny mumbled. She was curled on the dirt into a small ball and barely looked at Cienna.

"Are you okay?"

Penny finally looked up, fresh bruising evident all over her face.

"I'm so sorry." Cienna stroked the girl's hair. "You know I'm going to get us out of here—"

"Shut up." Penny startled Cienna. "You're the princess in the house, remember? I'm just the rat in the basement." It was the most words she'd spoken to Cienna ever. "Go away."

Cienna recoiled. Her heart broke for the girl. If Penny wouldn't accept help, Cienna could only help by distracting Mike more so that he spent less time in the crawlspace. Why had he been angry last night?

And why hadn't she spoken up? Told that driver they were in trouble? Ugh!

Cienna spent most of the day trying to figure how to speed up her escape plan. When she saw Mike's driver's license on the table and discovered that his birthday was that week, she decided luck was on her side. "I want to make you a special dinner for your birthday. We can celebrate tomorrow. I insist."

"Fine. Make a list." He grunted.

"But if I give you a list, it won't be a surprise!" She pouted and begged. She cleaned extra, did additional chores, and gave him a special favor in bed. And after that, he groggily agreed that she could go to the store with him, if she kept her mouth shut while there.

He found her new, tight jeans. She practiced wearing heels. He gave her some makeup from a drawer in another bedroom. By the time she paraded by his side to town, everyone who glanced would assume Cienna was a girlfriend. They would never suspect she was a fourteen-year-old slave.

Eager to learn more about the area in which they lived and how to get out, Cienna stared outside as they drove. Unfortunately, Mike had waited until after dinner. Darkness was coming soon. She saw a "Welcome to Hillsboro" sign. Hillsboro. She racked her brain. Familiar. Yes, she and her family would stop there for berries and peaches at the fruit stands on the way to the beach.

The blacktop roads, which took quite a time to reach,

boasted some homes and some small businesses. Gradually, there was a highway, then restaurants and strip malls. Finally, they stopped at the post office. They walked into the semi-dark lobby together. Mike used a key to open a small post office box. He crammed the mail under his arm. They returned to the truck, nodding at a man who held the lobby door open for them.

When the truck stopped at the grocery store, WinLand, Cienna tried to jump out. Mike clamped his hand down on her thigh. "Now listen here, sweetheart. Yer with me as my girl. Ya got that? Ya better act like it too. And no talking to people or sneaking off."

Cienna nodded quickly, not caring about his terms. She was at the store. She remembered her mission. To make Mike a special birthday dinner and cake. And then she would get him happy and drunk, find his keys, unchain Penny, pull her out of the crawl space, and get them both to safety. She tried to memorize the route as the truck drove and hoped she wouldn't get them lost. Maybe as she drove, she could flag down another car.

She noted that the truck didn't have a stick to move around and was grateful for that. She barely remembered her first trip in this truck. It was dark, and she was terrified. But her dad always said that with a stick in the middle, it was harder to drive. "When you get your permit, you'll learn on an automatic."

Mike's truck seemed pretty automatic. Cienna determined to make it happen.

Mike clenched her thigh hard, and she yelped.

"I said yes."

He laughed. "No, ya didn't. But even if ya had, I would want to hear it again. No talking!"

Cienna turned to him. She wanted to spit in his face. Obedient Cienna smiled. "Of course, I'll be good. I'm just excited to go into a store. It's been a while."

Mike chuckled as he got out of the truck. "What girl doesn't like to shop?"

Cienna hopped down from the seat. Mike came around to take her arm, and they entered the store. The sudden exposure to bright lights and many colors made Cienna blink. She shrunk back. Overwhelming. Music played loudly, and people pushed shopping carts to the left, where it seemed all who entered WinLand had to travel first. She saw several displays for Halloween candy and items. Her family was probably home in Beaverton by now—not so far away. Summer was definitely done.

A piece of her broke inside. She'd been on Mike's farm for four months. Although he walked next to her, she felt alone. Panic welled up in her stomach.

Mike placed a few things in the basket from the first aisle. Chips, soda, cheese dip and a couple of cans of hash. He grabbed a bottle of vegetable oil and snickered at Cienna, who was staring wide-eyed at everything in the store.

"Where the heck is yer list, girl? Wake up."

Her list! Her list was in the truck. No matter. Cienna smiled at him and took his arm as she sauntered next to him. She pointed at her head. "All here. No worries." Whoops. What if some of the things had been in the sale aisle, now behind them? It looked like you weren't supposed to go back there. All the shopping carts were being moved toward produce like they were on tracks or something. Like the doors on hangers in *Monsters, Inc.*

They rounded the corner, and Mike let her choose strawberries and bananas. "But not too many. They aren't cheap." Since most of their vegetables came from Mike's garden and Cienna had preserved a lot of them, they didn't spend much time in that section.

They moved on to the meat. Mike had mentioned salmon, so she picked that out for his birthday meal and grabbed a nearby sauce that said it was good with fish. She had no idea how to cook it. But she would figure it out. Mike had to be full, happy and sleepy for the plan to work.

Mike grumbled at the cost, but she reminded him it was for a special occasion. She smiled at him, and he reached over and ruffled her hair. They headed to the dairy aisle and picked out milk, eggs, and butter. She asked politely for a yogurt and he declined her.

They spent a bit of time in the baking aisle, and she picked out a cake mix and frosting. They were low on pancake mix, so he added that. And then, as they rounded the corner, they found themselves in the feminine products section.

Mike stopped the cart. "Don't ya need anything here? Sorry I forget that I should grab that stuff when I shop since the missus died."

Cienna blushed violently. Shook her head. She actually hadn't needed any. She felt sick to her stomach. It had been quite a while in fact. What did that mean? She shook her head to clear it, and Mike took that as confirmation that all was good. They moved onto paper supplies as Cienna tried to remember when she'd had her last period.

The final section of the store contained the alcohol shelves. She quickly recovered from her pondering.

"Come on, choose your fave. It's for your birthday, and that's a special day." She smiled at him and touched his arm.

"Eh, but yer only fourteen. I shouldn't drink so much with ya in the house."

Cienna shook her head. "No, this a very special occasion. I swear it's not a problem. We'll have fun. I'll have some too. Come on, Mike."

After he finally chose several bottles of wine and a pack of beer, she breathed a sigh of relief. There was alcohol at the house, but she needed enough to make this plan work.

They picked a checkout line and soon stood in front of the register . . . with a chatty cashier.

"How are you, honey? Haven't see you here before." She smiled at Cienna.

Cienna looked at Mike. She wasn't supposed to talk. He gave a brief nod, and she realized that it would be more awkward if she was silent. She stared at the woman's name tag, which read "Donna." Blunt Cienna wanted to bust it all out. "That's because he keeps me locked up all the time, Donna." But compliant Cienna found herself nodding. "Good. Thanks." She remembered her manners. "And you?"

"I'm doing really good. Thank you!" Donna grabbed more items and swiped them across the glass plate. Beep. Beep. Beep. Silence. "Oops. The strawberries didn't scan. Now how do I find those numbers? Sorry." She blushed. "I'm still learning." She kept looking at Cienna funny, as if she knew her from somewhere.

Mike started tapping his fingers impatiently against the handle of the shopping cart. Donna turned to her laminated book and flipped through it. "Organic strawberries . . . hmmm."

"Organic?" Mike exploded. "Them strawberries ain't organic."

A couple with a baby and a full shopping cart lined up behind them.

"Sir, I'm sorry." Donna smiled patiently. "These ones have an organic sticker. What I can't figure out is why their number isn't right on the package with it. Usually it is." She sighed. "Oh dear." As she looked through the book, she kept glancing at Cienna as though trying to figure something out. She chewed her lip. Donna was taking forever.

"Forget the strawberries." Mike was loud. "Take them back. We don't want 'em." The woman behind them shifted uncomfortably. The baby whimpered.

"No." Cienna gave Mike a sweet smile. "Please?" She'd really missed fruit. Maybe he'd let her eat some in the truck on the way back. She should get some to Penny, too.

Mike frowned at her.

She thought quickly. What were strawberries famous for?

Vitamin C? That was it. "I . . . I feel like my vitamin C is a little low." She spoke quietly so only Donna and Mike could hear her. "I would like them." She looked at the ground. "Please?"

She meekly and quickly glanced at Donna with her head still lowered. Suddenly something changed in the woman's face. She turned to glare at Mike. "This girl needs her vitamins. And you, sir, need to be a gentleman and get to bagging these groceries." She pointed down to the end of the belt where bags hung ready, and a kneepad was strategically placed to advance the belt. "While you do that, I'll find the code, and maybe we can find you a coupon for a discount on them."

Mike huffed loudly. He pushed his way past Cienna and the cart, squeezing her hip tightly on the way. Cienna bit back a startled gasp. But then he did as he'd been told. A small smile tugged at her lips. Mike being bossed around was funny, even more so since he had actually obeyed Donna. Hopefully, Cienna wouldn't get in too much trouble later.

"Now let's see here." Donna frowned. She turned her back and busied herself with a piece of paper, apparently looking for a coupon for the fruit. She wrote something quickly, still talking up a storm, and slid the piece of paper across the counter to Cienna. "Are you okay?" it read. There was a phone number. Cienna's eyes widened and flew up to meet Donna's concerned gaze.

Oh my gosh. Donna knew. Donna knew who she was.

Now Cienna would really be in trouble. She glanced at Mike, but he was busy double wrapping the wine. Quickly, Cienna tucked the piece of paper in the pocket of her too-tight jeans and pasted a smile on her face.

"Found it!" Donna turned to the folks who were lining up behind Cienna. "Sorry, everyone. I'm new. User error." And then to Mike, "I found the code." She triumphantly punched the code into the register and the screen listed the price. "And I also have a discount code. Guess everybody will want that discount." She smiled but kept eyeing Cienna and chattering as she scanned the salmon and the sauce and passed them down to Mike. "Almost time for Halloween. Any plans? What's your name, honey?"

"Cienna." She slapped her hand over her mouth. Crap.

From the end of the checkout belt, Mike straightened up and glared at her. Oh, she was in trouble for sure! But it WAS her name. And it had popped out. How was that her fault? But then she thought she better answer the other question too. "Nah. Who likes to trick or treat anymore? The little kids are annoying." Donna and the people waiting in line laughed, and she laughed along with them. She would have given anything to trick or treat this year. Anything at all.

The groceries were scanned and bagged. Red-faced Mike came to swipe his card. As they exited the store, he made Cienna push the cart. He put his arm tightly around her shoulder and squeezed hard.

Donna

As soon as they left, Donna grabbed her training notebook. "Excuse me. I'm so sorry. Be right back." Just as she'd suspected, this was one of the kidnapped girls. She looked a little different from the poster, but alike enough to be her. Donna was sure. And her name was Cienna, not a name you hear every day and just like the girl on the poster. That cinched it.

Maybe she'd be fired, but it didn't matter. She scooted out the door behind Mike and Cienna. She hovered behind the cement pillar in front of the store, peering out as the two approached Mike's truck. She saw Mike take Cienna by the shoulders and shake them hard before he pulled the tailgate down. She clearly heard him bellow. "Get your butt in the truck now." She sighed. This girl was in trouble tonight. It was Donna's fault.

As soon as Mike slammed the tailgate shut and headed to the driver's side, Donna stuck her head out from behind the pillar again. She read the license plate number. Fortunately, they had parked under one of the lights in the parking lot. The truck was dirty but not too dirty to read the plate. She jotted what she remembered in her notebook before heading back into the store, back to her station, and picking up the phone.

CHAPTER FORTY-FIVE
Cienna

CIENNA KNEW SHE WAS IN BIG TROUBLE. Mike had not stopped yelling since they left the store. And each time a streetlight gave her a glimpse of his face, he looked furious. He gripped the steering wheel tightly.

"Ya want Roger?" He growled. "Ya want to spend more time with him? That's what yer getting tonight! Yes, siree! Straight to the barn! He'll give ya what ya deserve. Stupid, stupid girl! All was fine until ya told her yer name. What the heck?"

Roger would kill her this time.

Cienna huddled close to the passenger door. She could not survive Roger's anger again. At the next stoplight, she would open the door and run. In the darkness of the truck, she managed to wiggle off her heels. Mike was still yelling. He didn't hear a thing.

A sudden thought struck her. What about Penny? She had promised to save her, to come back for her. If Cienna got away, Penny would indeed suffer at the hands of Roger and an angry Mike. She doubted that the little girl, already given minimal food and water, could survive much more. Cienna slumped back. She had to go back. Had to do what she could to survive a few days in the barn with Roger, and somehow save little Penny, who was waiting for her to come.

She had promised.

Sudden lights and sirens behind the truck caused Mike to swerve. He swore when a police car came up to the side of the truck. More than one! The second one sped up and pulled in front of the truck sideways. Mike slammed on the brakes, almost hitting the patrol car.

The truck had barely stopped before he scrambled out and ran. He was knocked to the ground by two large officers, who handcuffed him and hustled him to the back of a patrol car. As Cienna sat astounded in the truck, she could hear them reading him his rights, just like in a cop show. Mike was yelling obscenities the entire time.

Had Mike run a red light? What had happened?

She reached for the passenger side door handle to open it. She could run now. She would run—as fast as she could go. She would tell someone where to find Penny, too.

A female police officer with short blond hair opened the door from the outside. "Are you Cienna?"

Cienna almost fell off the seat of the truck. Not sure if she could say her name without the wrath of someone, she nodded.

The officer smiled gently. Held out her hand. After she helped Cienna out to stand up, she placed a hand briefly on her shoulder. "I'm glad to meet you. I'm Officer Cherie Hubble. We've been looking for you. You've done nothing wrong. We're here to help you."

Cienna looked up at her angel in blue . . . and smiled.

CHAPTER FORTY-SIX
Melissa

ON THE DAY MELISSA ALLOWED KAI to return to Harvest Elementary School, her phone rang at noon. It was late October. School had already been in session for nine weeks. She had hoped he could adapt quickly and find his friends from last year. Hopefully, he didn't feel like an oddball. They had chatted about guardian angels and how Kai's would attend school with him. Would it ease his nerves? Would the other students be kind?

"Mrs. Rydal, we need you to come pick up Kai."

Well, that was fine. She'd practically been pacing the floor all day anyway. But wait. "Why?"

The principal sighed. "I'm sorry for your family's pain. I know it won't ever go away. But today Kai threw a book at another student in the library, so he'll need to go home on suspension for the day."

She texted Jimmy brief information, and now in her car, impatiently waiting for the light to change, she looked for a better route on her GPS to get there quickly.

Comfort was what he needed. Not punishment. She needed to pick him up and bring him home for good. She clicked to choose a faster route. She should know all the routes by heart, but since Cienna disappeared, she seemed unable to conjure up the roadmaps in her head.

A sullen Kai met her when she entered the school office.

"Who did he hit? Are they okay?"

The lady gave her a name of a boy and confirmed that he was in the nurse's room with an ice pack. But, yes, he would be okay.

Melissa hugged Kai. Left with him in tow. "Get in the car, please."

He did and buckled his seat belt. He sighed loudly.

"What happened?" She glanced at him in her rearview mirror.

Kai shrugged.

Okay, he wasn't ready to talk about it.

At home, Kai worked on a puzzle and read a book. "Can I watch TV?"

"No." She ruffled his hair. "I know you're sad, honey, and I am too. But we can't hurt other people, even when we're sad."

He nodded. Later he fell asleep on the couch.

She covered him with a blanket. When Jimmy came home, Kai was grudgingly cleaning his room.

In the kitchen, Jimmy greeted her with a kiss. "What happened?"

Melissa shrugged. "I still don't know. He won't say. He threw a book at another kid who now has a black eye. That's all I know."

"Maybe after dinner he'll be ready to talk."

"Hope so. I told him no TV and that we can't hurt people, even when we're sad. I'm not taking him back there, Jimmy."

"I know." He gathered plates and cutlery to set the table for dinner.

Dinner was quiet. Melissa saw Kai eye Cienna's former

place at the table several times. He'd never been violent. In her heart, she knew it was related. "Kai, did you get your feelings hurt today?"

"He said she deserved it!" He burst into tears.

Melissa and Jimmy looked at each other.

"Who deserved what?"

Kai grabbed his napkin, wiped his face, and stared at his lap. "He said she deserved to get kid-kidnapped."

Understanding and anger dawned. Melissa fought to keep her emotion controlled.

Jimmy reached over and took Kai's hand. "I'm sorry, son. That boy doesn't understand. No one deserves to be kidnapped. That was wrong of him."

"She-She didn't deserve that." Kai sniffed. "She was-is my sister, and I love her. Even when we fight sometimes."

"You're right. She didn't deserve it. No one does. That boy was wrong. And I know he hurt your feelings when he said that. But, Kai, you were also wrong. What could you have done instead of throwing a book?"

Kai crossed his arms and stared at the floor.

Melissa signed. "Kai! Could you have told the teacher or the librarian instead of hurting him?" Her voice pitched higher.

Kai pushed back his chair and stood up, glaring at them both. "You don't get it. No one can talk bad about my sister! She's probably dead anyway, and I don't care!" He burst into tears again and ran to his bedroom, slamming his door.

Melissa shook her head.

Jimmy placed his hand over hers. "Let's just give him some time."

"Time like Cienna apparently has?" Melissa shoved her chair back abruptly. She picked up several dishes to take to the kitchen. Her poor babies. Both of them. And she couldn't fix it.

Carrying the casserole dish, Jimmy joined her in the

kitchen. "I'm sorry, hon. This is rough. But he must know that despite . . . in spite of our issues, he still has choices. He could have responded differently. He should have responded differently."

"I know." Melissa wiped a tear from her eye. "But I don't really understand. If my sister was missing, I think I might throw a book too! Like she could deserve it." She washed a plate furiously, letting her tears fall into the sink. "Stupid jerk heads! How could they? How could they take the girls like that?" The dish brush dropped from her grasp. She covered her face with soapy hands. "I can't do this anymore, Jimmy! I can't do this nightmare! I miss her so bad!" She sobbed, tears echoing off the kitchen walls, loud and piercing.

"Shh." Jimmy pulled her close. "Go to bed, honey. I'll finish this. Okay? It's okay . . . "

"It's not okay." She sobbed and hiccupped as he led her down the hallway. Even with his help, she bumped into the walls twice.

In their bedroom, Jimmy pulled back the covers. Melissa crawled in and grabbed her extra pillow, holding it close. Both pillows had absorbed many tears in the past several months. "I'm-I'm sorry Jimmy. Bad night, I guess."

Jimmy smoothed her hair back from her face. "I know. It's okay. Get some sleep. Some nights are bad. And it's okay."

A few hours later, her cell phone rang, and then Jimmy's. She drowsily poked at him, trying to shake herself out of sleep.

"Phone." She sat up, arms flailing, and knocked her prescription anti-depressant off her nightstand. "Jimmy, your phone!"

He jolted awake. Grabbed his phone. "Hi. Hello?" He covered the mouthpiece. "It's Miller." As he listened, his face grew as white as the sheets that covered their bed. His eyes filled. He blinked and hung up without saying a word to the detective. "They found them." His hand shook so hard his phone landed on the floor instead of his nightstand. "Cienna is okay and in a Portland hospital. She's okay! We have to go. Now!"

Melissa screamed in pure joy. Bounced out of the bed.

Scooping up Kai, they climbed into the car and headed toward the hospital. While Jimmy drove, Melissa listened to Detective Miller's voicemail on her phone. Her hands shook violently.

"Call me back." Relief was evident in Detective Miller's voice. "We've found the girls. They're safe."

After she'd listened at least seven times on speaker phone, Jimmy cleared his throat.

"I think we got the message."

The girls were safe. She could hear it a hundred times and still would never tire of the words. Cienna's guardian angel had finally come through.

CHAPTER FORTY-SEVEN
Mari

WHILE KEN DOZED IN HIS RECLINER, Mari headed to bed. This happened more and more often now. Sometimes he awoke later and came to bed, but there had been mornings recently when she awoke and found his side untouched. She sighed. Things had been rough lately. She couldn't even remember their last kiss. When Jasmine disappeared, the bottom had dropped out of their world.

She trudged to their room. Pulling her nightgown over her head, she noted that their bedroom was messy and stacks of things continued to appear next to the bed, the dresser, the vanity. Books, papers, folders, and files. Surely there was a drawer he could cram it all in instead. She'd have to find an empty one tomorrow.

Ken

Ken opened one eye and peered down the hallway. Finally, Mari had headed to bed. Didn't she know he could feel it when she kept checking, no, staring at him in the recliner? When she paused at the doorway or, worse, right next to the chair as if making sure he was still breathing? Irritating. He wanted left alone.

He could hear Seth's video game in the other room and occasionally heard him talking. He'd wanted a headset for his birthday. These days, Seth got pretty much what he wanted without a lot of questions being asked. It was just easier. Then again, it was past 11 at night. Good thing tomorrow was Saturday.

"Oh man." Seth swore. "Dude, you totally missed that one. What's the problem?"

Ken shook his head. He really should pop his head in, correct the boy, and send him to bed, but he didn't have the energy. Life was different now. He even found himself swearing here and there. In fact, he had sworn at Mari when she insisted he move his stacks of papers and books out of the living room. Couldn't she see that having his things close by made him feel better? Apparently, that didn't matter.

When his phone rang, Ken ignored it. It was in the kitchen, and he wouldn't reach it in time anyway. When it started ringing for a third time, he decided that he needed a beer anyway and got up to get it.

Mollie. Mollie times three. Suddenly his heartrate doubled, and he broke out in a sweat. Did he want to take this call? Had they finally found Jasmine's remains? He shuddered. But they needed to know. Everyone needed closure.

He picked up the phone hesitantly.

"Ken?" Mollie's voice was controlled but rushed. "Take a deep breath. We found both the girls. They're safe now at the hospital."

He dropped the phone to the floor and fell on his hands and knees, fumbling for it.

"I'm sorry. I'm sorry. Mari! Mari! Seth!"

His fingers located the phone under the refrigerator where it had spun. He pulled it out, scratched and dusty now but still connected. "Mollie?" He stayed on the floor as the room swam around him. "I'm sorry. I dropped the phone. Where is she? Where do we go? Thank you."

Tears dripped on his arm. He looked up to see Mari standing in the kitchen doorway, her hand covering her mouth. He imitated writing in the air with his finger. She hurried a pen and a piece of mail over to him. He listened more, jotted down a Portland hospital, and hung up after thanking Mollie again.

Mari sat down next to him, her back against the cupboard. She looked solemn . . . and suddenly very controlled. Her face tightened. "They are . . . ?" It was obvious to Ken that she was expecting the worst, like he had.

"Safe."

With that word, she collapsed against his shoulder.

He patted her arm. "Safe," he said again, to convince himself. A deep shudder started somewhere in his knees and worked all the way up to his stomach, then his head. Mari put both her arms around his shoulder and hugged him.

"I can't believe it." She started crying.

He texted Seth in the other room. His son was pretty much deaf with that headset. **Come to the kitchen now.**

In a minute I can.

No. NOW.

Seth appeared, frowning. "Why are you on the floor? Gross. I'm in the middle of a game."

"We know." His son was way too absorbed online. He himself had been too absorbed in collecting things and living in the recliner. His family had slowly been dying inside. He was supposed to be the strong one and supporting them all. It was time for a change.

Seth's expression sobered. "What happened? Jasmine?"

"She's alive. So is Cienna. We are heading to Portland. I have no idea when we'll be able to bring her home. Maybe not right away. Maybe you should stay home until we learn more. Your sister is safe, Seth. She's going to be okay. We'll have her call you from the hospital, okay?"

Seth's shoulders slumped. He covered his face with both his hands and turned to the wall.

Mari got to her feet and wrapped her arms around him as he cried into her shoulder. "I know, I know. But it's okay. We're all going to be okay."

He gently pushed her away and went quietly to his room, closing his door.

"He'll sleep now." Mari rushed to gather her purse, still in her nightgown.

"Yes." Ken pulled himself off the floor. "Get changed, honey. Let's call Amelie now and go get Jasmine."

Amelie

Amelie sat across from Mitch at a local fast-food place and picked at her breaded chicken. They had needed a late-night snack after studying biology for hours. This place was the only one open still in their Seattle neighborhood.

He swallowed a bite of burger. "Does it suck?"

"No." She dipped it in dressing and took a larger bite, washing it down with a sip of soda. "I just keep thinking about what you said."

Mitch covered her hand with his. "I shouldn't have brought it up. I'm sorry."

"No, no, it's not that." She shrugged. "Good you did. I just-I'm scared. What if Jasmine was trafficked? She could be dead by now."

"It sounds like the investigators considered that and are following up. I guess all we can do is let them do their jobs."

"Yeah. Guess so." Amelie finished her French fries and sat back in her seat. She glanced at her phone. How was it past midnight already? She should probably leave and get some sleep. When her phone started ringing, she ignored it. Her mom called every day. In fact, she had talked to her this morning. She probably was having trouble sleeping and was being needy. Amelie would let it ring. She wanted some non-homework time with Mitch.

CHAPTER FORTY-EIGHT
Mollie

IN A LARGE PORTLAND HOSPITAL, Cienna and Jasmine were cared for and examined gently. Before the parents saw the girls, they would need information. Mollie was going to meet with them all at once, along with Carisa, a counselor whom the hospital kept on call.

Carisa had worked in other situations involving trafficking and volunteered with many local, noteworthy organizations. Other professionals and recovery classes would likely be pulled in for the aftercare of the girls, too.

Mollie told Jasmine that Cienna had also been rescued and was at the same hospital. Plus, her parents were on the way. Jasmine cried when she heard. She asked Mollie to stay with her. Mollie happily complied.

A woman doctor examined Jasmine with the lady social worker nearby. The social worker explained that they would be using a Rape Kit that would help collect DNA evidence. She also offered her medication that might prevent sexually transmitted diseases. Did she want a pill to make sure she didn't get pregnant? Jasmine nodded and accepted it with a glass of water.

When the exam was finally finished, Jasmine took Mollie's hand. "I don't feel so good."

"No wonder." Mollie squeezed her fingers.

"At the farm, they gave us pills."

"Do you know what kind?" Rob had told Mollie about the narcotics, anti-anxiety meds, and birth-control pills they'd found when they arrested Sam and Kella Tindell. But she wanted to know what Jasmine knew.

"Birth-control. Some others. One of them made me feel real good." She gave Mollie a pleading look. "I sure could use some now. It's past time."

Mollie shook her head. "The doctor will prescribe something much better for you, honey."

After giving her a reassuring hug, Mollie stopped by the nurse's station to report what Jasmine had told her. "Can you help her with her nausea?"

"We can. She's going through withdrawals, and her blood pressure is on the high side. We'll need to wean her down from those drugs they were giving her. I was just about to page the doctor to get approval."

Over an hour later, when Jasmine was throwing up into a bed pan, the nurse brought a shot to add to her IV.

Within minutes, Jasmine smiled sleepily at Mollie. "I feel better." Her eyelids drooped, and she snuggled under clean white sheets and three warm blankets.

A lump came to Mollie's throat as she watched sweet Jasmine fall asleep.

Cienna

Cienna worried about Penny, still under Mike's house, and resisted the exam and pills. "Don't touch me!"

"It's okay. They're not going to hurt you." Mollie, the lady who'd visited her earlier, stood at the end of the bed. "Is there anything you can tell us about your time at Mike's?"

"Did you find Penny?"

"Penny?" The lady turned pale.

Cienna told her everything she knew. "I promised to help her. She's under the house. Please . . . "

"Don't you worry. We'll take care of her." Mollie smiled. "Right away."

After she left, Cienna agreed to the exam and pictures, but refused the pills they tried to give her. She laughed when the nurse told her the medical staff could be trusted. "Never again," she muttered as the woman left the room.

Mollie

Mollie and Carisa waited in the lobby of the ER for the Rydals and the Jensens to arrive. Before long, the two couples rushed in, looking panicked and happy at the same time.

"Where are they?" Jimmy looked flushed.

Mollie steered them into a conference room down the hallway from the ER waiting room. Rob Miller came in and greeted them. The smiles around the room were contagious. The girls were safe.

The hard job fell to Mollie, Carisa, and Rob that night. Although all four parents were grateful beyond words that the girls were coming home, they now learned their daughters had been through hell. Even the professionals didn't have all the details. But they knew the basics, and the parents needed to know them, too. There were tears and anger around the conference table as understanding, then horror, dawned on them. Melissa sobbed. Jimmy tried in vain to comfort her. Mari seemed too controlled. Ken impatient.

Rob told them about the arrests as the parents dried their tears. "Sam and Kella Tindell, the ones who held Jasmine, are in custody." Rob looked at Mari and Ken. "They called your daughter Bay. There was a man who occasionally helped with driving and on the farm, but we've not found him yet. Jasmine's housemates, Charli, Amber, Nia, Bee, Martha, and Maria are safe and in other local hospitals. Jasmine worked at a club while there. The club has been closed, the owners arrested. In return for being an informant, Eddie, a staff member, will be charged minimally, and will likely just receive probation."

Mollie nodded. "Eddie was a huge help and has seen what part he played. He's remorseful and his wife just had a baby girl. I think that helped him relate to these girls a little bit."

"Well, thank you, Eddie." Mari's tone was dry. Mollie couldn't tell whether she was being sarcastic or genuine.

She saw Ken squeeze Mari's hand.

Next Rob addressed Jimmy and Melissa. "While Cienna was being held, she discovered a girl imprisoned under Mike's house. Unfortunately, we just received word that Penny didn't make it, but Cienna doesn't know that yet. Penny passed before we got out to the house. Looks like things had been pretty rough for her."

Rob had told Mollie the sickening details. Thankfully, he didn't explain to these folks that the little girl had been completely naked and her ribs stuck out. They found her chained to one of the support posts under the house. Her poor heart had probably just finally given up. They were already searching for Penny's parents or family.

Rob explained that Devon James, who had initially assisted with the kidnapping, was jailed after his admission of guilt. Mike Bender was secured in a jail cell in Hillsboro. But unfortunately, Roger Wyatt was still nowhere to be found. "I don't expect you to remember all of this. We as a team are still here. We'll finish the investigation and arrests and are available to talk."

That was enough for today.

CHAPTER FORTY-NINE
Jasmine

J ASMINE AWOKE TO HER MOTHER stroking her cheek and her father standing nearby, tears streaming down his cheeks.

"Oh, my darling." Mom shook her head, unable to speak more. Jasmine threw her arms around her neck and sobbed uncontrollably.

"Mom, Mom. You're here!" This time, it was no dream. "I'm sorry. I'm so sorry. I've been so bad."

"Oh, honey." Mom hugged her tightly. "You're not bad. You've never been bad. We love you. None of this was your fault. Or Cienna's fault. I promise you. You are the best Jasmine ever. And now . . . now you'll be able to dance again." She ran her hands down Jasmine's hair. "It's so long and beautiful. I'm so glad to hold you again. It's a dream come true." She pulled back and looked into Jasmine's eyes. Searched them.

Dad nodded. He seemed unable to speak too. He moved forward. Hugged them both tightly. Jasmine giggled. A group hug was difficult in a hospital bed with the goofy rails on each side. It was almost comical as they all balanced carefully.

He sat on the edge of the bed toward the bottom of it and reached out to touch her leg, He pulled back before making contact, like maybe he was worried she wouldn't like it. "Your mom is right. None of this was your fault, Jasmine. You're not bad."

Jasmine started crying again. Buried her face in her arms. "She said I was bad. So bad. I thought-I thought maybe you sent me away. I didn't understand."

"They were very, very bad people." Mom fiercely wiped a tear, her voice rising. "Now they're in jail where they belong. They lied to you, Jasmine. They are liars and horrible, horrible people."

Jasmine quieted, although she still whimpered. "You don't understand. They made me . . . they made me . . . I won't ever be the same. They took-they took everything. Even-even my name. And they took Rose too. They hurt me. I'm so sorry."

Dad looked at Jasmine tenderly. He reached out tentatively. She grasped his hand. Then she looked down quickly. "Jasmine. Honey."

She looked into Dad's eyes and saw nothing but love. Love for her.

"There is nothing in the entire world or the entire heavens or even hell that would make us stop loving you. Nothing. It's not even possible. No matter what has happened, we'll always love you and accept you just like you are. Do you understand? You mean everything to us. And to your brother and sister too."

Jasmine managed a nod.

Dad touched her shoulders. "Believe me, honey. Please."

She nodded again. "I'll try."

Jasmine watched Mom walk to the window. She stared out. Wiped tears off her cheeks. Jasmine would need to heal—and help her parents heal too. How was it possible? How could they all ever heal from this horror? She shuddered.

"Are you up to texting your brother?" Ken interrupted her thoughts. "He's probably asleep, but he'll get it when he wakes up. I know he'd like to hear from you. Amelie, too."

"Amelie didn't pick up." Mari turned from the window. "I'll slip out in the hallway and try again. She's probably asleep too."

Jasmine nodded and smiled through her tears. She borrowed her dad's phone.

"We'll get you another one soon." He ruffled her hair.

Hey bro. The cell phone felt odd in her hands. **I'm at the hospital for now. Everyone's nice, but hospitals still suck. Can't wait to come home. C U soon. Love u. Jazz**

Despite Dad's caution that Mom should tell Amelie about her rescue first, Jasmine scrolled to her number and sent a quick text. **Hey sis. I'm okay and at hospital. Dad says I can get a new phone later. Can u come? Love Jazz.** She added a heart emoticon and hit "send."

The answer from the other side was quick. **Jazz?????? Really? OMG. I'm so glad you are okay!!!!!!! Be there soon. Where are you?** She'd added about twenty smiley faces and two hearts.

Dad took the phone back. "I'll let her know where and tell her to answer your mother." He typed out the message and then slipped the phone into his pocket. "She'll be three hours at least if she hits I-5. Maybe they'll even have you released by then."

"You need to sleep." Mom pulled up Jasmine's blankets when she came back into the room. "We'll be right here, honey. Not going anywhere."

Mari

Jasmine went to sleep within seconds. It was pure bliss to sit here quietly with Ken and watch the blankets move up and down with her daughter's steady breathing. When a nurse came in to check her vitals, Jasmine barely stirred. Decisions about her care would come later when they knew more.

Her phone beeped. A text from Amelie, finally.

Sorry, Mom. Not ignoring you. Was out with Mitch. Is she really okay? REALLY? Tell me the truth. Please.

Mitch?

Yes, as much as she can be. Much to the story. She'll have healing to do emotionally in particular. Maybe some physical. Still waiting for test results. Looking forward to seeing you. PLEASE drive safe and don't text and drive.

Not! Leaving now. Gtg.

Mari turned to Ken. "Who's Mitch?"

"Oh yeah, Mitch." He grimaced apologetically. "Should have told you. I guess he's someone she's dating." He dropped his voice to a whisper. "Mitch talked to Amelie about human trafficking. He thought the signs fit . . . " His voice drifted off. He buried his face in his hands.

Mari sighed and rubbed his back gently, knowing she could respond a few different ways. She was mad that Ken hadn't mentioned anyone name Mitch. For that matter, neither had Amelie. And she was mad that this Mitch had been right. Their poor little girl. "Why didn't you tell me?" She whispered. "He was right. He was right! Maybe if we had told Detective Miller or Mollie."

Ken clasped her hand. "They're a smart team. I know they were checking all avenues anyway. And Mitch didn't have proof. He's just been reading up on it apparently. Human Services major." He snorted softly.

Mari shook her head. It seems they weren't communicating in more ways than one. She moved her chair over by her daughter's bed and held her hand as she slept.

CHAPTER FIFTY
Cienna

CIENNA AWOKE TO A ROOM full of people, or so it seemed. And she had to pee. Would someone bring her a bucket? Then she remembered. She was in a hospital, and Mike wasn't there.

She slowly pulled herself to a sitting position.

People rushed to her bedside so quickly, you'd have thought she'd been brought back from the dead. Mom, crying and touching her hair. Dad, first balancing on one foot and then the other, back and forth, awaiting his turn. Kai seated on the end of her bed, practically bouncing, wearing the biggest smile she'd ever seen. A nurse adjusting something on a machine attached to her arm.

"Hey, Mom, Dad, Kai." Despite the gratitude in her heart at seeing them, she pushed at Mom. "Sorry, sorry. I gotta pee."

The nurse helped her out of bed, making sure she didn't disconnect from her IV, which hung on a pole that could be wheeled into the bathroom. There she closed the door and leaned on it, breathing deeply. Too many people. But they were her family. As she sat on the toilet, tears started rolling down both cheeks.

No more Mike. No more Roger. Where was Penny? Safe?

"Honey?" Mom called through the door.

Cienna flushed. Washed her hands. Opened the door and stepped into Mom's arms, holding on for a long time. Dad took a turn and blinked back tears for the first time ever. Kai was a little shyer, so Cienna reached out to hug him quickly and rub his hair. Mom helped her back into bed and adjusted her IV line and hospital gown.

When Cienna was settled, Mom pulled her blankets up for her and held her hand.

"I'm okay, Mom."

Mom seemed to be fighting tears. "Are you hungry, baby?"

Cienna nodded. "Not sure when I ate the last time."

Mom caressed Cienna's face, pausing at one cheekbone, a troubled look in her eyes.

"Yeah, I know. I've lost weight."

Mom kissed her cheek. "You're still our beautiful daughter."

"We have good news for you." Dad cleared his throat. "Jasmine's here and safe too." His voice cracked, and he coughed into his fist. "I'm just so grateful . . . so grateful." He gently squeezed her shoulder.

"I know." Cienna leaned back against the pillow. "Me, too. I hope Jazz is okay." She remembered her promise. "What about Penny? I found a girl . . . "

Dad cleared his throat. "Yes, we-uh, heard about Penny too. We can talk about that later."

"Why? I need to know now. Did they find her? I promised..."

Dad inclined his head toward Kai, now sitting near the window with his game system in his hands.

Right. Okay. Not with Kai there. "Can I see Jazz?"

"I'm sure you will." Mom patted her arm. "Right now, time to eat. What sounds good?"

She took the menu from the bedside table and set it on Cienna's lap.

The pictures of pork chops and chicken breasts made Cienna's stomach roll. She pushed the menu away. "Um . . . beef?"

"Here's a steak sandwich or a burger with veggies." Mom pointed to more appetizing pictures.

"Sandwich."

Mom ordered it on the bedside phone, with pickles and mayo, just the way Cienna liked it.

"Where's my phone?"

Mom produced it from her purse. "I'm sorry, but I had to look at your accounts. You were . . . just *gone*. We didn't know. Every potential clue was important."

"I know, Mom." Cienna scrolled through her Instagram, the last photo she was tagged in was a photo of her and Jasmine up on the cliff at the campground. She groaned. If only it had done some good. In the end, it was a trip to the store and Mike getting pulled over that saved her. She should probably update her followers, but she didn't know what to say. Besides, anything she wrote would bring more questions from her online friends. She briefly reviewed her text messages and then powered her phone off.

Dad stood and beckoned to Kai. "Hey, pal. Let's go explore the place. Maybe we can find a milkshake."

Kai unwound himself from the chair and tucked his game system in his jacket pocket. He hugged Cienna on the way out.

"I'm not going anywhere." She tweaked his nose, and he returned a grin. "Bye, Dad."

Dad paused at the door. "We aren't going anywhere either." He raised his eyebrows at her, eyes twinkling. "Back soon."

The sudden silence of the room hit her. "Mom, where's Penny? Did they find her?"

"They did." Mom swallowed hard. "Honey, there's no easy way to tell you. She-she didn't make it, hon. I'm so sorry."

"W-What?" Cienna choked. "She had to. I brought her food as much as I could . . . " Tears scalded her eyes. She angrily brushed them away. "She was so little. She reminded me of my babysitting girls. I-I tried to help her. I was too late."

"No, no." Mom's voice was thick with emotion. "Cienna, you did the very best you could. I can't believe how very brave you are. So brave and strong. There's no excuse for those awful men taking you and holding Penny there, too. No excuse. They're at fault, not you. This is all their fault. You . . . and Penny did the best you could."

"She-she must have been there a long time." Cienna used her sheet to wipe her damp cheeks, but it was no use. Tears kept coming. "Before me, I think. Poor Penny. She probably doesn't even know that I tried. I did try. I had a plan. It would have worked, but it took a long time to get Mike to take me anywhere."

Mom pulled her into her arms and rocked her gently as Cienna sobbed. "I'm sure she knows. I'm sure she does. She isn't sick and in pain anymore. She can eat all she wants, and she isn't tied to a pole."

They cried together for several minutes.

"I'm sorry." Mom smoothed her bouncy curls. "I don't know how much detail to tell you. What to say and what not to say. They're telling us to let you take it at your own pace, and that's good. We'll work on that. What's important is that you're finally safe and coming home. Jasmine too." Mom glanced at the door. "Hey now, here's your food. Yum." She pulled gently away from Cienna as a young girl in scrubs entered the room with a tray.

"Hi there." The girl's sunny disposition radiated from her dark brown eyes. "I hear you wanted a sandwich. Made special just for you." She opened the dome on the plate and whisked it away, setting the tray on the rolling hospital table. "And how about a milkshake?"

"That sounds okay." Cienna wiped her tears, a vision of a naked and bound Penny forever imprinted in her brain. She shuddered.

The girl pushed the tray over to Cienna's bed, and Mom helped her arrange things for easy reach. Cienna picked at the sandwich and finally just ate the bread and carrot sticks. The meat just didn't sound good. The vanilla milkshake tasted delicious though. She thought of the last time she had ice cream with Jazz, and her heart hurt. She pushed it away, halfway done.

Cienna reclined the bed after eating and closed her eyes. She opened them when Dad and Kai returned.

Kai brought her a big teddy bear from the gift shop. "This is your bodyguard." He crammed it between her side and the bed railing.

"Thanks, pest." Cienna wondered where Mike and Roger were. Would she ever see them again? She had more questions. But she was too tired to do it now. Instead, she fell asleep and dreamed of the rolling waves at the beach and searching for sand dollars.

When she awoke, Kai was sitting close to her head.

She smiled. "Where's Mom and Dad?"

Looking relieved, he smiled back. "Dad went to get food, and Mom's in the bathroom. I threw a book at someone at school and got in trouble."

"You did what?" Cienna propped herself up on one elbow and studied her brother. "Why would you do that?"

His face drooped. "Mom said I shouldn't say." She could barely hear him.

"Moms in the bathroom." She reminded him quietly.

"He said you deserved to be kidnapped. Stupid jerk."

Cienna barely had time to register that before Mom

came out of the bathroom, humming a tune. Kai didn't usually hurt other people. He must have been seriously provoked. She squeezed his hand quickly, letting him know she wouldn't say anything.

After Mom kissed her on the cheek, she took a seat by the window and read messages on her phone.

"Can you tell me how Jasmine's doing?"

"She's doing okay." Mom kept reading and typing into her phone. "I need to text your grandpa. He's waiting to hear how you are. And I let Jasmine's mom know how you're doing. Hopefully she'll get back to us." After a minute, her phone dinged, and she read a message. "Grandpa says he loves you very much and can't wait to see you."

Cienna nodded and soon drifted off to sleep.

CHAPTER FIFTY-ONE
Jasmine

WHEN JASMINE AWOKE AGAIN, both her parents still hung out. Dad sat in a chair with his head flung back. His snoring had never sounded so good. Mom sat curled up in the other chair with a blanket that barely covered her. Jasmine treasured their presence.

A man knocked at the half-open door and poked his head in. "Hi. I'm Raphael." He entered and waved at Jasmine.

Mom blinked and sat up. "Hi."

Raphael shook her hand. "I'm the drug treatment counselor here at the hospital. Is this a good time for us to talk? I understand you're a doctor?"

"PhD."

"Great." He turned to Jasmine. "Hi. How are you feeling today?"

"I'm a little nauseated. Maybe I need to eat."

"For sure. We'll get right on that. Any headaches?" He checked her chart on the computer. "Looks like your blood pressure is still a little on the high side. Any stomach cramps? Or diarrhea?"

Blushing, Jasmine shrugged. She'd had stomach cramps the evening before. She hadn't mentioned it because it wasn't as bad as when the Witch-Devil made her sick by not giving her meds. Those were the times when she'd had to keep running to the bathroom between clients. Last night, the cramps were minimal compared to what she'd been through. "Yeah, cramps and diarrhea." Why he was asking all these questions? She wished he would just go away.

Instead, Raphael moved closer to her bed.

She shrank back.

He retreated. "I'm sorry. I don't want to upset you. I thought I could maybe check your blood pressure. Would that be okay, Jasmine?"

He stepped toward the bed again.

Jasmine pulled her covers tightly to her chin. "My name isn't Jasmine. It's Bay." She stared down at the sheet fisted in her hands.

Mom muffled a cry. "Is there a woman who could come instead?" She stood and moved between the bed and Raphael. "No offense to you, Raphael. But Jasmine . . . Jasmine might need just female practitioners for a while. Maybe we could chat in the hallway?"

Raphael nodded and followed Mom out to the hallway. Dad woke up, shook his head, and followed them.

When Dad and Mom returned, they moved their chairs closer to the bed.

"Honey." Dad reached out and touched her knee. "One of the things we have to deal with is that your body is addicted to the drugs those people gave you."

"We know you're not addicted in your heart." Mom added quickly. "And it's not your fault."

"It's a process. They're going to work at getting you off the medicine in a safe way."

Jasmine nodded and then shrugged. She really just wanted the pills the Witch-Devil had given her at the farmhouse. Why couldn't someone make that happen? Everything would be alright then.

Mom's phone dinged. "Amelie's here. I'll give her the room number."

In minutes, Amelie ran into the room and burst into tears. She sat on the bed and hugged Jasmine gently. "I'm so glad to see you, sis."

"Me, too." Jasmine's head started to ache. She leaned against Amelie's shoulder.

"Will you girls be all right if Mom and Kai and I get breakfast?"

Amelie grinned. "Go. I got this."

Then, for two straight hours, the sisters talked and cried and hugged.

CHAPTER FIFTY-TWO
Cienna

CIENNA AWOKE TO SEE MOM still in her chair by the window. "How long have I been here?"

"Two days. Seems like forever, I know."

"No. Forever is being locked in the barn with Roger visiting every day. Or locked in a room for an entire afternoon and trying to find a way out." She didn't realize she had spoken aloud until she looked up and saw the horror on Mom's face. "Sorry."

"Oh, no, darling. Don't be." Mom came to the bed. She blinked hard. Took Cienna's hand. "I'm the sorry one. This never should have happened."

"Well, it did. I don't want to talk about it." Cienna sighed.

"Okay, yes, I know. No problem." Mom returned to the chair. "We love you very much Cienna. Do you know that?" She seemed to be choosing her words carefully.

Cienna nodded, staring at the wall. "How's Jazz?" Her younger friend was her responsibility. And, boy, had she screwed that up . . . for both of them.

Mom frowned. "I didn't really hear back recently. But last I heard, she's recovering. I know her sister came from Seattle, and that seemed to help. Do you want to see her?"

Cienna shrugged. How could she even face Jazz?

Mom picked up a magazine a nurse had left. She huffed and then shoved it quickly into her purse. "Why don't you see what's on TV?"

"I want to go home. When can I go home?"

"Soon, we hope. We're meeting with the doctor shortly, so we should know more after that."

Cienna lifted her chin. "They should meet with me, too. It's not fair that they just meet with you. I'm an adult now, Mom."

Oh, how life had changed.

Mom stared out the window. "In a few more years. Getting closer. Should I call the social worker to help us? I know you've been through a lot Cienna, I know, but . . . "

Cienna groaned and glared at her mother. "No, Mom. No, you don't know. You have no idea."

Melissa

Melissa found Kai and Jimmy in the waiting area and sent Kai to sit with his sister. She peeked around the corner and made sure he actually entered the hospital room before they followed the nurse down the hallway to a small conference room.

Dr. Shaw soon bustled in. She was a small, older woman with grey hair piled high on her head and a firm handshake. The hospital's social worker, Jenna, was right behind her. She shook their hands and introduced herself.

Taking a seat nearest the computer, which was attached to the wall with a metal arm, Dr. Shaw pulled up Cienna's records. Melissa grabbed Jimmy's hand for support. Cienna seemed okay physically to them, but who knew what they'd found?

The doctor scrolled around a bit. Changed screens. "Cienna's been through a lot. But her tests were clear for sexually transmitted diseases. No HIV per the test here, although we will send that out for more extensive testing to make sure. She should get rechecked in a few months. She doesn't have interior damage from the abuse, thank goodness. I've seen much worse. However-" She turned from the computer. "There is an issue you should be aware of, and it can be taken care of. Cienna is pregnant."

Pregnant? Melissa lost focus and couldn't breathe. Their baby, pregnant? The room spun.

Jimmy grabbed her hand tightly, emotions fluttering across his face. He let go of her hand and pulled her close.

Melissa wanted to scream and yell. Push the computer off its weird-looking stand. "How can that be?" That was a dumb first question. She tried to calm her racing heart with a deep breath. Would anyone even know who the father was? How many men had taken advantage of Cienna over the four months? "How-how far along?"

"The fetus is measuring at almost eleven weeks." Dr. Shaw spoke kindly. "Still first trimester should you decide you want to terminate the pregnancy. You should talk to Cienna, of course. But it would mean surgery for her and possibly emotional consequences. For you all. On a good note, she can go home soon. Maybe even tomorrow. Any procedure you decide on to deal with the pregnancy would be on an outpatient basis."

"There are things to think about." Jenna leaned forward. "But you still have a little time to do that. I'm happy to help you talk things through. Then perhaps we could all go talk to Cienna."

"That's our-our grandchild." Melissa moaned.

Jimmy's face hardened. "Well, I don't see an option here. She's far too young to be a mother. And who knows who the father is? What about DNA? This child will have half the DNA of a very bad person. Whoever he is, he's a monster."

"There are other options to abortion." Jenna clicked her pen. "Many girls in this situation choose adoption. Give their baby a chance to be raised in a loving home. Especially when they're so young and still need to finish school."

"That means the monster DNA is still out there somewhere." Jimmy gritted his teeth.

"Jimmy." Surprised by his strong reaction, Melissa squeezed his hand. "It's our DNA, too. And half Cienna's. Good can overcome the bad. I know it can." Wow. Her daughter was pregnant at fourteen. She cradled her head in her hands. The room swirled. Every parent wondered if their daughter might experience pregnancy someday. But who wondered if that pregnancy might be the result of rape? At this age? With no idea of who the father was?

What should they do?

The doctor left, and the social worker offered to stay. Jimmy waved her off.

"Thank God, she's okay." Tears rolled down Melissa's cheeks. "Thank God. She could have HIV or another deadly disease. But she's healthy. Thank God, she's healthy."

"God sure didn't do a very good job watching out for her, did He?" Bitterness colored Jimmy's tone.

"How can you say that? She could be dead. Do you know how many kids never come home, Jimmy? Do you know how many parents are still looking for their children? Hundreds of thousands. Some die without ever knowing."

"I know. I know." He shoved his chair back and walked to the window overlooking the hospital parking lot. "We do have a lot to be grateful for. But what now?"

"We have to talk to her."

"And say what? 'Guess what. You got knocked up by those bastards, and we don't even know who the father is?"

Melissa glared at her husband. Grow up, Jimmy. He had to get a hold of himself.

A calming presence surrounded her, squeezed her shoulders, covering her in warmth. She looked for a ray of sunshine coming in the window, but there wasn't one. She turned her face toward the warmth with no obvious source and closed her eyes. Soaked it in.

She suddenly knew that it would be alright. Every child was precious. Every child deserved a chance. It was not this baby's fault.

The room righted itself a little bit, and although she still felt a little nauseated, Melissa went to Jimmy and put her arms around his waist. His tears dripped on her hand. So much pain. Their daughter had been through so much, and now they had even more to work through.

"She's fourteen." Jimmy's voice broke. "She has no idea how to be a parent. How to be pregnant. How to deal with all of this. She doesn't want this baby. She didn't even have a boyfriend. It's not fair . . . "

"No, it's not fair. Grossly unfair." Melissa sighed. Why Cienna? Why did this happen to their daughter? Was it something they had done wrong? "We'll help her. There are organizations that can help us help her. She won't do this alone."

"Her friends might ostracize her. Never let her live it down."

"Her true friends will understand she's been to hell and back. Her true friends will stay close. The others may drift away like ours did when the girls disappeared. Maybe she'll make other friends of a different kind. We just don't know. She needs us even more now."

He turned to her, buried his face in her hair. "We can't even afford a baby."

Melissa smiled. Her husband, the eternal list-maker, was considering details. Then she grew solemn. "I know. I'll go back to work. We'll have to figure it out. She might not be able to go back to school anyway, you know. But, Jimmy, this baby is alive. It has a heartbeat, and it's our grandchild. I could never live with myself if we did away with it. I just couldn't."

Jimmy pulled back slightly. Wiped the tear on her cheek with his thumb. "I think we should let Cienna decide. She's been through so much. What if this baby is just a constant reminder of it all? What if she hates it? We have to talk to her."

With a heavy heart, Melissa took Jimmy's hand and let him lead her back to Cienna's room.

CHAPTER FIFTY-THREE
Amelie

THAT EVENING, Dr. Gregory asked Mom and Dad to step outside the room to hear further test results. Since Amelie was glued to Jasmine's side anyway, she agreed to sit with her sister. They decided to look for a movie. Jasmine claimed the right to select which one by holding the remote hostage. Easy to do since it was clipped to the side of her bed.

Amelie pulled up her chair very close to Jasmine's side. She found herself staring at her sister in wonder several times.

"I need food."

Thrilled that her sister was hungry, Amelie pushed the menu over. "Here. Pick out what you want. I'll eat too."

"You're not the patient."

Amelie laughed. "Well, good. We don't need two of us in bed, huh? I can order too, I think. If not, I'll snack off yours or go to the café when Mom and Dad come back. Do you want to see if they can make a no-cheese pizza?"

After being told the menu was only for patients, they ordered a hamburger and salad from the dairy-free menu. Jasmine grumbled that there were no fries. The medicine they gave her made her crave starchy stuff. Bread, potatoes, pie, whatever.

As Jasmine was choosing a movie, Amelie texted Mitch. **Hey. I'm here. We talked for hours today. I can't even tell you all she's been through. I'm so scared she won't be able to get through all of this. It's insane!**

His reply came quickly. **I know she's glad you're there.**

I don't know what to tell her. Her fingers flew over the keyboard. **SO stuck for words. How could all that happen to her? How is it possible? And there are still kids out there suffering! It's crazy. But she's okay, I think. I hope. My parents are talking to the doctor now.**

Maybe just do a lot of listening then. Maybe that's what she needs. How's Cienna?

Don't know yet. Her mom and my mom are texting, but Mom's mostly just focused on Jazz.

K. When you back?

Idk. Amelie was considering taking a leave from school, but she hadn't told Mitch or her parents yet. After glancing at Jasmine, who still seemed absorbed in finding a movie, she scrolled over to Seth's number.

Seth, all good here. How's it going at home? Jasmine's having a burger. Lucky girl. I might highjack it . . . Oops. She backed-spaced over "highjack" and sighed. **I think I might share it,** she typed instead.

Seth sent rolling smiley face. **Wait til she turns her head and take a bite. Bet she doesn't notice.**

She sent a smiley face back. **You're smarter than you look.**

What? Hey I look smarter than you and Jazz combined.

Yeah okay. She deserved that. **That's because you are.** She sent him a heart. He didn't reply.

Settled on a comedy, Jasmine put the remote down.

Amelie shoved her phone in her purse. Seth was likely

now back to playing his video games. Mom and Dad said if Jasmine was in the hospital much longer, one of them should drive home and pick him up. She didn't mind the assignment. All she wanted was to be with her family and help her sister get through this. She supposed seeing Seth might help Jasmine with that.

Amelie had a hard time focusing on the movie. With her sister's life now shattered, she had to distract herself from picturing the details Jasmine had shared. What a nightmare. Would Jasmine ever sleep peacefully again? And what was the doctor telling her parents?

She pulled out her phone again. She should update her friends. She took a selfie of them with their heads together and posted it to all her accounts. **My sister is safe!** She tucked her phone back in her pocket and tried again to focus on the movie.

Jasmine fell asleep, so Amelie turned the TV off. She sat by the window and texted Mitch again. She sent her concerns about returning to school. He understood.

Still asleep, Jasmine began to toss violently back and forth, shouting. "Cienna, don't go! I'll save you. No, Rose. No. Rose, please don't leave me." She awoke with tears streaming down her face.

Startled by her outburst, Amelie smoothed back her sister's hair and spoke quietly in her ear. "You're okay, Jazzy. You're safe. I'm here."

But who was Rose?

Mari

In the conference room, Dr. Gregory pulled up records on a computer screen Mari and Ken could not see. "We have test results back. Blood work looks good. A little low on iron and magnesium, which we can fix. Seems like she was eating well enough, although I know she's underweight. But I have some concerns about the CT scan of her pelvic area. It looks like we have some internal damage from the way she was treated. You probably know that in these situations the girls are not treated well and sometimes violently. No broken bones but definite internal damage."

"You mean forced sex of various types?" Mari hated to say the words but had to know the truth.

"Yes. I'm afraid so. It was obviously forced on her. Many times. I imagine it was very painful." He paused. "I'm very sorry. The result is a lot of scarring and some fresh wounds, too. But she's not pregnant."

Ken sighed and ran his fingers through his hair. "HIV?" He dreaded the answer. Surely working in a farmhouse brothel with all those men . . .

"No HIV. Well, I'll just say the fast test we have in our lab shows no HIV, but we'll send that out for a more thorough testing just to make sure. Does look like she got an STD and a urinary tract infection we can treat with antibiotics. We'll start those tonight and make sure they are better before she leaves."

"The scarring . . . " Mari's voice trailed off.

"Can it be fixed surgically?" Ken crossed his arms.

"Not at this point. She just needs to heal. She may have scar tissue that develops later that will need to be removed. And it might affect her fertility. Something she should be aware of."

He stood and gathered his files. "All and all, you are a lucky family. I'm sorry she went through all of this. But she's here, alive, and most of this is treatable. She's strong. Things will get better."

"How long will she have to stay?" They had both wondered.

Dr. Gregory smiled. "Not long now. Our job now is to get the infections treated and get her completely weaned off the narcotics. A couple more days for that. By then we'll be able to tell if the antibiotics are doing their job. At that point, we'll give her oral prescriptions. Then you can take your girl home." He shook their hands. "If you don't have any more questions, I'll head on over to my next appointment."

Leaving the conference room, Mari and Ken grabbed coffee in the hospital café and sat for a few minutes digesting the news. Their daughter had suffered unimaginable terrors. But no HIV. No pregnancy. Nothing untreatable, although she might not be able to have a family. Soon they could take her home. Perhaps then they could break those odds and give her a healthy life after all.

CHAPTER FIFTY-FOUR
Melissa

KAI WAS AGAIN BOUNCING on the foot of Cienna's mattress when Melissa and Jimmy returned.

"Kai!" Melissa hurried over to the bed. "Your sister has healing to do."

Kai pouted. Cienna laughed.

He pulled out his game system and headed to the chair by the window. "She wouldn't let me change the channel."

"I don't want to watch stupid cartoons." Cienna rolled her eyes. "Sheesh."

Melissa and Jimmy traded a look. He was probably thinking the same thing she was. As irritating as it could be, at least brother and sister could now bicker as usual. A blessing they wouldn't soon forget.

"Hey, she's the patient. You have your game, Kai." Melissa moved close to Cienna, a feeling of protectiveness filling her heart. "How are you doing, sweetie?" She smoothed back her daughter's hair. "How about a shower? I can help you."

The panic that flitted across Cienna's face startled her. "Am I-am I dirty?" Her voice hitched.

Melissa shook her head. "No, honey. Not dirty. Although your hair could use washing."

"I can do it myself." More panic in her voice.

Melissa nodded, puzzled. "Of course you can."

Cienna crossed her arms.

Melissa glanced at Cienna's abdomen and blinked rapidly. "So Kai." She cleared her throat. "You and Daddy are going for a walk now. Get some exercise. Mommy wants to talk to Cienna."

Kai grumbled but unwound himself from the chair and turned his game system off.

"Come on, sport." Jimmy gave Melissa a hug and a nod before leaving with Kai. He patted Cienna's arm. They'd agreed on the way back to the room it was best for mother and daughter to talk alone.

"You've been through so much."

"You have no idea."

"I know I don't. I wish I knew more. But I don't want to force you to talk. I'm here when you're ready. The good news is that the doctor says you're healthy. No infections or anything. Great news. At this rate, you can go home pretty soon. Maybe even tomorrow, she said."

Cienna nodded and yawned. "Okay. What's the bad news? I need a nap."

Melissa laughed nervously. "Bad news?"

"Mom, you said 'the good news is—' That means there's bad news, too. Come on. I'm not stupid."

"Far from stupid." She paused, gathering courage. "Cienna, it's not your fault." She pulled the chair close to the bed and sat as near to her daughter as she dared, then drew a deep breath. Pushed back sudden tears. "The doctor says . . . the doctor says you're going . . . to have a baby."

Cienna turned a stony glare on her. "She's full of crap."

Melissa placed her hand on Cienna's arm. Cienna shook it off. "I'm so sorry. They did bloodwork and an ultrasound. They say . . . they say the baby is about eleven weeks. Don't be afraid . . . "

"I'm not pregnant." Cienna turned back to the wall. "I can't be."

"Please, Cienna, we have to talk about this. Not now if you don't feel up to it. But soon. There are decisions to make. We'll help you. I promise. I know this sucks. I'm so sorry. But it isn't your fault, and we will do whatever we can to support you. We love you. And this is our grandchild. We-we love it, too." Tears spilled down her cheeks, and she grabbed a tissue from the bedside table. "It doesn't matter who the father is, sweetie. This baby is yours and ours. We'll get it all figured out."

A rustling sound at the door caught Melissa's attention.

Mollie stood there and with her a very large, although well-behaved German shepherd.

"I'm sorry, Mollie." Melissa dabbed at her tears. "This isn't the best time."

Cienna burst into laughter. She squealed. "Coal! Hi, Mollie." Melissa sighed but nodded at Mollie.

Mollie entered the room and told Coal to sit. He obeyed, wagging his tail vigorously.

"Don't tell anyone." Mollie grinned. "I knew you wanted to meet him, and I had to let a couple of nurses in on the secret because he's so big. I couldn't hide him in a bag."

Cienna giggled and tossed off her blanket. She sat on the edge of the bed.

Melissa stood and stepped out of the way so Cienna could greet her canine visitor.

Mollie unclipped the leash, and the dog leaned forward. Cienna put her hands behind his ears and started scratching them. His tail thumped loudly.

"Hi, Coal." Cienna slid off the bed, sat on the floor, and wrapped both her arms around him, hugging him tightly. "Thanks for helping to find me, Coal. I hear you found the last clue they needed. Good boy."

Coal tilted his head sideways. Melissa was almost sure he nodded in agreement.

"I'm sure he'll take all the credit you want to give him," Mollie warned. "He has a big head."

Laughter filled the room. Cienna continued to stroke the dog, who was now leaning heavily against her, bliss in his big brown eyes.

"A dog!" Kai shouted from the doorway.

"Shh." Melissa ushered him and Jimmy into the room. "It's a secret, Kai." She closed the door behind them.

Kai dropped to the floor and joined Cienna in showering Coal with attention.

The adults shared a smile.

"Hi, Mollie. Nice to see you." Jimmy shook her hand.

"You, too. Under wonderful circumstances."

Jimmy questioned Melissa with raised eyebrows. She nodded. Then she shrugged. Jimmy glanced at Cienna, a puzzled look on his face.

A nurse bustled in to take Cienna's vitals. "Okay, Mollie, not sure how much longer we can keep your secret. Probably time to move along to the other patient, although you're certainly the most popular visitor today."

Mollie grinned. "We've outworn our welcome already, Coal." She snapped on his leash, much to Cienna's and Kai's disappointment. "Don't worry. We'll see you again. We'll visit after you get home, okay?"

Cienna hugged the dog goodbye. Melissa was glad to see her daughter smile. Mollie had come along at the perfect time. After she and Coal left, Cienna agreed to a shower and locked herself in the bathroom.

Melissa pulled Jimmy out of the room, leaving Kai to play his game.

Jimmy

"She doesn't believe me that she's pregnant," Melissa whispered urgently.

"What? How? She must know . . . "

"I don't know. Denial, I guess? Maybe believing it's true reminds her of all the bad things, like you said. You talk to her, okay? Kai can come with me to get snacks."

"Okay."

"But if you convince her, please don't influence any decisions. Please, Jimmy. We agreed. That's our grandchild."

"We agreed it's up to her."

"No, you said it's up to her. I didn't agree. I think it's a family decision. She's way too young to be a mom, I know. But, just please, stay neutral for now, okay? Please?" Her eyes held unshed tears.

"Fine." He crossed his arms over his chest, much like his daughter.

Melissa shook her head as she entered the room to get Kai. He followed her out the door toward the coffee stand in the lobby.

Cienna returned from the restroom wearing clothes Melissa had purchased the day before. Jimmy winced when he remembered what Cienna had been wearing when the police found her. His daughter looked clean and comfortable now in stretchy pants and a long-sleeved tee-shirt. She insisted on sitting in the chair by the window instead of crawling back into bed.

"How are you feeling?" Jimmy asked.

"I'm good." She looked out the window. "Why am I still here?"

"We'll go home soon. Your mom, um, chatted with you earlier. Do you remember what she told you?"

Cienna nodded. She walked to the bed and lay down, pulling the blanket all the way to her chin. "I'm tired." She shuddered.

"I'm sure you are." Jimmy sat down and cradled his chin in his hands, studying his daughter. He remembered her as a baby, remembered holding her tightly, bouncing her on his knees, and later pushing her on the swing in their backyard. Fourteen years had flashed by in a wink. "So, what did your mom tell you?"

Cienna yawned again. "Going home tomorrow." Her breathing steadied and slowed, and Jimmy knew she was asleep. Or pretending to be.

CHAPTER FIFTY-FIVE
Jasmine

Sitting in bed, Jasmine awaited Amelie and Seth's arrival. She wanted to see her brother. In the meantime, her parents insisted on chatting. She mostly tuned it out. They were giving her medications for an infection, she heard. She was healthy but had scars inside. They asked her if she was hurting, and she shook her head. Mom looked relieved.

"You can come home soon." Dad tucked his wallet in his pocket. "We just need to make sure the medicine is working, and you can go without any of . . . the other stuff."

The other stuff.

Yeah, that was the stuff that had helped Jasmine/Bay survive. It made her body relax and her mind go numb. She missed the feeling, especially when she felt overwhelmed or emotional. Sometimes she still wanted to turn her head to the wall and sleep like she had in the TC Room. The medicine helped her do that, as well as not care so much when people were hurting her.

She wondered how the other girls at the farmhouse were doing. Where were they? Were they still getting meds? Had they seen their families? She wondered if their parents were forgiving and kind, as hers had been. She hoped so.

Jenna, the hospital social worker, had visited twice now and apparently was coming again. Jenna liked to sit next to her and ask her how she was feeling, which Jasmine thought was stupid. She felt glad to be rescued, happy to see her parents, sad about Rose, mad at Sam and the Witch-Devil, uh Kella. Sometimes mad at herself. And she wanted to go home. Oh, and sometimes she wanted the meds back.

That about summed it up.

Jenna spent fifteen minutes talking about her pets and a variety of other things Jasmine cared nothing about. She smiled. "Do you want to talk about what happened to you?"

"Why would I want to do that?"

Jenna smiled again gently. "Don't you ever feel better after talking about something? Sometimes people do."

Jasmine shrugged. "I had good friends. I miss them, especially Rose. I don't miss scrubbing the floors."

She was glad when Jenna finally left.

Seth and Amelie appeared at the door, and Seth allowed a brief hug. "Glad you're back." His voice was gruff. "That took a while."

Jasmine mulled over his words, thought about life at the farm, in the shed, at the club. "Felt like a year. Was it?"

"No, silly, it's still the same year."

"That's good. I don't want to miss Christmas." She grinned at him.

Mom and Dad glanced at each other and smiled.

Seth sat near the bed. "I-I don't know what to say. Missed you. You, uh, feel okay?"

She nodded. "I'm okay. I have an infection, but you can't get it."

As they talked, Amelie joined in. Jasmine saw Mom pull her phone out of her purse and start texting.

Mari

Mari punched on her keyboard. **How's it going over there?**

Melissa's text back was quick. **Good. Getting discharged soon. YEAH!**

Today?

YES.

Mari felt deflated. **Congrats. Happy for you all.** She was happy for them, but sad that Jasmine couldn't go home yet. Time dragged.

Still have a lot to work through. Ci's preggers. Yeah, I know. It's crazy. Don't tell anyone. Still trying to figure things out.

Pregnant! Mari sucked in her breath. Poor Cienna. And Melissa and Jimmy. Their journey was far from over. **I'm so sorry. Wow. Hard news, I'm sure. How far along?**

11 wks. Still digesting it. She's refusing to believe it. It's a tough one. How's it with you all? Jazz ok?

Yes. Off all the meds as of today except an antidepressant. Antibiotics worked! Hopefully out of here tomorrow. Can't wait to get her home!

She put her phone in her purse and stared at the window. Cienna pregnant. What would their friends do? Would they get rid of the pregnancy? Fourteen was far too young to be a mother. She pulled her phone back out and typed quickly. **Here if you need to talk, k?** She put her phone away again and turned to Ken. "Thank God it's not Jasmine," she muttered.

He raised his eyebrows at her.

"Tell you later."

Her phone rang. Her mom, calling to get an update. She stepped into the hallway to take the call. That reminded her, she had a new cell phone for Jasmine in her purse. Hopefully it would cheer her daughter to feel in contact with the outside world again.

When she returned to the room, Amelie and Seth headed to the cafeteria for a snack. She suspected they were getting milkshakes but didn't tell their sister that. Maybe a good thing. Jasmine had missed out on so many things these past several months. Ken followed them a moment later, saying he was in desperate need of caffeine.

Jasmine's eyes lit up as Mari pulled the cell phone out of her purse and handed it to her. "All set up and ready to go. Same number."

The phone had a bright pink cover. "Now you can find it easily if you drop it or it lands in the bushes somewhere." Mari winced. Shoot. "I mean, I mean, you know at home it sometimes gets buried under your schoolbooks and stuff."

She needed lessons on how talk to her daughter now. She had just royally screwed it up.

"Thanks, Mom." Jasmine hugged her. Mari held on tight. "I didn't drop it, okay? I-I was trying to text you back. He . . . someone pulled it out of my hands." Her arms around Mari tightened, too.

"I know, honey. I'm so sorry. I didn't mean . . . I wasn't trying to bring up a bad memory. I'm so sorry." Mari was suddenly grateful for life. The ability to live, the privilege of breathing. Choosing to love and making a difference. The list was endless. They had a second chance as a whole family. She would make the best possible life for all of them from here on out, starting with some amazing holidays. She and Melissa had talked about volunteering for some of the organizations in their community focused on safe families. She'd heard of one called ARMS, for Abuse Recovery Ministry & Services. She vowed to start as soon as she could.

Jasmine pulled away, excited to get on her phone. She quickly went to her texting screen and pulled up Cienna's number. Then she paused. "Mom, what if Cienna doesn't want to talk to me?"

Mari had also wondered about the girls' future relationship, and her and Ken's friendship with Melissa and Jimmy. From her professional experience, she knew things could get awkward. Truly it could go either way. Could Jasmine withstand the hurt of her best friend withdrawing from her if that's what happened?

"I'm sure she wants to hear from you." She said what her heart was telling her to say. "You might as well try. But keep in mind she's still healing too and might not be talking much to anyone right now."

"Yeah." Jasmine sighed and looked at the phone. She texted her dad instead. Mari could see the screen clearly and smiled. **Hey can you bring me a doughnut? LOL.** She set the phone next to her on the table. Maybe Cienna would text her instead.

CHAPTER FIFTY-SIX
Cienna

ONE WEEK LATER, both the girls were home from the hospital, safe in their homes in Beaverton. Life had not yet returned to normal. Cienna refused school, and no one was pushing her to go. Her parents dragged her to counseling sessions twice a week and made sure she wasn't home alone. Twice she awoke to find her brother sleeping on her bedroom floor next to her bed. Curious neighbors dropped by, and cars would often slow in front of the house. The family sometimes closed their curtains even before darkness fell.

In her head, Cienna pictured a tour bus driving by. "Now here on the right lives a girl who was kidnapped and abused. Sold to a guy who she at first thought was nice but then learned otherwise. Then the guy who took her came back—"

Cienna had an appointment that day, and she wanted Jasmine to come with her. After arguing with Mom about it, Mom finally agreed.

Cienna sent a text. **Hey Jazz. I wondered how u r doing? Also do u want to go to a doc appoint w me today?**

I've missed you and been wondering. I'm so sorry, so sorry bout the long ways back. A teary face flashed on the screen. Animated. Huh.

Not ur fault. c u at 3?

Mom said OK. Hey, seen the news?

Cienna sighed heavily. **They won't let me. So stupid.**

Um. Did u meet a Roger Wyatt?

Cienna's heart started pounding hard. Growing lightheaded, she grabbed the edge of her headboard. He'd bashed her forehead against a similar one in those awful days in the barn.

WHY?

Cuz the news said they caught everyone except him. Don't know who he is but he sure is butt ugly.

Cienna dropped her phone on the bed and flopped down next to it. She tried to catch her breath. No one had told her ugly Roger was still out there. No one. No wonder they were keeping such a close eye on her. He could come and take her again. He still owned her, right? He and Mike? She closed her eyes. Hiccupped as tears came. No Mike now to protect her. Even though sometimes he hadn't done that so well. At least in Mike's home, Roger had stayed away. She threw her pillow against the wall and then her stuffed bear. She stood and closed the shades on her bedroom window. She left her room. Checked every door and window in the house. All locked. She ran to the bathroom. She threw up. Then huddled on the bathroom floor between the toilet and wall. Mom came and found her.

"What are you doing? Are you okay?" Mom knelt. "Are you sick? Cienna, what's going on?"

"You didn't-didn't tell me about Roger . . . " Her teeth chattered.

Mom's face wrinkled like she was trying not to cry. "I'm sorry, sweetie. I wasn't sure how much to tell you. How much you want to know. Detective Miller is still working hard on the case, and I know that they'll get him. I just know it. I'm so sorry."

She tried to pull Cienna out of her tight corner. Cienna pushed at her, coughing and choking. She barely had time to lift the toilet lid before she threw up again. On and on it went as Mom smoothed back her hair and murmured words Cienna couldn't even hear.

Finally, with nothing left in her stomach, the painful dry heaves started. Mom flushed it all down. Cienna watched it go. The heaving finally stopped. Her eyes streamed with tears. Snot ran down her face. She sat back and took a deep breath. Then she picked up her phone and texted back to Jasmine.

He's the one who took us.

She pushed Mom out of her way, ran to her room, and slammed her door.

Thirty minutes later, Cienna glanced at her phone. Mom again. Argh.

Almost time to go. Want a sandwich? Ginger Ale?

A few moments later, Cienna opened her door, visited the bathroom, and clumped down the stairs. She was dry-eyed but wouldn't look at Mom. She ate and drank with her eyes on the table.

"I'm sorry, Cienna." Mom sounded wounded. "I should have told you more."

Cienna shrugged.

At the clinic a nice receptionist asked Cienna for her name. Mom filled out a bunch of paperwork. She took it to the counter with her ID and health insurance card. When Jasmine and Mari came in, Cienna stood and hugged her friend tightly. Jazz looked different. She wondered if she looked different, too. Maybe she looked like a monster. No words could convey what they felt and all they had been through. The girls sat in silence, holding hands.

Mari was extra chatty, apparently trying to fill the silence. "After the appointment, we're getting our nails done. You guys want to join us?" No one answered her, so she continued to talk about other things.

All four entered the exam room. Cienna had to go pee in a cup but was soon back.

When the doctor entered the room, she looked at all of them and laughed. "Okay, who's my patient?"

Jasmine giggled.

Mom shook the doctor's hand. "Hi, I'm Melissa, and this is Cienna, my daughter. She's the patient. She wanted her friend Jasmine to come along. This is Mari, Jasmine's mom."

"All right then. I'm Dr. Mizel. Cienna, why don't you hop up here on the table for me?"

Cienna rolled her eyes but obeyed.

The doctor took her blood pressure and pulse and listened to her breathe. "I understand you're declining the internal exam."

"Right. I'm not pregnant. Tell my mom that, please."

"Hmm." Dr. Mizel wrapped the stethoscope around her neck. "Okay. Well, we do have an ultrasound for you today, so please follow me. I'll have you put on a gown, but no worries. Pants stay on. We'll only uncover your belly, I promise. You want everyone along?"

Cienna nodded.

"I'll wait in the lobby." Mari scooted out.

Mom and Jasmine followed them down the hallway where Cienna entered a small room and pulled the curtain shut. She took her clothes off, put the gown on, and came back into the hallway.

Dr. Mizel led them into the ultrasound room. "Usually, I have a tech do this, but I want to have a peek first, okay? After I'm finished, I'll have the tech come in and look at the screen too. They take measurements of things."

"Okay." Cienna hiccupped. "Sorry. Annoying."

Mom's face relaxed. The doctor helped Cienna onto the table and pulled the gown up just enough. "Can we unbutton the top button of your jeans?" She reached for them and Cienna shoved her hand away.

"Cienna." Mom said gently. Cienna glared. The doctor sighed. Cienna reached down and unbuttoned them herself. She turned her head away.

"Can you tell me why you think you aren't pregnant?" Dr. Mizel took some gel out of a container. She squirted it on Cienna's tummy. It was warm, but she still squirmed. The doctor placed the ultrasound wand on her stomach, moving it around.

The monitor made a strange *wa-woosh, wa-woosh, wa-woosh* sound.

Mom's hand flew over her mouth.

"Do you know what that sound is?" The doctor addressed Cienna.

Cienna shook her head. She glanced at Jasmine, whose eyes widened, then back at the doctor, who had turned the screen so she could see it.

"That's your baby's heartbeat, Cienna."

Looking at the screen, Cienna saw a perfectly formed human, who lifted a hand like it was waving at them. It had a head, arms, legs. She could even see its fingers. She reached up in wonder. Touched the screen. "Inside me?"

"Inside you." The doctor smiled gently. "You're going to be a mama."

Tears rolled down Cienna's face.

Mom moved closer. "What a beautiful baby, Cienna. It looks just like you."

While the technician came in and measured the baby, Mom held Cienna's hand. The girl was young and chatty, but still focused.

Mom wiped the tears from Cienna's face and whispered words of encouragement. "It'll be okay, I promise you. All will be well. You're doing a wonderful job, honey. Don't worry." At the same time, she stared at the monitor.

The technician printed several 3D pictures of the baby and handed them to Cienna. She clutched them for a moment, then handed them to Mom while she changed back into her clothes. She stared out the window. Her tears dried. Determination lined her features. Jasmine squeezed her hand several times.

All the way home, Cienna held onto the pictures and looked at them. A baby. But she didn't believe Mom. The baby probably wouldn't look like her at all. She stared out the window and wondered. Would the baby look more like Mike or like ugly Roger?

CHAPTER FIFTY-SEVEN
Two Years Later
Jasmine

JASMINE LEANED AGAINST THE SIDE OF THE BUILDING in downtown Portland. She anxiously watched for the bicycle. Checking her phone, she hit reply and texted. **Anytime now!!!** It was a full five minutes before she saw Ang weaving her way through the cars. When she saw Jasmine, Ang hopped off her bike and walked it into an alleyway across the street. Jasmine casually checked for traffic before crossing and sauntered confidently into the dark shadows. "It's 'bout time."

"Shut up!" Ang huffed, her breath making clouds in the air. "You play by my rules or none at all, yeah?" She took a baggie out of her jacket pocket and waved it at Jasmine. "Where's my money?"

When Jasmine saw the small blue pills, her mouth watered. Her eyes fixated, she pulled bills from her jeans pocket and shoved them at Ang.

Ang quickly counted them. "Five short."

Jasmine groaned. "No. No, it's all there. I swear."

Her dealer grinned. "My rules. You want these babies or no?" She again waved the baggie back and forth.

Jasmine snatched them from her hand. Opening the baggie, she popped one in her mouth, swallowing it dry. "Fine." She pulled a fiver from her other pocket and tossed it at Ang. The girl could dive for it for all she cared. "Hey, when you gonna get a real car?" She laughed as she walked out of the alley.

Blinding colored lights suddenly surrounded Jasmine. She lifted her arm to cover her eyes as she stumbled. She'd been caught! She swore. Turned to run back into the alley.

A cop stepped in her way. He called her by name, grabbed her arms and confiscated the baggie. He very politely put her under arrest as he placed her in the back of his patrol car. His radio crackled. Once she was in the backseat, practically lying sideways, he picked up the mic.

"Apprehended Jasmine Leah Jensen. Transporting to station now. Over." She groaned. But as the pill took effect, she felt warmth spread inside her and grew brave.

"Give me my pills!" She called him a name Mom would have cringed at.

The cop laughed. He started the car and turned off his flashing lights. "Jasmine Jensen. Been awhile, but here you are again."

Always a screwup.

"Only because you're an a-hole! Bastard. What the heck did I do to you? You're preying on the innocent. I didn't do anything. I should be recording this. Where's Ang, huh? She's the one who sells me these stupid things."

The cop glanced in his rearview mirror. He pulled the car over on the side of the road.

Jasmine panicked. Looked around for a way to escape. What would he do to her? She shouldn't have yelled.

He turned halfway around and met her eyes. "Jasmine." His voice was quiet but held a firm authority. "I know you don't believe or trust me now. But we're only here to help you. Someday you'll see this. I hope you'll want to make something better of yourself. You deserve much better than this, even after all you've been through. You're not a monster, you know. Nor are you a real drug user. It's up to you what you make of the rest of your life. Only you."

Jasmine flopped back against the seat, feeling deflated, although she really wanted to tell the cop where to shove it. How dare he bring up anything about her. She was not *that* Jasmine anymore.

"Can I have my pills?"

He shook his head and pulled the patrol car back on the road.

She watched the buildings flash by as they made their way to the station. Her parents, she knew, would be waiting.

She looked at the floor as they entered the station and at the ceiling when the cop guided her to a chair. "Where's my mom?"

He left without answering.

She looked around the room for a way to escape. Those were her pills. Bought them fair and square. She wouldn't leave without them. She squirmed. Could she wiggle her way out of the handcuffs? She'd done it before. "Hey." She noted a lady typing at a computer nearby. "Where's my mom?"

"Hello, Jasmine. I can't say it's good to see you here again." The female cop sat back against her chair, crossing her arms over her chest.

Jasmine thought her uniform was too tight as parts of her upper body strained against it. But she wasn't as fat as the Witch-Devil. "What's it to you?"

The woman pushed back her rolling chair. "Well, some people around here actually care about you and what you've been through."

Jasmine swore. Loudly. "Forget about it. Just forget about it. How come everyone brings that up? It's stupid. I hate it. Hate everyone."

The woman raised one eyebrow and went back to her computer. "You're right. None of my business. But I have a feeling the judge won't be so easy on you this time. Your parents aren't here, Jasmine. I don't know if they're coming this time."

Jasmine thought about that a moment, then dismissed it. She shrugged. "What about my pills?"

"Your pills are no longer your property. They were confiscated during a crime and are now in Evidence. Now, I suggest you sit back and relax. We'll get you processed soon enough."

Jasmine groaned and leaned back in her chair. Of all the rotten luck. She had babysat and even used some of her birthday money to buy those pills. And they were gone. Just like that. Boy, did that cop owe her.

Mari

Mari's phone dinged. She sighed. Would she never stop expecting bad news?

"Hello?"

"Mrs. Jensen. Hi. This is Officer Victoria Gells calling. Do you have a moment?"

"Yes." She checked the clock on her desk. Seven-oh-nine. Where had the time gone? Dinner would have to be take-out since she had forgotten to put anything in the crockpot that morning. "Is Jasmine okay?"

"Yes. She's with us and safe," Officer Gells paused. "But we did pick her up downtown. Portland."

Mari felt anger rise. "What now? Sorry, officer. I'm sorry."

"I understand. No worries. Jasmine was purchasing narcotics from a known dealer down on 82nd. I know she's a juvenile, but being this isn't her first offense—"

Mari groaned and rubbed her eyes with the back of her hand. Since Jasmine returned home, her life had not returned to the longed-for normalcy. Sometimes Mari wanted to shake her daughter for all she kept putting her and her family through. "Are you sure?"

"Very sure. Officer Hendricks witnessed the transaction, although the dealer did get away."

"What should I do?" Mari whispered. Call Ken, of course. But she and Ken hadn't been on the best of terms. In fact, he wasn't even living at home right now. Of course, she should still let him know. Had their marital issues messed Jasmine up even more?

"I'd suggest you let her spend the night here at the station. She's got quite the attitude going. I think it might help her think a little bit. Call your attorney. They will likely arraign her tomorrow sometime. She's safe here, Mrs. Jensen. I promise."

She was supposed to be safe walking to the store in River Falls. Mari shuddered. Their lives truly would never be the same. And if anyone ever hurt Jasmine again, she would personally make sure they couldn't move afterward. "Okay. Let me call my husband and call you back."

Jasmine

Officer Gells hung up the phone, walked down the hallway, and helped Jasmine to her feet.

As soon as she was upright, Jasmine yanked backward. "Don't touch me."

Officer Gells shrugged. "Suit yourself. Come with me, please."

"Where's my mom?"

"I just talked to her. Follow me, please." She led the girl to a holding cell.

As soon as Jasmine saw the bars, she threw herself on the floor, thrashing about and shedding very real tears. "You wouldn't dare lock me up."

Officer Gells called for assistance. Another female officer came, and together they helped Jasmine into the cell and locked it. Jasmine sniffed. Tears rolled down her cheeks. She sat on the cot. "Another trouble couch."

"I'll bring you a snack later." Officer Gells left. A door slammed.

"Wait!" But it was too late. No one heard her. Jasmine curled up to sleep.

In the middle of a bad dream, Bay woke up. Why was she in jail?

CHAPTER FIFTY-EIGHT
Melissa

MELISSA SCOOPED UP A HANDFUL OF TOYS and tossed them into the toybox. The place looked like Romper Room. But it was worth it. The little girl sitting next to her and looking more and more like Cienna every day was completely worth it. Life had certainly taken some huge and unexpected turns.

She ruffled her granddaughter's dark curls. At eighteen months, baby Grace was curious about everything. Fairly firm on her once wobbly feet, she explored mostly with her hands. And her mouth, of course.

"Gam . . . " She pulled a toy from her mouth and offered it to Melissa, whose heart warmed with love.

"Thanks, love." She shook her head no.

Grace's shoulders drooped, and she wrinkled her face, about to cry.

Melissa reached for a dry part of the toy and set it next to her. "Thank you."

They laughed.

Grace toddled to the bookshelf and pulled out a book, three more tumbling down with it.

Melissa sighed. It was just like when her kids were young. The mess never ended. But as she scooted over and leaned against the couch, waiting for Grace to bring the chosen book, she wouldn't trade it for anything. They almost hadn't had Grace. And although the little one was as unplanned as they come and a result of violence in Cienna's life, Melissa was grateful to know her granddaughter. "Thank you," she whispered into Grace's soft hair as they opened the book.

"Da." Grace poked her chubby finger at the smiling dog on the first page. Her beautiful blue eyes widened as she turned for affirmation.

"That's right. Dog. Good girl." Melissa was so proud of her. Like Cienna, Grace was a fast learner.

Her cell phone buzzed, and she put her hand behind her, feeling around on the seat of the big leather couch. It was Jimmy. "Hi honey. Grace and I are reading about Skip the puppy."

He laughed. "That sounds better than classes."

Feeling a moment of regret, Melissa sighed. With the added expenses of an unexpected granddaughter, Jimmy had sought and received a promotion to general manager of a local hotel chain. It appeared that human resources, filling the rooms, and counting the numbers took most of his time now. The unfortunate part was that he traveled quite a bit to the corporate offices and other hotels.

"When are you home?" She cradled the phone on her shoulder. Helped curious Grace stand up.

"One more training class, then I'll be hitting the airport. So, eleven? Where's Ci?"

"I dropped her off to take her GED exam."

"She was okay with being there without you?"

"Jimmy, yes. Someone has to watch the baby." She raised her eyebrows at Grace, who promptly giggled.

"I thought she agreed to finish at the alternative school and graduate."

"Well." Melissa thought for a moment. "She's a mother. She's sixteen but grown up now. You know that. She's feeling stuck and wants to help support Grace more."

"Her job prospects would be better with a high school diploma and some college."

"Yes." This was a frequent discussion in their house, but in the end, what could they do? In a very short time, Cienna had become a woman. And although they were working hard to be a team, some things she would have to learn on her own. "But we're here for them both, aren't we now, Gracie Leah."

Her voice rose to a higher pitch as she talked to the toddler. Grace plopped back on her lap. Turned the page of the book. Maybe Grace would think she was reading if she kept her voice sing-songy while she talked to Jimmy. Grace stuck her thumb in her mouth and settled back against Melissa, sighing in contentment. Melissa had missed cuddling a little one since Kai had grown up so much.

"I love you, honey." Jimmy's voice turned gruff. "Tell Kai hello. Grace too. I'll be home soon."

"Love you, Jim. See you soon." Melissa punched "end" and tossed the phone on the couch, away from curious fingers and drool. "Oh, look at Skip! What's he doing now?"

She had just tucked Grace into her crib in Cienna's room and walked back out when her phone buzzed again. She looked at the piles of toys and dishes and sighed. When she sat on the couch and reached for her phone, she didn't want to get up again. Maybe all the mess could wait until tomorrow.

Hey. She typed quickly back to Mari. **How's it going? What's word on Jazz?**

Jazz or Bay? A crying face appeared. **She . . . they? They said they would send her to rehab at a house with a bunch of other girls on lockdown?! CAN U IMAGINE?! WHAT is wrong with them? She'll never be able to leave Bay behind in that kind of place. Anyway, the judge said today she is going to the Greenwood Center instead.**

Heard good things about it. Maybe they can help her?

The little bubble showed that Mari was texting back. The phone dinged. **Hope so. They have experience in both the narcotics and dissociative disorder. That's what they call multiple personalities now.**

Melissa made a crying face too. **I'm so sorry. This has been so hard. For Jazz/Bay and all of you too.** She added praying hands to the text. **Cienna is taking GED test. Here's Grace for you.** She sent a picture of Grace holding a ball and smiling.

AWWWW. Precious. She's amazing!

Yes. Melissa quickly typed back. **She is a gift. Something the angels reserved just for us.**

Cienna came home and flopped on the couch without checking on Grace in her crib. Instead, she buried her face in the pillow and mumbled at her mother.

Laughing, Melissa sat next to her and rubbed her back. "If you think I can understand you . . . "

Cienna mumbled again.

Melissa smiled. "How about some ice cream?" That earned her one eye peering out from the fluff of the pillow.

"Raw-rerry?" Cienna looked up. "We have strawberry?"

"We do." Melissa got up to get it. Now it appeared cleaning up the house would have to wait for sure.

Cienna rose and shuffled into the kitchen behind Melissa. "When's Dad home?"

"After midnight. He has one more class, then will be on the plane. Jazz is going into rehab."

"I know."

"How was the test?"

"I don't know. I think I screwed up on the math. But they said I passed."

Melissa smiled. "I knew you would do well."

Cienna had discovered most of the people in her GED classes needed help. Some barely spoke English, and things like math seemed a mystery. She'd spent time helping many of them with the basics so they would be able to pass the test as well.

"When do you get your card?" Melissa asked.

"They mail that." Cienna yawned before shoving a large spoonful of strawberry ice cream into her mouth. "Did Grace behave herself?"

Melissa was tempted to lie but resisted. "Well, let's see. Two scream-fests. She refused a nap and threw food on the floor. But tonight she was snuggly and all smiles, and we read a book before bed."

"Sounds kind of typical." Cienna laughed.

"Sounds kind of like you."

Cienna tilted her head to the side and grinned. "Yeah." She sobered. "But you don't have to remind me every day."

"You're right. I'm sorry." Melissa finished her ice cream. "But just because Grace is done for the day doesn't mean we are. Want the dishes or the playroom?"

Cienna yawned again and moaned. "Mom, I'm too tired."

Melissa tossed her daughter a look.

Cienna stood, not bothering to take her bowl to the sink. "Playroom." She shuffled from the room. Shortly after, Melissa heard toys being tossed roughly into the toybox.

"I want you to know I'm proud of you." Melissa paused at the door. "I know it's hard to get out there now, but you're doing what you need to do to make things better for Grace and yourself. You're doing a great job. Really, honey."

Cienna gritted her teeth. "Not a great job, or none of this ever would have happened." She waved her hand at the mess in the playroom. "How will I ever get her past the fact of her birth?" Tears welled in her eyes. "I was stupid. An idiot."

"No, you're not. It's not your fault, Cienna. You don't get her past that fact. You can't. When the time is right, we'll be as honest as we can be with her. We'll get advice. We'll figure it out." She paused, considering her daughter's repeated remarks about who Grace's father was. "Do you want to know?"

Cienna threw the last book onto the shelf and turned to face her, her hands on her hips. "What?"

"Do you . . . do you want to find out who Grace's father is? Mike's in prison. They did get DNA from him. We would just need to request it and sign papers."

Cienna walked out of the room. "I'll just pretend I didn't hear that."

Melissa sighed with relief and went back to face the mountain of dishes in the sink.

CHAPTER FIFTY-NINE
Jasmine

JASMINE ENTERED THE COMMUNITY ROOM at Greenwood, a smile on her face. Her entire family, Cienna's family, and Detective Miller and Mollie were there to greet her. Jasmine plunked her suitcase on the ground and carefully set down some treasures that would always remind her of her rescue . . . and recovery.

While Mom wiped tears from her eyes, Dad enveloped Jasmine in a large hug. "I love you, Daddy."

"Love you too." He grinned. "Let's go celebrate you kicking this place to the curb."

Jasmine and Cienna hugged each other.

"I'm so grateful to be done." Jasmine felt a huge burden lift.

"I think Roger's dead." Cienna whispered in her friend's ear. "I overheard my folks talking to Miller on the phone."

Jasmine nodded, ready to forget that creep. They pulled apart. "Did you see the rock on Mollie's hand?" Cienna giggled. "She and Detective Miller look so cute together. So romantic."

"Yeah." Jasmine blinked back more tears. With her past, would she ever find love like that?

Then she laughed, calling goodbyes to the staff members whom she saw on the way out. They were all going to celebrate with dinner at The Lighthouse.

Cienna squeezed into a seat of Jasmine's family's van with Seth, Amelie, and Mitch. They chatted all the way to the restaurant. Grace rode with her grandparents.

Amelie and Mitch had progressed in locating Rose's hometown and tracking her life before her daughter. They shared updates as they traveled along. Jasmine looked forward to helping them find out more and to keeping her promise to Rose to make sure that her daughter was well and being treated kindly. She couldn't wait to help someone else.

The meal was going well, and the families were talking about volunteering activities when Jasmine surprised everyone and asked if she and Cienna could go for a walk. Instant wariness crossed their mothers' faces. The restaurant had a large back deck that overlooked a river and a trail. The girls told their parents that they would stay in sight this time. Both took their cell phones.

In the sudden quiet of the hushed woods around them, Cienna brushed off a chill. "I'm a little nervous." She glanced back and saw Jasmine's mom sitting on the deck, sipping her iced tea, and watching them.

"I know." Jasmine put her hair in a scrunchie she kept on her wrist. "Who would ever have thought it would be scary just to go on a walk?" Tears filled her eyes. "I feel so bad, Ci. It wouldn't have happened if I hadn't insisted on changing our original plan of just going to the store and back. What was I thinking?"

"Geez, Jazz, it was our normal camping trip. Every year at the same place. And it was just to the store and back. No way you could have known."

"I know, I know. But I still have to work on forgiving myself for all the horrible things that happened. We were laughing about Sasquatch, and then . . . then he got us."

Cienna hugged Jazz, and they held each other for a long time.

"I needed to say that I'm sorry, Ci. And I love you. I don't know about all the hell you went through, but I would have taken it on if I could. I was so worried when I woke up on the TC and you weren't around."

"I know." Cienna picked up a rock. She flicked it into the river where it skipped four times. "I was worried about you too but then just tried to survive."

A warm breeze suddenly wrapped itself around the girls. A bright light poked through the clouds and placed a beam directly on them. The evening light brightened as Jasmine shrugged off her light jacket. "What the hey?" Cienna laughed.

Jasmine nodded firmly. "They're here. Our angels. Ci, there was a reason that we survived this."

Cienna nodded slowly. Seemed to consider. "Penny didn't make it. But I did. Why?"

"Rose died too. And she was amazing. I wish you could have known her, Ci. She got me through some really hard times. I want to be like her. She even left a notebook. Poems and prayers. And through it all, she just wanted to help the others." Jasmine looked at the sky, into the bright light. "I hope she knows now that none of us in that house would have survived without her there. Maybe her angel passed that job to me now."

They considered.

"Most of us never come home." Cienna mused. "Most of us die out there. Why are we different?" She thought again of Penny tied under the house. "I tried to save her. I really did." A tear dripped down her cheek. She angrily brushed it away.

"You couldn't, Ci. It's not your fault. But we survived." Jasmine shook her head. "We were meant for greater things. And Grace. They saved all three of us. Can you see that?"

"I see something for sure. I see horrible days of starvation, beatings, and rapes in a barn. I see a little girl who I couldn't do enough for. I see that I was stupid and trusting of one man who took me from another but in retrospect also really hurt me. What do I do with that? All these horrible thoughts running through my head! There are nights I can't face it. I have awful nightmares! I hate it. I'm so sorry! I'm the oldest, but I couldn't even take care of you!" Cienna started sobbing.

Jasmine took her hand. She got it. "We're healthy and well, Ci. There is a plan. A reason that we're alive. Will you find that with me, Cienna? Search with me? Please?"

Cienna slowly nodded her head, wiped her tears, and took her friend's hand. Her tears dried. Despite all they had been through, the joy of playing together again triumphed. They skipped more rocks, looked back at the restaurant porch to wave occasionally, giggled at the antics of the squirrels . . . and enjoyed playing as girls once again.

The beginning of healing felt good to them both.

THE END

To be continued in "A Solitary Path: Guardians of Grace, Book 2."

A Solitary Path: Guardians of Grace, Book 2

Pre-Order "A Solitary Path: Guardians of Grace, Book 2" now. Releases Fall of 2022. Paperbacks are available at a discounted price of $12.00, including shipping within the USA.

Here's a sneak peek—

Jem has fled with her infant sister Jade from their abusive home. On her way to find her maternal grandmother, they live on the streets—under overpasses and in homeless camps where the nights are long and horror besieges. When she meets a friend, Jet, she clings to him and believes that he will help her find the way.

Getting to safety isn't all it's cracked up to be. Jem finds not safety—but terrifying consequences for leaving home. She is not old enough to parent her sibling. Her drug-addicted mom is making a case to get her sister back. During this, she discovers that her mom isn't even related to her. Can finally meeting Cienna and Jasmine help her untangle this mess?

Will she take Jade from her new home and run again? Jem must finally come to a resolution in her own mind. She must learn a new life, one that is safe for them both. Letting go is the hardest thing she has ever faced. As she loses the fight to keep her sister safe, Jem learns who she can lean on, and whom she can't. Then angels intervene and change their family unit, and destiny, forever.

Preorder "A Solitary Path" signed paperback at https://juliebonnblank.com and pay there for the discounted price.

A NOTE FOR YOU

Did you have a favorite book as a child? Mine was "The Giving Tree" by Shel Silverstein. I must not be the only one as it was reprinted several times and translated into many languages. Although at times the message resonated sadness, as an adult I see much more. I see a generous tree who loves to a fault and gives until he/she dies, all in the name of love. I see a reflection of what my Heavenly Father has done for me.

I also see grace in "The Giving Tree." You see, Grace is more than a little girl in this book. Grace reflects how my angels stepped into my life and turned some bad decisions into amazing joy (although please note, Cienna did not make these bad choices, she was a victim of other's bad choices). I cannot imagine my life without my "Grace," and I would encourage you to not become discouraged if you have made some bad choices. You are forgiven if you have asked. Any reminders of your bad choices can be tossed into the ocean and released. Time to move forward.

Human Trafficking is a subject long placed on my heart as a topic that needs more attention. Over a million children a year are trafficked and placed into deplorable conditions—both overseas and in the United States. Although it is true that most trafficking does not happen because of kidnapping (most happens through what we call intimate partner relationships), it does happen and there are bad people in this world who believe that other humans can be owned and have no rights. They believe they have the right to use, abuse and sell them to the highest bidder. Our poor children pay the price. Because it's so heart-breaking, many avoid learning more about trafficking. Indeed, it can be very hard to envision what these kids and adults go through.

It's time to talk about it. It is my hope that "Innocent Lives" gives people a starting place to learn and talk more about human trafficking. Perhaps it might even be the beginning of a new journey for you—if you're so called.

This book wouldn't have been possible without the support of many. Thanks to Ben Kadolph, Administrative Sergeant/CALEA Manager of the Oak Brook, Illinois police department for reviewing endless sections of verbiage and making sure I was accurate with the role of law enforcement in a trafficking situation. Although this is a work of fiction, accuracy is very important to me. Thank you to my amazing daughter, Megan Heath, and to Melissa Jane, Sandi Harrington and author Kathi Macias for early reading. Kathi also has some fiction novels on trafficking, and you should pick those up! Thanks to Sandi for some early edits. You were a true friend and I miss you. Thank you to Carmen Leal, an early cheerleader of my work who encourages me often. And thank you to my wonderful and amazing editor, Louise M. Gouge. Thank you to the entire team at Write to Publish, 2018. That was my first full writer's conference and I left incredibly encouraged. God told me multiple times at that conference that I was on the right path. Thanks to Oregon Christian Writers and West Coast Christian Writers. Thank you to the group I facilitate, North Coast Christian Writers. I love each one of you. Numerous validations of my work have happened through the grace of these people and I'm grateful. Thank you to longtime family friend, Cathie Blackstock, for proofreading the final when my eyes were weary. A second set of eyes are the best! Thank you to the ministry of my heart, ARMS/Abuse Recovery Ministry Services and those there who helped me work through my own trauma to full and complete healing. I didn't think I could heal. I am so grateful to actually be wrong. Thank you to our Family Justice Center/Family Peace Center of Washington County and to our Domestic Violence Resource Center for your support and for being there for those who can hardly think for themselves, due to their abusive trauma. They need you. Please don't ever forget. Thank you also to suspense author Brandilyn Collins.

After her "Fantastic Fiction" retreat, I was able to edit even more, making lasting changes with incredible impact. I highly recommend her retreat!

I want to thank all of our children. Their support throughout all my journeys have been vital. Thanks to my Middle. When I expressed frustration that there are always stories running through my head and every situation frames another one, he said patiently, "Mom, that's because you're a writer." To my Oldest, who picked up on her mother's desire and shakes the pom-poms on a regular basis. Once when I stopped writing this book for several weeks (months?) she told me, "Mom, when we talk next weekend, I want one paragraph done." I complied—the night before we talked again—and that one paragraph turned into pages and started another whirlwind. To my Youngest, who is the most humorous, loving adult-kid ever. Thanks for listening endlessly to plots and giving me ideas. Thanks for helping me shape things by sharing what happens in your life. Thanks for watching all the musicals with me. I hope that you'll write someday. Because you can. But I of course will support whatever path you choose. Thanks to my lovely Daughter-Through-My-Marriage, whose great strength and tenacity reminds me each day that I can do more than I thought possible. I only need to keep pushing through.

Thanks to my Parents. Your support and encouragement are endless. I am so grateful for you both. (Thanks, Dad, for letting me know that Moses didn't start his destiny until he was eighty. I'm glad to be a few years ahead of that milestone).

Thanks to my amazing "second chance," Bill. Life sure turned upside down when we lost Marty and Glenda. A piece is forever gone for us and our families. The trauma is real and the journey never forgotten. But our angels so carefully orchestrated our dance that there's no doubt that they were deep into the details and planned our reunion twenty-five years after we had met. Thank you, Bill. You not only are convinced that I can do this, but your support shows that you mean it. The truth is, I couldn't do it without your support, and I love you always and forever. I'll always be the luckiest girl.

Thank you, readers. I presently feel called to write about difficult subjects. The publishing market is not always so accepting of this. This means that I need you a BUNCH! If you liked this book, please consider leaving a review on Amazon, Facebook (https://www.facebook.com/Innocent-Lives108836794921520) GoodReads or elsewhere. If you have a blog or website, please consider highlighting it there. It's a huge help. I hope that you will join me for this series as it continues through North Beach Books. Feel free to connect with me through social media or on my website at https://juliebonnblank.com

Julie Bonn Blank

Made in the USA
Columbia, SC
21 March 2022

57881087R00172